BLUEBEARD'S EGG

Whether they are set in remote parts of northern Quebec and Ontario, in other countries, or in downtown Toronto, these vignettes and narratives focus on relationships—some partially flawed, others quite bizarre. There's the jealous wife and her mysterious husband, a political activist and his kidnapped cat, a woman and her dead psychiatrist, a potter and the group of poets who live with her and mythologize her. Finally, there are the very telling relationships among parents and children in this brilliant collection of stories whose dramatic range between the desolate and the hilarious prove Margaret Atwood to be a true master of this genre.

"Atwood displays polished craftsmanship and rare insight in the stories in this collection. They are the work of an author in full control of her considerable talents."
—*Globe and Mail*

"Enter this Atwood country warily, prepared to expose your own hidden agendas, your precious mythologies, your perceptions of yourself as narrator in good faith. Atwood is nothing if not clairvoyant."
—*The Whig-Standard*

Bluebeard's Egg

Margaret Atwood

SEAL BOOKS
McClelland and Stewart-Bantam Limited
Toronto

*This low-priced Seal Book
has been completely reset in a type face
designed for easy reading, and was printed
from new plates. It contains the complete
text of the original hard-cover edition.*
NOT ONE WORD HAS BEEN OMITTED.

BLUEBEARD'S EGG

*A Seal Book / published by arrangement with
McClelland and Stewart Limited*

PRINTING HISTORY

McClelland and Stewart edition published October 1983

Seal edition / August 1984

*Art by Heather Cooper,
courtesy of Margaret Atwood.*

*Seal Books are published by McClelland and Stewart-Bantam Limited.
Its trademark, consisting of the words "Seal Books" and the portrayal
of a seal, is the property of McClelland and Stewart-Bantam Limited, 60
St. Clair Avenue East, Suite 601, Toronto, Ontario M4T 1N5 Canada.
This trademark has been duly registered in the Trademarks Office of
Canada. The trademark, consisting of the word "Bantam" and the
portrayal of a rooster, is the property of and is used with the consent of
Bantam Books, Inc. 666 Fifth Avenue, New York, New York 10103. This
trademark has been duly registered in the Trademarks Office of Canada
and elsewhere.*

PRINTED IN CANADA

COVER PRINTED IN U.S.A.

U   0 9 8 7 6 5 4 3 2 1

ACKNOWLEDGEMENTS

Material in this collection has been previously published as follows:

"Significant Moments in the Life of My Mother" in *Queen's Quarterly*; "Betty" and "Bluebeard's Egg" in *Chatelaine*; "Loulou; or, The Domestic Life of the Language" in *Saturday Night*; "The Sin Eater" on the CBC Radio program *Anthology* and its printed anthology, *Small Wonders*; and "Unearthing Suite" in a limited edition by Grand Union Press.

For My Parents

Contents

Significant Moments in the Life of My Mother

❧

When my mother was very small, someone gave her a basket of baby chicks for Easter. They all died.

"I didn't know you weren't supposed to pick them up," says my mother. "Poor little things. I laid them out in a row on a board, with their little legs sticking out straight as pokers, and wept over them. I'd loved them to death."

Possibly this story is meant by my mother to illustrate her own stupidity, and also her sentimentality. We are to understand she wouldn't do such a thing now.

Possibly it's a commentary on the nature of love; though, knowing my mother, this is unlikely.

My mother's father was a country doctor. In the days before cars he drove a team of horses and a buggy around his territory, and in the days before snow ploughs he drove a team and a sleigh, through blizzards and rainstorms and in the middle of the night, to arrive at houses lit with oil lamps where water would be boiling on the wood range and flannel sheets warming on the plate rack, to deliver babies who would subsequently be named after him. His office was in the house, and as a child my mother would witness people arriving at the office door, which was reached through the front porch, clutching parts of themselves—thumbs, fingers, toes, ears, noses—which had accidentally been cut off, pressing these severed parts to the raw stumps of their bodies as if they could be stuck there like dough, in the mostly

1

vain hope that my grandfather would be able to sew them back on, heal the gashes made in them by axes, saws, knives, and fate.

My mother and her younger sister would loiter near the closed office door until shooed away. From behind it would come groans, muffled screams, cries for help. For my mother, hospitals have never been glamorous places, and illness offers no respite or holiday. "Never get sick," she says, and means it. She hardly ever does.

Once, though, she almost died. It was when her appendix burst. My grandfather had to do the operation. He said later that he shouldn't have been the person to do it: his hands were shaking too much. This is one of the few admissions of weakness on his part that my mother has ever reported. Mostly he is portrayed as severe and in charge of things. "We all respected him, though," she says. "He was widely respected." (This is a word which has slipped a little in the scale since my mother's youth. It used to outrank *love*.)

It was someone else who told me the story of my grandfather's muskrat farm: how he and one of my mother's uncles fenced in the swamp at the back of their property and invested my mother's maiden aunt's savings in muskrats. The idea was that these muskrats would multiply and eventually be made into muskrat coats, but an adjoining apple farmer washed his spraying equipment upstream, and the muskrats were all killed by the poison, as dead as doornails. This was during the Depression, and it was no joke.

When they were young—this can cover almost anything these days, but I put it at seven or eight—my mother and her sister had a tree house, where they spent some of their time playing dolls' tea parties and so forth. One day they found a box of sweet little bottles outside my grandfather's dispensary. The bottles were being thrown out, and my mother (who has always hated waste) appropriated them for use in their dolls' house. The bottles were full of yellow liquid, which they left in because it looked so pretty. It turned out that these were urine samples.

"We got Hail Columbia for that," says my mother. "But what did we know?"

My mother's family lived in a large white house near an apple orchard, in Nova Scotia. There was a barn and a carriage-house; in the kitchen there was a pantry. My mother can remember the days before commercial bakeries, when flour came in barrels and all the bread was made at home. She can remember the first radio broadcast she ever heard, which was a singing commercial about socks.

In this house there were many rooms. Although I have been there, although I have seen the house with my own eyes, I still don't know how many. Parts of it were closed off, or so it seemed; there were back staircases. Passages led elsewhere. Five children lived in it, two parents, a hired man and a hired girl, whose names and faces kept changing. The structure of the house was hierarchical, with my grandfather at the top, but its secret life—the life of pie crusts, clean sheets, the box of rags in the linen closet, the loaves in the oven—was female. The house, and all the objects in it, crackled with static electricity; undertows washed through it, the air was heavy with things that were known but not spoken. Like a hollow log, a drum, a church, it amplified, so that conversations whispered in it sixty years ago can be half-heard even today.

In this house you had to stay at the table until you had eaten everything on your plate. "'Think of the starving Armenians,' mother used to say," says my mother. "I didn't see how eating my bread crusts was going to help them out one jot."

It was in this house that I first saw a stalk of oats in a vase, each oat wrapped in the precious silver paper which had been carefully saved from a chocolate box. I

thought it was the most wonderful thing I had ever seen,
and began saving silver paper myself. But I never got
around to wrapping the oats, and in any case I didn't
know how. Like many other art forms of vanished
civilizations, the techniques for this one have been lost
and cannot quite be duplicated.

"We had oranges at Christmas," says my mother.
"They came all the way from Florida; they were very
expensive. That was the big treat: to find an orange in
the toe of your stocking. It's funny to remember how
good they tasted, now."

When she was sixteen, my mother had hair so long she
could sit on it. Women were bobbing their hair by then;
it was getting to be the twenties. My mother's hair was
giving her headaches, she says, but my grandfather, who
was very strict, forbade her to cut it. She waited until
one Saturday when she knew he had an appointment
with the dentist.

"In those days there was no freezing," says my mother.
"The drill was worked with a foot pedal, and it went
grind, grind, grind. The dentist himself had brown
teeth: he chewed tobacco, and he would spit the tobacco
juice into a spittoon while he was working on your
teeth."

Here my mother, who is good mimic, imitates the
sounds of the drill and the tobacco juice: "*Rrrrr! Rrrrr!
Rrrrr! Phtt! Rrrrr! Rrrrr! Phtt!* It was always sheer
agony. It was a heaven-sent salvation when gas came in."

My mother went into the dentist's office, where my
grandfather was sitting in the chair, white with pain. She
asked him if she could have her hair cut. He said she
could do anything in tarnation as long as she would get
out of there and stop pestering him.

"So I went out straight away had it all chopped off,"
says my mother jauntily. "He was furious afterwards, but
what could he do? He'd given his word."

My own hair reposes in a cardboard box in a steamer trunk in my mother's cellar, where I picture it becoming duller and more brittle with each passing year, and possibly moth-eaten; by now it will look like the faded wreaths of hair in Victorian funeral jewellery. Or it may have developed a dry mildew; inside its tissue-paper wrappings it glows faintly, in the darkness of the trunk. I suspect my mother has forgotten it's in there. It was cut off, much to my relief, when I was twelve and my sister was born. Before that it was in long curls: "Otherwise," says my mother, "it would have been just one big snarl." My mother combed it by winding it around her index finger every morning, but when she was in the hospital my father couldn't cope. "He couldn't get it around his stubby fingers," says my mother. My father looks down at his fingers. They are indeed broad compared with my mother's long elegant ones, which she calls boney. He smiles a pussy-cat smile.

So it was that my hair was sheared off. I sat in the chair in my first beauty parlour and watched it falling, like handfuls of cobwebs, down over my shoulders. From within it my head began to emerge, smaller, denser, my face more angular. I aged five years in fifteen minutes. I knew I could go home now and try out lipstick.

"Your father was upset about it," says my mother, with an air of collusion. She doesn't say this when my father is present. We smile, over the odd reactions of men to hair.

I used to think that my mother, in her earlier days, led a life of sustained hilarity and hair-raising adventure. (That was before I realized that she never put in the long stretches of uneventful time that must have made up much of her life: the stories were just the punctuation.) Horses ran away with her, men offered to, she was continually falling out of trees or off the ridgepoles of barns, or nearly being swept out to sea in rip-tides; or, in a more minor vein, suffering acute embarrassment in trying circumstances.

Churches were especially dangerous. "There was a guest preacher one Sunday," she says. "Of course we had to go to church every Sunday. There he was, in full career, preaching hellfire and damnation"—she pounds an invisible pulpit—"and his full set of false teeth shot out of his mouth—*phoop!*—just like that. Well, he didn't miss a stride. He stuck his hand up and caught them and popped them back in his mouth, and he kept right on, condemning us all to eternal torment. The pew was shaking! The tears were rolling down our faces, and the worst of it was, we were in the front pew, he was looking right at us. But of course we couldn't laugh out loud: father would have given us Hail Columbia."

Other people's parlours were booby-trapped for her; so were any and all formal social occasions. Zippers sprang apart on her clothes in strategic places, hats were unreliable. The shortage of real elastic during the war demanded constant alertness: underpants then had buttons, and were more taboo and therefore more significant than they are now. "There you would be," she says, "right on the street, and before you knew it they'd be down around your galoshes. The way to do was to step out of them with one foot, then kick them up with your other foot and whip them into your purse. I got quite good at it."

This particular story is told only to a few, but other stories are for general consumption. When she tells them, my mother's face turns to rubber. She takes all the parts, adds the sound effects, waves her hands around in the air. Her eyes gleam, sometimes a little wickedly, for although my mother is sweet and old and a lady, she avoids being a sweet old lady. When people are in danger of mistaking her for one, she flings in something from left field; she refuses to be taken for granted.

But my mother cannot be duped into telling stories when she doesn't want to. If you prompt her, she becomes self-conscious and clams up. Or she will laugh and go out into the kitchen, and shortly after that you will hear the whir of the Mixmaster. Long ago I gave up attempting to make her do tricks at parties. In gatherings of unknown people, she merely listens intently, her head tilted a little, smiling a smile of glazed politeness. The secret is to wait and see what she will say afterwards.

At the age of seventeen my mother went to the Normal School in Truro. This name—"Normal School"—once held a certain magic for me. I thought it had something to do with learning to be normal, which possibly it did, because really it was where you used to go to learn how to be a schoolteacher. Subsequently my mother taught in a one-room school house not far from her home. She rode her horse to and from the school house every day, and saved up the money she earned and sent herself to university with it. My grandfather wouldn't send her: he said she was too frivolous-minded. She liked ice-skating and dancing too much for his taste.

At Normal School my mother boarded with a family that contained several sons in more or less the same age group as the girl boarders. They all ate around a huge dining-room table (which I pictured as being of dark wood, with heavy carved legs, but covered always with a white linen tablecloth), with the mother and father presiding, one at each end. I saw them both as large and pink and beaming.

"The boys were great jokers," says my mother. "They were always up to something." This was desirable in boys: to be great jokers, to be always up to something. My mother adds a key sentence: "We had a lot of fun."

Having fun has always been high on my mother's agenda. She has as much fun as possible, but what she means by this phrase cannot be understood without making an adjustment, an allowance for the great gulf across which this phrase must travel before it reaches us.

It comes from another world, which, like the stars that
originally sent out the light we see hesitating in the sky
above us these nights, may be or is already gone. It is
possible to reconstruct the facts of this world—the
furniture, the clothing, the ornaments on the mantelpiece, the jugs and basins and even the chamber pots in
the bedrooms, but not the emotions, not with the same
exactness. So much that is now known and felt must be
excluded.

This was a world in which guileless flirtation was
possible, because there were many things that were
simply not done by nice girls, and more girls were nice
then. To fall from niceness was to fall not only from
grace: sexual acts, by girls at any rate, had financial
consequences. Life was more joyful and innocent then,
and at the same time permeated with guilt and terror, or
at least the occasions for them, on the most daily level. It
was like the Japanese haiku: a limited form, rigid in its
perimeters, within which an astonishing freedom was
possible.

There are photographs of my mother at this time,
taken with three or four other girls, linked arm in arm or
with their arms thrown jestingly around each other's
necks. Behind them, beyond the sea or the hills or
whatever is in the background, is a world already
hurtling towards ruin, unknown to them: the theory of
relativity has been discovered, acid is accumulating at
the roots of trees, the bull-frogs are doomed. But they
smile with something that from this distance you could
almost call gallantry, their right legs thrust forward in
parody of a chorus line.

One of the great amusements for the girl boarders and
the sons of the family was amateur theatre. Young
people—they were called "young people"—frequently
performed in plays, which were put on in the church
basement. My mother was a regular actor. (I have a stack
of the scripts somewhere about the house, yellowing
little booklets with my mother's parts checked in pencil.

They are all comedies, and all impenetrable.) "There was no television then," says my mother. "You made your own fun."

For one of these plays a cat was required, and my mother and one of the sons borrowed the family cat. They put it into a canvas bag and drove to the rehearsal (there were cars by then), with my mother holding the cat on her lap. The cat, which must have been frightened, wet itself copiously, through the canvas bag and all over my mother's skirt. At the same time it made the most astonishingly bad smell.

"I was ready to sink through the floorboards," says my mother. "But what could I do? All I could do was sit there. In those days things like that"—she means cat pee, or pee of any sort—"were not mentioned." She means in mixed company.

I think of my mother driven through the night, skirts dripping, overcome with shame, the young man beside her staring straight ahead, pretending not to notice anything. They both feel that this act of unmentionable urination has been done, not by the cat, but by my mother. And so they continue, in a straight line that takes them over the Atlantic and past the curvature of the earth, out through the moon's orbit and into the dark reaches beyond.

Meanwhile, back on earth, my mother says: "I had to throw the skirt out. It was a good skirt, too, but nothing could get rid of the smell."

"I only heard your father swear once," says my mother. My mother herself never swears. When she comes to a place in a story in which swearing is called for, she says "dad-ratted" or "blankety-blank."

"It was when he mashed his thumb, when he was sinking the well, for the pump." This story, I know, takes place before I was born, up north, where there is nothing underneath the trees and their sheddings but sand and bedrock. The well was for a hand pump, which in turn was for the first of the many cabins and houses my parents built together. But since I witnessed later wells being sunk and later hand pumps being installed, I know how it's done. There's a pipe with a point at one end. You pound it into the ground with a sledge hammer, and as it goes down you screw other lengths of pipe onto it, until you hit drinkable water. To keep from ruining the thread on the top end, you hold a block of wood between the sledge hammer and the pipe. Better, you get someone else to hold it for you. This is how my father mashed his thumb: he was doing both the holding and the hammering himself.

"It swelled up like a radish," says my mother. "He had to make a hole in the nail, with his toad-sticker, to ease the pressure. The blood spurted out like pips from a lemon. Later on the whole nail turned purple and black and dropped off. Luckily he grew another one. They say you only get two chances. When he did it though, he turned the air blue for yards around. I didn't even know he knew those words. I don't know where he picked them up." She speaks as if these words are a minor contagious disease, like chicken pox.

Here my father looks modestly down at his plate. For him, there are two worlds: one containing ladies, in which you do not use certain expressions, and another one—consisting of logging camps and other haunts of his youth, and of gatherings of acceptable sorts of men—in which you do. To let the men's world slip over verbally into the ladies' would reveal you as a mannerless boor, but to carry the ladies' world over into the men's brands you a prig and maybe even a pansy. This is the word for it. All of this is well understood between them.

This story illustrates several things: that my father is no pansy, for one; and that my mother behaved properly by being suitably shocked. But my mother's eyes shine with delight while she tells this story. Secretly, she thinks it funny that my father got caught out, even if only

once. The thumbnail that fell off is, in any significant
way, long forgotten.

There are some stories which my mother does not tell
when there are men present: never at dinner, never at
parties. She tells them to women only, usually in the
kitchen, when they or we are helping with the dishes or
shelling peas, or taking the tops and tails off the string
beans, or husking corn. She tells them in a lowered
voice, without moving her hands around in the air, and
they contain no sound effects. These are stories of
romantic betrayals, unwanted pregnancies, illnesses of
various horrible kinds, marital infidelities, mental break-
downs, tragic suicides, unpleasant lingering deaths.
They are not rich in detail or embroidered with incident:
they are stark and factual. The women, their own hands
moving among the dirty dishes or the husks of vegetables, nod solemnly.

Some of these stories, it is understood, are not to be
passed on to my father, because they would upset him. It
is well known that women can deal with this sort of thing
better than men can. Men are not to be told anything
they might find too painful; the secret depths of human
nature, the sordid physicalities, might overwhelm or
damage them. For instance, men often faint at the sight
of their own blood, to which they are not accustomed.
For this reason you should never stand behind one in the
line at the Red Cross donor clinic. Men, for some
mysterious reason, find life more difficult then women
do. (My mother believes this, despite the female bodies,
trapped, diseased, disappearing, or abandoned, that
litter her stories.) Men must be allowed to play in the
sandbox of their choice, as happily as they can, without
disturbance; otherwise they get cranky and won't eat
their dinners. There are all kinds of things that men are
simply not equipped to understand, so why expect it of

them? Not everyone shares this belief about men; nevertheless, it has its uses.

"She dug up the shrubs from around the house," says my mother. This story is about a shattered marriage: serious business. My mother's eyes widen. The other women lean forward. "All she left him were the shower curtains." There is a collective sigh, an expelling of breath. My father enters the kitchen, wondering when the tea will be ready, and the women close ranks, turning to him their deceptive blankly smiling faces. Soon afterwards, my mother emerges from the kitchen, carrying the tea pot, and sets it down on the table in its ritual place.

"I remember the time we almost died," says my mother. Many of her stories begin this way. When she is in a certain mood, we are to understand that our lives have been preserved only by a series of amazing coincidences and strokes of luck; otherwise the entire family, individually or collectively, would be dead as doornails. These stories, in addition to producing adrenalin, serve to reinforce our sense of gratitude. There is the time we almost went over a waterfall, in a canoe, in a fog; the time we almost got caught in a forest fire; the time my father almost got squashed, before my mother's very eyes, by a ridgepole he was lifting into place; the time my brother almost got struck by a bolt of lightning, which went by him so close it knocked him down. "You could hear it sizzle," says my mother.

This is the story of the hay wagon. "Your father was driving," says my mother, "at the speed he usually goes." We read between the lines: *too fast*. "You kids were in the back." I can remember this day, so I can remember how old I was, how old my brother was. We were old enough to think it was funny to annoy my father by singing popular songs of a type he disliked, such as "Mockingbird Hill"; or perhaps we were imitating bagpipe music by holding our noses and humming, while hitting our Adam's apples with the edges of our hands. When we became too irritating my father would say, "Pipe down." We weren't old enough to know that his irritation could be real: we thought it was part of the game.

"We were going down a steep hill," my mother continues, "when a hay wagon pulled out right across the road, at the bottom. Your father put on the brakes, but nothing happened. The brakes were gone! I thought our last moment had come." Luckily the hay wagon continued across the road, and we shot past it, missing it by at least a foot. "My heart was in my mouth," says my mother.

I didn't know until afterwards what had really happened. I was in the back seat, making bagpipe music, oblivious. The scenery was the same as it always was on car trips: my parents' heads, seen from behind, sticking up above the front seat. My father had his hat on, the one he wore to keep things from falling off the trees into his hair. My mother's hand was placed lightly on the back of his neck.

"You had such an acute sense of smell when you were younger," says my mother.

Now we are on more dangerous ground: my mother's childhood is one thing, my own quite another. This is the moment at which I start rattling the silverware, or ask for another cup of tea. "You used to march into houses that were strange to you, and you would say in a loud voice, 'What's that funny smell?'" If there are guests present, they shift a little away from me, conscious of their own emanations, trying not to look at my nose.

"I used to be so embarrassed," says my mother absentmindedly. Then she shifts gears. "You were such an easy child. You used to get up at six in the morning and play by yourself in the play room, singing away. . . ." There is a pause. A distant voice, mine, high and silvery, drifts over the space between us. "You used to talk a blue streak. Chatter, chatter, chatter, from morning to night." My mother sighs imperceptibly, as if wondering why I have become so silent, and gets up to poke the fire.

Hoping to change the subject, I ask whether or not the crocuses have come up yet, but she is not to be diverted. "I never had to spank you," she says. "A harsh word, and you would be completely reduced." She looks at me sideways; she isn't sure what I have turned into, or how. "There were just one or two times. Once, when I had to go out and I left your father in charge." (This may be the real point of the story: the inability of men to second-guess small children.) "I came back along the street, and there were you and your brother, throwing mud balls at an old man out of the upstairs window."

We both know whose idea this was. For my mother, the proper construction to be put on this event is that my brother was a hell-raiser and I was his shadow, "easily influenced," as my mother puts it. "You were just putty in his hands."

"Of course, I had to punish both of you equally," she says. Of course. I smile a forgiving smile. The real truth is that I was sneakier than my brother, and got caught less often. No front-line charges into enemy machine-gun nests for me, if they could be at all avoided. My own solitary acts of wickedness were devious and well concealed; it was only in partnership with my brother that I would throw caution to the winds.

"He could wind you around his little finger," says my mother. "Your father made each of you a toy box, and the rule was—" (my mother is good at the devising of rules) "—the rule was that neither of you could take the toys out of the other's toy box without permission. Otherwise he would have got all your toys away from you. But he got them anyway, mind you. He used to talk you into playing house, and he would pretend to be the baby.

Then he would pretend to cry, and when you asked what he wanted, he'd demand whatever it was out of your toy box that he wanted to play with at the moment. You always gave it to him."

I don't remember this, though I do remember staging World War Two on the living-room floor, with armies of stuffed bears and rabbits; but surely some primal patterns were laid down. Have these early toy-box experiences—and "toy box" itself, as a concept, reeks with implications—have they made me suspicious of men who wish to be mothered, yet susceptible to them at the same time? Have I been conditioned to believe that if I am not solicitous, if I am not forthcoming, if I am not a never-ending cornucopia of entertaining delights, they will take their collections of milk-bottle tops and their mangy one-eared teddy bears and go away into the woods by themselves to play snipers? Probably. What my mother thinks was merely cute may have been lethal.

But this is not her only story about my suckiness and gullibility. She follows up with the *coup de grâce*, the tale of the bunny-rabbit cookies.

"It was in Ottawa. I was invited to a government tea," says my mother, and this fact alone should signal an element of horror: my mother hated official functions, to which however she was obliged to go because she was the wife of a civil servant. "I had to drag you kids along; we couldn't afford a lot of babysitters in those days." The hostess had made a whole plateful of decorated cookies for whatever children might be present, and my mother proceeds to describe these: wonderful cookies shaped like bunny rabbits, with faces and clothes of coloured icing, little skirts for the little girl bunny rabbits, little pants for the little boy bunny rabbits.

"You chose one," says my mother. "You went off to a corner with it, by yourself. Mrs. X noticed you and went over. 'Aren't you going to eat your cookie?' she said. 'Oh, no,' you said. 'I'll just sit here and talk to it.' And there you sat, as happy as a clam. But someone had made the mistake of leaving the plate near your brother. When they looked again, there wasn't a single cookie left. He'd eaten every one. He was very sick that night, I can tell you."

Some of my mother's stories defy analysis. What is the moral of this one? That I was a simp is clear enough, but on the other hand it was my brother who got the stomach ache. Is it better to eat your food, in a straightforward materialistic way, and as much of it as possible, or go off into the corner and talk to it? This used to be a favourite of my mother's before I was married, when I would bring what my father referred to as "swains" home for dinner. Along with dessert, out would come the bunny-rabbit cookie story, and I would cringe and twiddle my spoon while my mother forged blithely on with it. What were the swains supposed to make of it? Were my kindliness and essential femininity being trotted out for their inspection? Were they being told in a roundabout way that I was harmless, that they could expect to be talked to by me, but not devoured? Or was she, in some way, warning them off? Because there is something faintly crazed about my behaviour, some tinge of the kind of person who might be expected to leap up suddenly from the dinner table and shout, "Don't eat that! It's alive!"

There is, however, a difference between symbolism and anecdote. Listening to my mother, I sometimes remember this.

"In my next incarnation," my mother said once, "I'm going to be an archaeologist and go around digging things up." We were sitting on the bed that had once been my brother's, then mine, then my sister's; we were sorting out things from one of the trunks, deciding what could now be given away or thrown out. My mother believes that what you save from the past is mostly a matter of choice.

At that time something wasn't right in the family; someone wasn't happy. My mother was angry: her good cheer was not paying off.

This statement of hers startled me. It was the first time I'd ever heard my mother say that she might have wanted to be something other than what she was. I must have been thirty-five at the time, but it was still shocking and slightly offensive to me to learn that my mother might not have been totally contented fulfilling the role in which fate had cast her: that of being my mother. What thumb-suckers we all are, I thought, when it comes to mothers.

Shortly after this I became a mother myself, and this moment altered me.

While she was combing my next-to-impossible hair, winding it around her long index finger, yanking out the snarls, my mother used to read me stories. Most of them are still in the house somewhere, but one has vanished. It may have been a library book. It was about a little girl who was so poor she had only one potato left for her supper, and while she was roasting it the potato got up and ran away. There was the usual chase, but I can't remember the ending: a significant lapse.

"That story was one of your favourites," says my mother. She is probably still under the impression that I identified with the little girl, with her hunger and her sense of loss; whereas in reality I identified with the potato.

Early influences are important. It took that one a while to come out; probably until after I went to university and started wearing black stockings and pulling my hair back into a bun, and having pretentions. Gloom set in. Our next-door neighbour, who was interested in wardrobes, tackled my mother: "'If she would only *do* something about herself,'" my mother quotes, "'she could be *quite attractive*.'"

"You always kept yourself busy," my mother says charitably, referring to this time. "You always had something cooking. Some project or other."

It is part of my mother's mythology that I am as cheerful and productive as she is, though she admits that these qualities may be occasionally and temporarily concealed. I wasn't allowed much angst around the house. I had to indulge it in the cellar, where my mother wouldn't come upon me brooding and suggest I should go out for a walk, to improve my circulation. This was her answer to any sign, however slight, of creeping despondency. There wasn't a lot that a brisk sprint through dead leaves, howling winds, or sleet couldn't cure.

It was, I knew, the *zeitgeist* that was afflicting me, and against it such simple remedies were powerless. Like smog I wafted through her days, dankness spreading out from around me. I read modern poetry and histories of Nazi atrocities, and took to drinking coffee. Off in the distance, my mother vacuumed around my feet while I sat in chairs, studying, with car rugs tucked around me, for suddenly I was always cold.

My mother has few stories to tell about these times. What I remember from them is the odd look I would sometimes catch in her eyes. It struck me, for the first time in my life, that my mother might be afraid of me. I could not even reassure her, because I was only dimly aware of the nature of her distress, but there must have been something going on in me that was beyond her: at any time I might open my mouth and out would come a language she had never heard before. I had become a visitant from outer space, a time-traveller come back from the future, bearing news of a great disaster.

Hurricane Hazel

The summer I was fourteen, we lived in a one-room cabin, on a hundred acres of back-concession scrub farmland. The cabin was surrounded by a stand of tall old maples, which had been left there when the land was cut over, and the light sifted down in shafts, like those in pictures I had seen in Sunday school, much earlier, of knights looking for the Holy Grail, helmets off, eyes rolled up purely. Probably these trees were the reason my parents had bought the land: if they hadn't, someone else would have bought it and sold off the maples. This was the kind of thing my parents were in the habit of doing.

The cabin was of squared timber. It hadn't been built there originally, but had been moved from some other location by the people who had owned it before us, two high-school teachers who were interested in antiques. The logs had been numbered, then dismantled and put back together in the original order, and the cracks had been re-chinked with white cement, which was already beginning to fall out in places; so was the putty on the small panes of the windows. I knew this because one of my first jobs had been to wash them. I did this grudgingly, as I did most jobs around the house at the time.

We slept on one side of the room. The sleeping areas were divided off by parachutes, which my father had bought at the war-surplus store, where he often bought things: khaki-coloured pants with pockets on the knees, knife, fork, and spoon sets which locked together and snapped apart and were impossible to eat with, rain

capes with camouflage markings on them, a jungle
hammock with mosquito-netting sides that smelled like
the inside of a work sock and gave you a kink in the back,
despite which my brother and I used to compete for the
privilege of sleeping in it. The parachutes had been cut
open and were hung like curtains from lengths of thick
wire strung from wall to wall. The parachutes inside the
house were dark green, but there was a smaller orange
one set up outside, like a tent, for my three-year-old
sister to play in.

I had the cubicle in the southeast corner. I slept there
on a narrow bed with wire coil springs that squeaked
whenever I turned over. On the other side of the cabin,
the living side, there was a table coated with ruined
varnish and a couple of much-painted chairs, the paint
now cracked like a dried mud flat so that you could see
what colours had been used before. There was a dresser
with plates in it, which smelled even mustier than the
rest of the things in the cabin, and a couple of rocking
chairs, which didn't work too well on the uneven boards
of the floor. All this furniture had been in the cabin when
we bought it; perhaps it was the schoolteachers' idea of
pioneer décor.

There was also a sort of counter where my mother
washed the dishes and kept the primus stove she cooked
on when it was raining. The rest of the time she cooked
outdoors, on a fireplace with a grate of iron rods. When
we ate outside we didn't use chairs: instead we sat on
rounds of logs, because the ground itself was damp. The
cabin was in a river valley; at night there was heavy dew,
and the heat of the morning sunlight made an almost
visible steam.

My father had moved us into the cabin early in the
summer. Then he'd taken off for the forests on the north
shore of the St. Lawrence, where he was doing some
exploration for a pulp-and-paper company. All the time
we were going through our daily routine, which re-
volved mainly around mealtimes and what we would eat

at them, he was flying in bush planes into valleys with sides so steep the pilot had to cut the engine to get down into them, or trudging over portages past great rocky outcrops, or almost upsetting in rapids. For two weeks he was trapped by a forest fire which encircled him on all sides, and was saved only by torrential rains, during which he sat in his tent and toasted his extra socks at the fire, like weiners, to get them dry. These were the kinds of stories we heard after he came back.

My father made sure before he went that we had a supply of split and stacked wood and enough staples and tinned goods to keep us going. When we needed other things, such as milk and butter, I was sent on foot to the nearest store, which was a mile and a half away, at the top of an almost perpendicular hill which, much later, got turned into a ski resort. At that time there was only a dirt road, in the middle of what I thought of as nowhere, which let loose clouds of dust every time a car went past. Sometimes the cars would honk, and I would pretend not to notice.

The woman at the store, who was fat and always damp, was curious about us; she would ask how my mother was getting along. Didn't she mind it, all alone in that tumbledown place with no proper stove and no man around? She put the two things on the same level. I resented that kind of prying, but I was at the age when anybody's opinion mattered to me, and I could see that she thought my mother was strange.

If my mother had any reservations about being left alone on a remote farm with a three-year-old, no telephone, no car, no electricity, and only me for help, she didn't state them. She had been in such situations before, and by that time she must have been used to them. Whatever was going on she treated as normal; in the middle of crises, such as cars stuck up to their axles in mud, she would suggest we sing a song.

That summer she probably missed my father, though she would never say so; conversations in our family were not about feelings. Sometimes, in the evenings, she would write letters, though she claimed she could never think of what to say. During the days, when she wasn't cooking or washing the dishes, she did small tasks which could be interrupted at any time. She would cut the grass, even though the irregular plot in front of the house was overgrown with weeds and nothing would make it look any more like a lawn; or she would pick up the fallen branches under the maple trees.

I looked after my little sister for part of the mornings: that was one of my jobs. At these times my mother would sometimes drag a rocking chair out onto the bumpy grass and read books, novels of historical times or accounts of archaeological expeditions. If I came up behind her and spoke to her while she was reading, she would scream. When it was sunny she would put on shorts, which she would never wear when other people were around. She thought she had bony knees; this was the only thing about her personal appearance that she showed much awareness about. For the most part she was indifferent to clothes. She wanted them to cover what they were supposed to cover and to stay in one piece, and that was all she expected from them.

When I wasn't taking care of my sister, I would go off by myself. I would climb one of the maples, which was out of sight of the house and had a comfortable fork in it, and read *Wuthering Heights;* or I would walk along the old logging road, now grown up in saplings. I knew my way around in the weedy and brambly jungle back there, and I'd been across the river to the open field on the other side, where the next-door farmer was allowed to graze his cows, to keep down the thistles and burdock. This was where I'd found what I thought was the pioneers' house, the real one, though it was nothing now but a square depression surrounded by grass-covered ridges. The first year, this man had planted a bushel of peas, and

he'd harvested a bushel. We knew this from the
schoolteachers, who looked up records.

If my brother had made this discovery, he would have
drawn a map of it. He would have drawn a map of the
whole area, with everything neatly labelled. I didn't
even attempt this; instead, I merely wandered around,
picking raspberries and thimbleberries, or sunning myself in the tall weeds, surrounded by the smell of
milkweed and daisies and crushed leaves, made dizzy by
the sun and the light reflected from the white pages of
my book, with grasshoppers landing on me and leaving
traces of their brown spit.

Towards my mother I was surly, though by myself I
was lazy and aimless. It was hard even to walk through
the grass, and lifting my hand to brush away the
grasshoppers was an effort. I seemed always to be half
asleep. I told myself that I wanted to be doing something; by that I meant something that would earn money,
elsewhere. I wanted a summer job, but I was too young
for one.

My brother had a job. He was two years older than I
was, and now he was a Junior Ranger, cutting brush by
the sides of highways somewhere in northern Ontario,
living in tents with a batch of other sixteen-year-old
boys. This was his first summer away. I resented his
absence and envied him, but I also looked for his letters
every day. The mail was delivered by a woman who lived
on a nearby farm; she drove it around in her own car.
When there was something for us she would toot her
horn, and I would walk out to the dusty galvanized
mailbox that stood on a post beside our gate.

My brother wrote letters to my mother as well as to
me. Those to her were informative, descriptive, factual.
He said what he was doing, what they ate, where they
did their laundry. He said that the town near their camp
had a main street that was held up only by the telephone

wires. My mother was pleased by these letters, and read them out loud to me.

I did not read my brother's letters out loud to her. They were private, and filled with the sort of hilarious and vulgar commentary that we often indulged in when we were alone. To other people we seemed grave and attentive, but by ourselves we made fun of things relentlessly, outdoing each other with what we considered to be revolting details. My brother's letters were illustrated with drawings of his tent-mates, showing them with many-legged bugs jumping around on their heads, with spots on their faces, with wavy lines indicating smelliness radiating from their feet, with apple cores in the beards they were all attempting to grow. He included unsavoury details of their personal habits, such as snoring. I took these letters straight from the mailbox to the maple tree, where I read them over several times. Then I smuggled them into the cabin under my T-shirt and hid them under my bed.

I got other letters too, from my boyfriend, whose name was Buddy. My brother used a fountain pen; Buddy's letters were in blue ball-point, the kind that splotched, leaving greasy blobs that came off on my fingers. They contained ponderous compliments, like those made by other people's uncles. Many words were enclosed by quotation marks; others were underlined. There were no pictures.

I liked getting these letters from Buddy, but also they embarrassed me. The trouble was that I knew what my brother would say about Buddy, partly because he had already said some of it. He spoke as if both he and I took it for granted that I would soon be getting rid of Buddy, as if Buddy were a stray dog it would be my duty to send to the Humane Society if the owner could not be found. Even Buddy's name, my brother said, was like a dog's. He said I should call Buddy "Pal" or "Sport" and teach him to fetch.

I found my brother's way of speaking about Buddy

both funny and cruel: funny because it was in some ways accurate, cruel for the same reason. It was true that there was something dog-like about Buddy: the affability, the dumb faithfulness about the eyes, the dutiful way he plodded through the rituals of dating. He was the kind of boy (though I never knew this with certainty, because I never saw it) who would help his mother carry in the groceries without being asked, not because he felt like it but simply because it was prescribed. He said things like, "That's the way the cookie crumbles," and when he said this I had the feeling he would still be saying it forty years later.

Buddy was a lot older than I was. He was eighteen, almost nineteen, and he'd quit school long ago to work at a garage. He had his own car, a third-hand Dodge, which he kept spotlessly clean and shining. He smoked and drank beer, though he drank the beer only when he wasn't out with me but was with other boys his own age. He would mention how many bottles he had drunk in an offhand way, as if disclaiming praise.

He made me anxious, because I didn't know how to talk to him. Our phone conversations consisted mostly of pauses and monosyllables, though they went on a long time; which was infuriating to my father, who would walk past me in the hall, snapping his first two fingers together like a pair of scissors, meaning I was to cut it short. But cutting short a conversation with Buddy was like trying to divide water, because Buddy's conversations had no shape, and I couldn't give them a shape myself. I hadn't yet learned any of those stratagems girls were supposed to use on men. I didn't know how to ask leading questions, or how to lie about certain kinds of things, which I was later to call being tactful. So mostly I said nothing, which didn't seem to bother Buddy at all.

I knew enough to realize, however, that it was a bad tactic to appear too smart. But if I had chosen to show off, Buddy might not have minded: he was the kind of boy for whom cleverness was female. Maybe he would have liked a controlled display of it, as if it were a special kind of pie or a piece of well-done embroidery. But I never figured out what Buddy really wanted; I never figured out why Buddy was going out with me in the first place. Possibly it was because I was there. Buddy's world, I gradually discovered, was much less alterable than mine: it contained a long list of things that could never be changed or fixed.

All of this started at the beginning of May, when I was in grade ten. I was two or three years younger than most of the others in my class, because at that time they still believed in skipping you ahead if you could do the work. The year before, when I'd entered high school, I had been twelve, which was a liability when other people were fifteen. I rode my bicycle to school when other girls in my class were walking, slowly, langorously, holding their notebooks up against their bodies to protect and display their breasts. I had no breasts; I could still wear things I'd worn when I was eleven. I took to sewing my own clothes, out of patterns I bought at Eaton's. The clothes never came out looking like the pictures on the pattern envelopes; also they were too big. I must have been making them the size I wanted to be. My mother told me these clothes looked very nice on me, which was untrue and no help at all. I felt like a flat-chested midget, surrounded as I was by girls who were already oily and glandular, who shaved their legs and put pink medicated makeup on their pimples and fainted interestingly during gym, whose flesh was sleek and plumped-out and faintly shining, as if it had been injected under the skin with cream.

The boys were even more alarming. Some of them, the ones who were doing grade nine for the second time, wore leather jackets and were thought to have bicycle chains in their lockers. A few of them were high-voiced and spindly, but these of course I ignored. I knew the difference between someone who was a drip or a pill, on the one hand, and cute or a dream on the other. Buddy wasn't a dream, but he was cute, and that counted for a lot. Once I started going out with Buddy, I found I could pass for normal. I was now included in the kinds of conversations girls had in the washroom while they were putting on their lipstick. I was now teased.

Despite this, I knew that Buddy was a kind of accident: I hadn't come by him honestly. He had been handed over to me by Trish, who had come up to me out of nowhere and asked me to go out with her and her boyfriend Charlie and Charlie's cousin. Trish had a large mouth and prominent teeth and long sandy hair, which she tied back in a pony tail. She wore fuzzy pink sweaters and was a cheerleader, though not the best one. If she hadn't been going steady with Charlie, she would have had a reputation, because of the way she laughed and wiggled; as it was, she was safe enough for the time being. Trish told me I would like Buddy because he was so cute. She also mentioned that he had a car; Charlie didn't have a car. It's likely that I was put into Buddy's life by Trish so that Trish and Charlie could neck in the back seat of Buddy's car at drive-in movies, but I doubt that Buddy knew this. Neither did I, at the time.

We always had to go to the early show—a source of grumbling from Trish and Charlie—because I wasn't allowed to stay out past eleven. My father didn't object to my having boyfriends, as such, but he wanted them to be prompt in their pick-up and delivery. He didn't see why they had to moon around outside the front door when they were dropping me off. Buddy wasn't as bad in this respect as some of the later ones, in my father's opinion. With those, I got into the habit of coming in after the deadline, and my father would sit me down and explain very patiently that if I was on my way to catch a train and I was late for it, the train would go without me, and that was why I should always be in on time. This cut no ice with me at all, since, as I would point out, our house wasn't a train. It must have been then that I began to lose faith in reasonable argument as the sole measure of truth. My mother's rationale for promptness was more understandable: if I wasn't home on time, she would think I had been in a car accident. We knew without admitting it that sex was the hidden agenda at these discussions, more hidden for my father than for my mother: she knew about cars and accidents.

At the drive-in Buddy and Charlie would buy popcorn and Cokes, and we would all munch in unison as the pale shadowy figures materialized on the screen, bluish in the diminishing light. By the time the popcorn was gone it would be dark. There would be rustlings, creakings, suppressed moans from the back seat, which Buddy and I would pretend to ignore. Buddy would smoke a few cigarettes, one arm around my shoulders. After that we would neck, decorously enough compared with what was going on behind us.

Buddy's mouth was soft, his body large and comforting. I didn't know what I was supposed to feel during these sessions. Whatever I did feel was not very erotic, though it wasn't unpleasant either. It was more like being hugged by a friendly Newfoundland dog or an animated quilt than anything else. I kept my knees pressed together and my arms around his back. Sooner or later Buddy would attempt to move his hands around to the front, but I knew I was supposed to stop him, so I did. Judging from his reaction, which was resigned but good-natured, this was the correct thing to do, though he would always try again the next week.

It occurred to me very much later that Trish had selected me, not despite the fact that I was younger and less experienced than she was, but because of it. She needed a chaperone. Charlie was thinner than Buddy, better-looking, more intense; he got drunk sometimes, said Trish, with an already matronly shake of her head. Buddy was seen as solid, dependable, and a little slow, and so perhaps was I.

After I had been going out with Buddy for a month or so, my brother decided it would be in my own best interests to learn Greek. By that he meant he would teach it to me whether I liked it or not. In the past he had taught me many things, some of which I had wanted to know: how to read, how to shoot with a bow, how to skip flat rocks, how to swim, how to play chess, how to aim a rifle, how to paddle a canoe and scale and gut a fish. I hadn't learned many of them very well, except the reading. He had also taught me how to swear, sneak out of bedroom windows at night, make horrible smells with chemicals, and burp at will. His manner, whatever the subject, was always benignly but somewhat distantly pedagogical, as if I were a whole classroom by myself.

The Greek was something he himself was learning; he was two grades ahead of me and was at a different high school, one that was only for boys. He started me with the alphabet. As usual, I didn't learn fast enough for him, so he began leaving notes about the house, with Greek letters substituted for the letters of the English words. I would find one in the bathtub when I was about to take a bath before going out with Buddy, set it aside for later, turn on the tap and find myself drenched by the shower. (*Turn off the shower*, the note would read when translated.) Or there would be a message taped to the closed door of my room, which would turn out to be a warning about what would fall on me—a wet towel, a clump of cooked spaghetti—when I opened it. Or one on my dresser would announce a Frenched bed or inform me that my alarm clock was set to go off at 3 A.M. I didn't ever learn much real Greek, but I did learn to transpose quickly. It was by such ruses, perhaps, that my brother

was seeking to head me off, delay my departure from the
world he still inhabited, a world in which hydrogen
sulphide and chess gambits were still more interesting
than sex, and Buddy, and the Buddies to come, were still
safely and merely ridiculous.

My brother and Buddy existed on different layers
altogether. My brother, for instance, was neither cute
nor a pill. Instead he had the preternatural good looks
associated with English schoolboys, the kind who turned
out to be pyromaniacs in films of the sixties, or with
posters of soldiers painted at the time of World War One;
he looked as if he ought to have green skin and slightly
pointed ears, as if his name should have been Nemo, or
something like it; as if he could see through you. All of
these things I thought later; at the time he was just my
brother, and I didn't have any ideas about how he
looked. He had a maroon sweater with holes in the
elbows, which my mother kept trying to replace or
throw out, but she was never successful. He took her
lack of interest in clothes one step further.

Whenever I started to talk like what he thought of as a
teenager, whenever I mentioned sock hops or the hit
parade, or anything remotely similar, my brother would
quote passages out of the blackhead-remover ads in his
old comic books, the ones he'd collected when he was
ten or eleven: "Mary never knew why she was not
POPULAR, until. . . . Someone should tell her! Mary,
NOW there's something you can do about those UGLY
BLACKHEADS! *Later*. . . . Mary, I'd like to ask you to
the dance. (*Thinks*: Now that Mary's got rid of those UGLY
BLACKHEADS, she's the most POPULAR girl in the class.)" I
knew that if I ever became the most popular girl in the
class, which was not likely, I would get no points at all
from my brother.

When I told Buddy I would be away for the summer, he
thought I was "going to the cottage," which was what a

lot of people in Toronto did; those who had cottages, that is. What he had in mind was something like Lake Simcoe, where you could ride around in fast motorboats and maybe go water-skiing, and where there would be a drive-in. He thought there would be other boys around; he said I would go out with them and forget all about him, but he said it as a joke.

I was vague about where I was actually going. Buddy and I hadn't talked about our families much; it wouldn't be easy to explain to him my parents' preferences for solitude and outhouses and other odd things. When he said he would come up and visit me, I told him it was too far away, too difficult to find. But I couldn't refuse to give him the address, and his letters arrived faithfully every week, smeared and blobby, the handwriting round and laborious and child-like. Buddy pressed so hard the pen sometimes went through, and if I closed my eyes and ran my fingers over the paper I could feel the letters engraved on the page like braille.

I answered Buddy's first letter sitting at the uneven table with its cracked geological surface. The air was damp and warm; the pad of lined paper I was writing on was sticking to the tacky varnish. My mother was doing the dishes, in the enamel dishpan, by the light of one of the oil lamps. Usually I helped her, but ever since Buddy had appeared on the scene she'd been letting me off more frequently, as if she felt I needed the energy for other things. I had the second oil lamp, turned up as high as it would go without smoking. From behind the green parachute curtain I could hear the light breathing of my sister.

Dear Buddy, I wrote, and stopped. Writing his name embarrassed me. When you saw it on a blank sheet of paper like that, it seemed a strange thing to call someone. Buddy's name bore no relation to what I could really remember of him, which was mostly the smell of his freshly washed T-shirts, mixed with the smell of cigarette smoke and Old Spice aftershave. *Buddy*. As a word, it reminded me of *pudding*. I could feel under my hand the little roll of fat at the back of his neck, hardly noticeable now, but it would get larger, later, when he was not even that much older.

My mother's back was towards me but I felt as if she were watching me anyway; or listening, perhaps, to the absence of sound, because I wasn't writing. I couldn't think of what to say to Buddy. I could describe what I'd been doing, but as soon as I began I saw how hopeless this would be.

In the morning I'd made a village out of sand, down on the one small available sandbar, to amuse my sister. I was good at these villages. Each house had stone windows; the roads were paved with stone also, and trees and flowers grew in the gardens, which were surrounded by hedges of moss. When the villages were finished, my sister would play with them, running her toy cars along the roads and moving the stick people I'd made for her, in effect ruining them, which annoyed me.

When I could get away, I'd waded down the river by myself, to be out of range. There was a seam of clay I already knew about, and I'd gouged a chunk out of it and spent some time making it into beads, leaving them on a stump in the sun to harden. Some of them were in the shape of skulls, and I intended to paint these later and string them into a necklace. I had some notion that they would form part of a costume for Hallowe'en, though at the same time I knew I was already too old for this.

Then I'd walked back along the river bank, climbing over the tangles of fallen trees that blocked the way, scratching my bare legs on the brambles. I'd picked a few flowers, as a peace offering to my mother, who must have known I'd deserted her on purpose. These were now wilting in a jam jar on the dresser: bladder campion, jewelweed, Queen Anne's Lace. In our family you were supposed to know the names of the things you picked and put in jars.

Nothing I did seemed normal in the light of Buddy; spelled out, my activities looked childish or absurd. What did other girls the age people thought I was do when they weren't with boys? They talked on the telephone, they listened to records; wasn't that it? They went to movies, they washed their hair. But they didn't wash their hair by standing up to their knees in an ice-cold river and pouring water over their heads from an enamel basin. I didn't wish to appear eccentric to Buddy; I wished to disguise myself. This had been easier in the city, where we lived in a more ordinary way: such things as my parents' refusal to buy a television set and sit in front of it eating their dinners off fold-up trays, and their failure to acquire an indoor clothes dryer, were minor digressions that took place behind the scenes.

In the end I wrote to Buddy about the weather, and said I missed him and hoped I would see him soon. After studying the blotchy X's and O's, much underlined, which came after Buddy's signature, I imitated them. I sealed this forgery and addressed it, and the next morning I walked out to the main road and put it in our loaf-shaped mailbox, raising the little flag to show there was a letter.

Buddy arrived unannounced one Sunday morning in August, after we had done the dishes. I don't know how he found out where we lived. He must have asked at the crossroads where there were a few houses, a gas station, and a general store with Coca-Cola ads on the screen door and a post office at the back. The people there would have been able to help Buddy decipher the rural-route number; probably they knew anyway exactly where we were.

My mother was in her shorts, in front of the house, cutting the grass and weeds with a small scythe. I was carrying a pail of water up the slippery and decaying wooden steps from the river. I knew that when I got to the top of the steps my mother would ask me what I wanted for lunch, which would drive me mad with irritation. I never knew what I wanted for lunch, and if I did know there was never any of it. It didn't occur to me then that my mother was even more bored with mealtimes than I was, since she had to do the actual cooking, or that her question might have been a request for help.

Then we heard a noise, a roaring motor noise, exaggerated but muffled too, like a gas lawnmower inside a tin garage. We both stopped dead in our tracks and looked at one another; we had a way of doing that whenever we heard any machine-made sound out on the main road. We believed, I think, that nobody knew we were there. The good part of this was that nobody would come in, but the bad part was that somebody might, thinking our place uninhabited, and the sort of people who would try it would be the sort we would least want to see.

The noise stopped for a few minutes; then it started up again, louder this time. It was coming in, along our road. My mother dropped her scythe and ran into the house. I knew she was going to change out of her shorts. I continued stolidly up the steps, carrying the pail of water. If I'd known it was Buddy I would have brushed my hair and put on lipstick.

When I saw Buddy's car, I was surprised and almost horrified. I felt I had been caught out. What would Buddy think of the decaying cabin, the parachute curtains, the decrepit furniture, the jam jar with its drooping flowers? My first idea was to keep him out of the house, at least. I went to meet the car, which was floundering over the road towards me. I was conscious of the dead leaves and dirt sticking to my wet bare feet.

Buddy got out of the car and looked up at the trees. Charlie and Trish, who were in the back seat, got out too. They gazed around, but after one quick look they gave no indication that they thought this place where I was living was hardly what they had expected; except that they talked too loudly. I knew though that I was on the defensive.

Buddy's car had a big hole in the muffler, which he hadn't had time to fix yet, and Charlie and Trish were full of stories about the annoyed looks people in the back-roads villages had given them as they'd roared through. Buddy was more reserved, almost shy. "You got my letter, eh?" he said, but I hadn't, not the one that announced this visit. That letter arrived several days later, filled with a wistful loneliness it would have been handy to have known about in advance.

Charlie and Trish and Buddy wanted to go on a picnic. It was their idea that we would drive over to Pike Lake, about fifteen miles away, where there was a public beach. They thought we could go swimming. My mother had come out by this time. Now that she had her slacks on she was behaving as if everything was under control. She agreed to this plan; she knew there was nothing for them to do around our place. She didn't seem to mind my going off with Buddy for a whole day, because we would be back before dark.

The three of them stood around the car; my mother tried to make conversation with them while I ran to the cabin to get my swimsuit and a towel. Trish already had her swimsuit on; I'd seen the top of it under her shirt. Maybe there would be no place to change. This was the kind of thing you couldn't ask about without feeling like a fool, so I changed in my cubicle of parachute silk. My suit was left over from last year; it was red, and a little too small.

My mother, who didn't usually give instructions, told Buddy to drive carefully; probably because the noise made his car sound a lot more dangerous than it was. When he started up it was like a rocket taking off, and it was even worse inside. I sat in the front seat beside

Buddy. All the windows were rolled down, and when we reached the paved highway Buddy stuck his left elbow out the window. He held the steering wheel with one hand, and with the other he reached across the seat and took hold of my hand. He wanted me to move over so I was next to him and he could put his arm around me, but I was nervous about the driving. He gave me a reproachful look and put his hand back on the wheel.

I had seen road signs pointing to Pike Lake before but I had never actually been there. It turned out to be small and round, with flattish countryside around it. The public beach was crowded, because it was a weekend: teenagers in groups and young couples with children mostly. Some people had portable radios. Trish and I changed behind the car, even though we were only taking off our outer clothes to reveal our bathing suits, which everybody was going to see anyway. While we were doing this, Trish told me that she and Charlie were now secretly engaged. They were going to get married as soon as she was old enough. No one was supposed to know, except Buddy of course, and me. She said her parents would have kittens if they found out. I promised not to tell; at the same time, I felt a cold finger travelling down my spine. When we came out from behind the car, Buddy and Charlie were already standing up to their ankles in the water, the sun reflecting from their white backs.

The beach was dusty and hot, with trash from picnickers left here and there about it: paper plates showing half-moons above the sand, dented paper cups, bottles. Part of a hot-dog weiner floated near where we waded in, pallid, greyish-pink, lost-looking. The lake was shallow and weedy, the water the temperature of cooling soup. The bottom was of sand so fine-grained it was almost mud; I expected leeches in it, and clams, which would probably be dead, because of the warmth. I swam out into it anyway. Trish was screaming because she had walked into some water weeds; then she was splashing Charlie. I felt that I ought to be doing these things too, and that Buddy would note the omission. But instead I floated on my back in the lukewarm water, squinting up at the cloudless sky, which was depthless and hot blue and had things like microbes drifting across it, which I knew were the rods and cones in my eyeballs. I had skipped ahead in the health book; I even knew what a zygote was. In a while Buddy swam out to join me and spurted water at me out of his mouth, grinning.

After that we swam back to the beach and lay down on Trish's oversized pink beach towel, which had a picture of a mermaid tossing a bubble on it. I felt sticky, as if the water had left a film on me. Trish and Charlie were nowhere to be seen; at last I spotted them, walking hand in hand near the water at the far end of the beach. Buddy wanted me to rub some suntan lotion onto him. He wasn't tanned at all, except for his face and his hands and forearms, and I remembered that he worked all week and didn't have time to lie around in the sun the way I did. The skin of his back was soft and slightly loose over the muscles, like a sweater or a puppy's neck.

When I lay back down beside him, Buddy took hold of my hand, even though it was greasy with the suntan lotion. "How about Charlie, eh?" he said, shaking his head in mock disapproval, as if Charlie had been naughty or stupid. He didn't say Charlie and Trish. He put his arm over me and started to kiss me, right on the beach, in the full sunlight, in front of everyone. I pulled back.

"There's people watching," I said.

"Want me to put the towel over your head?" he said.

I sat up, brushing sand off me and tugging up the front of my bathing suit. I brushed some sand off Buddy too: his stuck worse because of the lotion. My back felt parched and I was dizzy from the heat and brightness. Later, I knew, I would get a headache.

"Where's the lunch?" I said.

"Who's hungry?" he said. "Not for food, anyways." But

he didn't seem annoyed. Maybe this was the way I was supposed to behave.

I walked to the car and got out the lunch, which was in a brown paper bag, and we sat on Trish's towel and ate egg-salad sandwiches and drank warm fizzy Coke, in silence. When we had finished, I said I wanted to go and sit under a tree. Buddy came with me, bringing the towel. He shook it before we sat down.

"You don't want ants in your pants," he said. He lit a cigarette and smoked half of it, leaning against the tree trunk—an elm, I noticed—and looking at me in an odd way, as if he was making up his mind about something. Then he said, "I want you to have something." His voice was offhand, affable, the way it usually was; his eyes weren't. On the whole he looked frightened. He undid the silver bracelet from his wrist. It had always been there, and I knew what was written on it: *Buddy*, engraved in flowing script. It was an imitation army I.D. tag; a lot of the boys wore them.

"My identity bracelet," he said.

"Oh," I said as he slid it over my hand, which now, I could tell, smelled of onions. I ran my fingers over Buddy's silver name as if admiring it. I had no thought of refusing it; that would have been impossible, because I would never have been able to explain what was wrong with taking it. Also I felt that Buddy had something on me: that, now he had accidentally seen something about me that was real, he knew too much about my deviations from the norm. I felt I had to correct that somehow. It occurred to me, years later, that many women probably had become engaged and even married this way.

It was years later too that I realized Buddy had used the wrong word: it wasn't an identity bracelet, it was an identification bracelet. The difference escaped me at the time. But maybe it was the right word after all, and what Buddy was handing over to me was his identity, some key part of himself that I was expected to keep for him and watch over.

Another interpretation has since become possible: that Buddy was putting his name on me, like a *Reserved* sign or an ownership label, or a tattoo on a cow's ear, or a brand. But at the time nobody thought that way. Everyone knew that getting a boy's I.D. bracelet was a privilege, not a degradation, and this is how Trish greeted it when she came back from her walk with Charlie. She spotted the transfer instantly.

"Let's *see*," she said, as if she hadn't seen this ornament of Buddy's many times before, and I had to hold out my wrist for her to admire, while Buddy looked sheepishly on.

When I was back at the log house, I took off Buddy's identification bracelet and hid it under the bed. I was embarrassed by it, though the reason I gave myself was that I didn't want it to get lost. I put it on again in September though, when I went back to the city and back to school. It was the equivalent of a white fur sweater-collar, the kind with pom-poms. Buddy, among other things, was something to wear.

I was in grade eleven now, and studying Ancient Egypt and *The Mill on the Floss*. I was on the volleyball team; I sang in the choir. Buddy was still working at the garage, and shortly after school began he got a hernia, from lifting something too heavy. I didn't know what a hernia was. I thought it might be something sexual, but at the same time it had the sound of something that happened to old men, not to someone as young as Buddy. I looked it up in our medical book. When my brother heard about Buddy's hernia, he sniggered in an irritating way and said it was the kind of thing you could expect from Buddy.

Buddy was in a hospital for a couple of days. After that I went to visit him at home, because he wanted me to. I felt I should take him something; not flowers though. So I took him some peanut-butter cookies, baked by my

mother. I knew, if the subject came up, that I would lie
and say I had made them myself.

This was the first time I had ever been to Buddy's
house. I hadn't even known where he lived; I hadn't
thought of him as having a house at all or living
anywhere in particular. I had to get there by bus and
streetcar, since of course Buddy couldn't drive me.

It was Indian summer; the air was thick and damp,
though there was a breeze that helped some. I walked
along the street, which was lined with narrow, two-
storey row houses, the kind that would much later be
renovated and become fashionable, though at that time
they were considered merely old-fashioned and inconve-
nient. It was a Saturday afternoon, and a couple of the
men were mowing their cramped lawns, one of them in
his undershirt.

The front door of Buddy's house was wide open; only
the screen door was closed. I rang the doorbell; when
nothing happened, I went in. There was a note, in
Buddy's blotchy blue ball-point writing, lying on the
floor: COME ON UP, it said. It must have fallen down from
where it had been taped to the inside of the door.

The hallway had faded pink rose-trellis paper; the
house smelled faintly of humid wood, polish, rugs in
summer. I peered into the living room as I went towards
the stairs: there was too much furniture in it and the
curtains were drawn, but it was immaculately clean. I
could tell that Buddy's mother had different ideas about
housework than my mother had. Nobody seemed to be
home, and I wondered if Buddy had arranged it this way
on purpose, so I wouldn't run into his mother.

I climbed the stairs; in the mirror at the top I was
coming to meet myself. In the dim light I seemed older,
my flesh plumped and flushed by the heat, my eyes in
shadow.

"Is that you?" Buddy called to me. He was in the front
bedroom, lying propped up in a bed that was much too
large for the room. The bed was of chocolate-coloured

varnished wood, the head and foot carved; it was this bed, huge, outmoded, ceremonial, that made me more nervous than anything else in the room, including Buddy. The window was open, and the white lace-edged curtains—of a kind my mother never would have considered, because of the way they would have to be bleached, starched, and ironed—shifted a little in the air. The sound of the lawn-mowers came in through the window.

I hesitated in the doorway, smiled, went in. Buddy was wearing a white T-shirt, and had just the sheet over him, pulled up to his waist. He looked softer, shorter, a little shrunken. He smiled back at me and held out his hand.

"I brought you some cookies," I said. We were both shy, because of the silence and emptiness. I took hold of his hand and he pulled me gently towards him. The bed was so high that I had to climb half onto it. I set the bag of cookies down beside him and put my arms around his neck. His skin smelled of cigarette smoke and soap, and his hair was neatly combed and still a little wet. His mouth tasted of toothpaste. I thought of him hobbling around, in pain maybe, getting ready for me. I had never thought a great deal about boys getting themselves ready for girls, cleaning themselves, looking at themselves in bathroom mirrors, waiting, being anxious, wanting to please. I realized now that they did this, that it wasn't only the other way around. I opened my eyes and looked at Buddy as I was kissing him. I had never done this before, either. Buddy with his eyes closed was different, and stranger, than Buddy with his eyes open. He looked asleep, and as if he was having a troublesome dream.

This was the most I had ever kissed him. It was safe enough: he was wounded. When he groaned a little I thought it was because I was hurting him. "Careful," he said, moving me to one side.

I stopped kissing him and put my face down on his shoulder, against his neck. I could see the dresser, which matched the bed; it had a white crocheted runner on it, and some baby pictures in silver stands. Over it was a mirror, in a sombre frame with a carved festoon of roses, and inside the frame there was Buddy, with me lying beside him. I thought this must be the bedroom of Buddy's parents, and their bed. There was something sad about lying there with Buddy in the cramped formal room with its heavy prettiness, its gaiety which was both ornate and dark. This room was almost foreign to me; it was a celebration of something I could not identify with and would never be able to share. It would not take very much to make Buddy happy, ever: only something like this. This was what he was expecting of me, this not very much, and it was a lot more than I had. This was the most afraid I ever got, of Buddy.

"Hey," said Buddy. "Cheer up, eh? Everything still works okay." He thought I was worried about his injury.

After that we found that I had rolled on the bag of cookies and crushed them into bits, and that made everything safer, because we could laugh. But when it was time for me to go, Buddy became wistful. He held onto my hand. "What if I won't let you go?" he said.

When I was walking back towards the streetcar stop, I saw a woman coming towards me, carrying a big brown leather purse and a paper bag. She had a muscular and determined face, the face of a woman who has had to fight, something or other, in some way or another, for a long time. She looked at me as if she thought I was up to no good, and I became conscious of the creases in my cotton dress, from where I had been lying on the bed with Buddy. I thought she might be Buddy's mother.

Buddy got better quite soon. In the weeks after that, he ceased to be an indulgence or even a joke, and became instead an obligation. We continued to go out, on the same nights as we always had, but there was an edginess about Buddy that hadn't been there before. Sometimes

Trish and Charlie went with us, but they no longer necked extravagantly in the back seat. Instead they held hands and talked together in low voices about things that sounded serious and even gloomy, such as the prices of apartments. Trish had started to collect china. But Charlie had his own car now, and more and more frequently Buddy and I were alone, no longer protected. Buddy's breathing became heavier and he no longer smiled good-naturedly when I took hold of his hands to stop him. He was tired of me being fourteen.

I began to forget about Buddy when I wasn't with him. The forgetting was deliberate: it was the same as remembering, only in reverse. Instead of talking to Buddy for hours on the phone, I spent a lot of time making dolls' clothes for my little sister's dolls. When I wasn't doing that, I read through my brother's collection of comic books, long since discarded by him, lying on the floor of my room with my feet up on the bed. My brother was no longer teaching me Greek. He had gone right off the deep end, into trigonometry, which we both knew I would never learn no matter what.

Buddy ended on a night in October, suddenly, like a light being switched off. I was supposed to be going out with him, but at the dinner table my father said that I should reconsider: Toronto was about to be hit by a major storm, a hurricane, with torrential rain and gale-force winds, and he didn't think I should be out in it, especially in a car like Buddy's. It was already dark: the rain was pelting against the windows behind our drawn curtains, and the wind was up and roaring like breakers in the ash trees outside. I could feel our house growing smaller. My mother said she would get out some candles, in case the electricity failed. Luckily, she said, we were on high ground. My father said that it was my decision, of course, but anyone who would go out on a night like this would have to be crazy.

Buddy phoned to see when he should pick me up. I said that the weather was getting bad, and maybe we should go out the next night. Buddy said why be afraid of a little rain? He wanted to see me. I said I wanted to see him, too, but maybe it was too dangerous. Buddy said I was just making excuses. I said I wasn't.

My father walked past me along the hall, snapping his fingers together like a pair of scissors. I said anyone who would go out on a night like this would have to be crazy, Buddy could turn on the radio and hear for himself, we were having a hurricane, but Buddy sounded as if he didn't really know what that meant. He said if I wouldn't go out with him during a hurricane I didn't love him enough. I was shocked: this was the first time he had ever used the word *love*, out loud and not just at the ends of letters, to describe what we were supposed to be doing. When I told him he was being stupid he hung up on me, which made me angry. But he was right, of course. I didn't love him enough.

Instead of going out with Buddy, I stayed home and played a game of chess with my brother, who won, as he always did. I was never a very good chess player: I couldn't stand the silent waiting. There was a feeling of reunion about this game, which would not, however, last long. Buddy was gone, but he had been a symptom.

This was the first of a long series of atmospherically supercharged break-ups with men, though I didn't realize it at the time. Blizzards, thunderstorms, heat waves, hailstorms: I later broke up in all of them. I'm not sure what it was. Possibly it had something to do with positive ions, which were not to be discovered for many years; but I came to believe that there was something about me that inspired extreme gestures, though I could never pinpoint what it was. After one such rupture, during a downpour of freezing rain, my ex-boyfriend gave me a valentine consisting of a real cow's heart with an actual arrow stuck through it. He'd been meaning to do it anyway, he said, and he couldn't think of any other girl who would appreciate it. For weeks I wondered whether or not this was a compliment.

Buddy was not this friendly. After the break-up, he never spoke to me again. Through Trish, he asked for his identification bracelet back, and I handed it over to her in the girls' washroom at lunch hour. There was someone else he wanted to give it to, Trish told me, a girl named Mary Jo who took typing instead of French, a sure sign in those days that you would leave school early and get a job or something. Mary Jo had a round, good-natured face; bangs down over her forehead like a sheepdog's, and heavy breasts, and she did in fact leave school early. Meanwhile she wore Buddy's name in silver upon her wrist. Trish switched allegiances, though not all at once. Somewhat later, I heard she had been telling stories about how I'd lived in a cowshed all summer.

It would be wrong to say that I didn't miss Buddy. In this respect too he was the first in a series. Later, I always missed men when they were gone, even when they meant what is usually called absolutely nothing to me. For me, I was to discover, there was no such category as absolutely nothing.

But all that was in the future. The morning after the hurricane, I had only the sensation of having come unscathed through a major calamity. After we had listened to the news, cars overturned with their drivers in them, demolished houses, all that rampaging water and disaster and washed-away money, my brother and I put on our rubber boots and walked down the old, pot-holed and now pitted and raddled Pottery Road to witness the destruction first-hand.

There wasn't as much as we had hoped. Trees and branches were down, but not that many of them. The Don River was flooded and muddy, but it was hard to tell whether the parts of cars half sunk in it and the mangled truck tires, heaps of sticks, planks, and assorted debris washing along or strewn on land where the water had already begun to recede were new or just more of the junk we were used to seeing in it. The sky was still overcast; our boots squelched in the mud, out of which no hands were poking up. I had wanted something more like tragedy. Two people had actually been drowned there during the night, but we did not learn that until later. This is what I have remembered most clearly about Buddy: the ordinary-looking wreckage, the flatness of the water, the melancholy light.

Loulou; or, The Domestic Life of the Language

Loulou is in the coach-house, wedging clay. She's wearing a pair of running shoes, once white, now grey, over men's wool work socks, a purple Indian-print cotton skirt, and a rust-coloured smock, so heavy with clay dust it hangs on her like brocade, the sleeves rolled up past the elbow. This is her favourite working outfit. To the music of *The Magic Flute*, brought to her by CBC stereo, she lifts the slab of clay and slams it down, gives a half-turn, lifts and slams. This is to get the air bubbles out, so nothing will explode in the kiln. Some potters would hire an apprentice to do this, but not Loulou.

It's true she has apprentices, two of them; she gets them through the government as free trainees. But they make plates and mugs from her designs, about all they're fit for. She doesn't consider them suitable for wedging clay, with their puny little biceps and match-stick wrists, so poorly developed compared with her own solid, smoothly muscled arms and broad, capable but shapely hands, so often admired by the poets. *Marmoreal*, one of them said—wrote, actually—causing Loulou to make one of her frequent sorties into the dictionary, to find out whether or not she'd been insulted.

Once she had done this openly, whenever they'd used a word about her she didn't understand, but when they'd discovered she was doing it they'd found it amusing and had started using words like that on purpose. "Loulou is so geomorphic," one of them would say, and when she would blush and scowl, another would take it up. "Not only that, she's fundamentally chthonic." "Telluric," a

47

third would pipe up. Then they would laugh. She's decided that the only thing to do is to ignore them. But she's not so dumb as they think, she remembers the words, and when they aren't watching she sneaks a look at the Shorter Oxford (kept in the study which really belongs to only one of them but which she thinks of as *theirs*), washing her hands first so she won't leave any tell-tale signs of clay on the page.

She reads their journals, too, taking the same precautions. She suspects they know she does this. It's her way of keeping up with what they are really thinking about her, or maybe only with what they want her to think they're thinking. The journals are supposed to be secret, but Loulou considers it her right and also a kind of duty to read them. She views it in the same light as her mother viewed going through the family's sock and underwear drawers, to sort out the clean things from the ones they'd already worn and stuffed back in. This is what the poets' journals are like. Socks, mostly, but you never know what you will find.

"Loulou is becoming more metonymous," she's read recently. This has been bothering her for days. Sometimes she longs to say to them, "Now just what in hell did you mean by that?" But she knows she would get nowhere.

"Loulou is the foe of abstract order," one would say. This is a favourite belief of theirs.

"Loulou is the foe of abstract ordure."

"Loulou is the Great Goddess."

"Loulou is the great mattress."

It would end up with Loulou telling them to piss off. When that didn't stop them, she would tell them they couldn't have any more baked chicken if they went on like that. Threatening to deprive them of food usually works.

Overtly, Loulou takes care to express scorn for the poets; though not for them, exactly—they have their points—but for their pickiness about words. Her mother

would have said they were finicky eaters. "Who cares
what a thing's called?" she says to them. "A piece of
bread is a piece of bread. You want some or not?" And
she bends over to slide three of her famous loaves, high
and nicely browned, out of the oven, and the poets
admire her ass and haunches. Sometimes they do this
openly, like other men, growling and smacking their
lips, pretending to be construction workers. They like
pretending to be other things; in the summers they play
baseball games together and make a big fuss about
having the right hats. Sometimes, though, they do it
silently, and Loulou only knows about it from the poems
they write afterwards. Loulou can tell these poems are
about her, even though the nouns change: "my lady,"
"my friend's lady," "my woman," "my friend's woman,"
"my wife," "my friend's wife," and, when necessary for
the length of the line, "the wife of my friend." Never
"girl" though, and never her name. *Ass* and *haunches*
aren't Loulou's words either; she would say *butt*.

Loulou doesn't know anything about music but she
likes listening to it. Right now, the Queen of the Night
runs up her trill, and Loulou pauses to see if she'll make
it to the top. She does, just barely, and Loulou, feeling
vicarious triumph, rams her fist into the mound of clay.
Then she covers it with a sheet of plastic and goes to the
sink to wash her hands. Soon the oven timer will go off
and one of the poets, maybe her husband but you never
know, will call her on the intercom to come and see
about the bread. It isn't that they wouldn't take it out
themselves, if she asked them to. Among the four or five
of them they'd likely manage. It's just that Loulou
doesn't trust them. She decided long ago that none of
them knows his left tit from a hole in the ground when it
comes to the real world. If she wants the bread taken out
when it's done but not overdone, and she does, she'll
have to do it herself.

She wonders who will be in the kitchen at the main
house by now: her first husband for sure, and the man

she lived with after that for three years without being married, and her second husband, the one she has now, and two ex-lovers. Half a dozen of them maybe, sitting around the kitchen table, drinking her coffee and eating her hermit cookies and talking about whatever they talk about when she isn't there. In the past there have been periods of strain among them, especially during the times when Loulou has been switching over, but they're all getting along well enough now. They run a collective poetry magazine, which keeps them out of trouble mostly. The name of this magazine is *Comma*, but among themselves the poets refer to it as *Coma*. At parties they enjoy going up to young female would-be poets ("proupies," they call them behind their backs, which means "poetry groupies"), and saying, "I'd like to put you in a *Coma*." A while ago *Comma* published mostly poems without commas, but this is going out now, just as beards are going out in favour of moustaches and even shaving. The more daring poets have gone so far as to cut off their sideburns. Loulou is not quite sure whether or not she approves of this.

She doesn't know whether the poets are good poets, whether the poems they write in such profusion are any good. Loulou has no opinion on this subject: all that matters is what they are writing about her. Their poems get published in books, but what does that mean? Not money, that's for sure. You don't make any money with poetry, the poets tell her, unless you sing and play the guitar too. Sometimes they give readings and make a couple of hundred bucks. For Loulou that's three medium-sized casseroles, with lids. On the other hand, they don't have her expenses. Part of her expenses is them.

Loulou can't remember exactly how she got mixed up with the poets. It wasn't that she had any special thing for poets as such: it just happened that way. After the first one, the others seemed to follow along naturally, almost as if they were tied onto each other in a long line with a piece of string. They were always around, and she was so busy most of the time that she didn't go out much to look for other kinds of men. Now that her business is doing so well you'd think she would have more leisure time, but this isn't the case. And any leisure time she does have, she spends with the poets. They're always nagging her about working too hard.

Bob was the first one, and also her first husband. He was in art school at the same time she was, until he decided he wasn't suited for it. He wasn't practical enough, he let things dry out: paint, clay, even the leftovers in his tiny refrigerator, as Loulou discovered the first night she'd slept with him. She devoted the next morning to cleaning up his kitchen, getting rid of the saucers of mummified cooked peas and the shrivelled, half-gnawed chicken legs and the warped, cracked quarter-packages of two-month-old sliced bacon, and the bits of cheese, oily on the outside and hard as tiles. Loulou has always hated clutter, which she defines, though not in so many words, as matter out of its proper place. Bob looked on, sullen but appreciative, as she hurled and scoured. Possibly this was why he decided to love her: because she would do this sort of thing. What he said though was, "You complete me."

What he also said was that he'd fallen in love with her name. All the poets have done this, one after the other. The first symptom is that they ask her whether Loulou is short for something—Louise, maybe? When she says no, they look at her in that slightly glazed way she recognizes instantly, as if they've never paid proper attention to her or even seen her before. This look is her favourite part of any new relationship with a man. It's even better than the sex, though Loulou likes sex well enough and all the poets have been good in bed. But then, Loulou has never slept with a man she did not consider good in bed. She's beginning to think this is because she has low standards.

At first Loulou was intrigued by this obsession with

her name, mistaking it for an obsession with her, but it turned out to be no such thing. It was the gap that interested them, one of them had explained (not Bob though; maybe Phil, the second and most linguistic of them all).

"What gap?" Loulou asked suspiciously. She knew her upper front teeth were a little wide apart and had been self-conscious about it when she was younger.

"The gap between the word and the thing signified," Phil said. His hand was on her breast and he'd given it an absent-minded squeeze, as if to illustrate what he meant. They were in bed at the time. Mostly Loulou doesn't like talking in bed. But she's not that fond of talking at other times, either.

Phil went on to say that Loulou, as a name, conjured up images of French girls in can-can outfits, with corseted wasp-waists and blonde curls and bubbly laughs. But then there was the real Loulou—dark, straight-haired, firmly built, marmoreal, and well, not exactly bubbly. More earthy, you might say. (Loulou hadn't known then what he meant by "earthy," though by now she's learned that for him, for all of them, it means "functionally illiterate.") The thing was, Phil said, what existed in the space between Loulou and her name?

Loulou didn't know what he was talking about. What space? Once she'd resented her mother for having saddled her with this name; she would rather have been called Mary or Ann. Maybe she suspected that her mother would really have preferred a child more like the name—blonde, thin, curly-headed—but had disappointingly got Loulou instead, short, thick, stubborn-jawed, not much interested in the frilly dolls' clothes her mother had painstakingly crocheted for her. Instead, Loulou was fond of making mud pies on the back porch, placing them carefully along the railing where people wouldn't step on them and ruin them. Her mother's response to these pies was to say, "Oh, Loulou!", as if *Loulou* itself meant mud, meant trouble and dismay.

"It's just a name," she said. "Phil is kind of a dumb name too if you ask me."

Phil said that wasn't the point, he wasn't *criticizing* her, but Loulou had stopped the conversation by climbing on top of him, letting her long hair fall down over his face.

That was early on; he'd liked her hair then. "Rank," he'd called it in a poem, quite a lot later. Loulou hadn't thought much of that when she looked it up. It could mean *too luxuriant* or *offensive and foul-smelling*. The effect of this poem on Loulou was to cause her to wash her hair more often. Sooner or later all the poets got into her hair, and she was tired of having it compared to horses' tails, Newfoundland dog fur, black holes in space and the insides of caves. When Loulou was feeling particularly enraged by the poets she would threaten to get a brushcut, though she knew it would be pushing her luck.

When she has dried her hands, Loulou takes off her smock. Underneath it she's wearing a mauve sweatshirt with RAVING OPTIMIST stencilled across the front. The poets gave it to her, collectively, one Christmas, because a few weeks before one of them had said, "Why are you so grumpy, Loulou?" and Loulou had said, "I'm only grumpy when you pick on me," and then, after a pause, "Compared to you guys I'm a raving optimist." This was true, though they made fun of her for it. In a group they can laugh, but it's only Loulou who has seen them one at a time, sitting in chairs for hours on end with their heads down on their arms, almost unable to move. It's Loulou who's held their hands when they couldn't make it in bed and told them that other things are just as important, though she's never been able to specify what. It's Loulou who has gone out and got drunk with them and listened to them talking about the void and about the terrifying blankness of the page and about how any art form is just a way of evading suicide. Loulou thinks this is a load of b.s.: she herself does not consider the making of

casseroles with lids or the throwing of porcelain fruit
bowls as an evasion of suicide, but then, as they have
often pointed out, what she's doing isn't an art form, it's
only a craft. Bob once asked her when she was going to
branch out into macramé, for which she emptied the
dust-pan on him. But she matches them beer for beer;
she's even gone so far as to throw up right along with
them, if that seemed required. One of them once told
her she was a soft touch.

The intercom buzzes as Loulou is hanging up her
smock. She buzzes back to show she has heard, takes her
hair out of the elastic band and smooths it down, looking
in the round tin-framed Mexican mirror that hangs over
the sink, and checks up on little Marilyn, her new
apprentice, before heading out the door.

Marilyn is still having trouble with cup handles.
Loulou will have to spend some time with her later and
explain them to her. If the cup handles aren't on straight,
she will say, the cup will be crooked when you pick it up
and then the people drinking out of it will spill things
and burn themselves. That's the way you have to put it
for trainees: in terms of physical damage. It's important
to Loulou that the production pieces should be done
right. They're her bread and butter, though what she
most likes to work on are the bigger things, the
amphora-like vases, the tureens a size larger than
anyone ought to be able to throw. Another potter once
said that you'd need a derrick to give a dinner party with
Loulou's stuff, but that was jealousy. What they say about
her mostly is that she doesn't fool around.

Loulou flings her pink sweater-coat across her shoulders, bangs the coach-house door behind her to make it
shut, and walks towards the house, whistling between
her teeth and stomping her feet to get the clay dust off.
The kitchen is filled with the yeasty smell of baking
bread. Loulou breathes it in, revelling in it: a smell of
her own creation.

The poets are sitting around the kitchen table, drinking coffee. Maybe they're having a meeting, it's hard to tell. Some nod at her, some grin. Two of the female poets are here today and Loulou isn't too pleased about that. As far as she's concerned they don't have a lot to offer: they're almost as bad as the male poets, but without the saving grace of being men. They wear black a lot and have cheekbones.

Piss on their cheekbones, thinks Loulou. She knows what cheek-bones mean. The poets, *her* poets, consider these female poets high-strung and interesting. Sometimes they praise their work, a little too extravagantly, but sometimes they talk about their bodies, though not when they are there of course, and about whether or not they would be any good in bed. Either of these approaches drives Loulou wild. She doesn't like the female poets—they eat her muffins and condescend to her, and Loulou suspects them of having designs on the poets, some of which may already have been carried out, judging from their snotty manner—but she doesn't like hearing them put down, either. What really gets her back up is that, during these discussions, the poets act as if she isn't there.

Really, though, the female poets don't count. They aren't even on the editorial board of *Comma*; they are only on the edges, like mascots, and today Loulou all but ignores them.

"You could've put on more coffee," she says in her grumpiest voice.

"What's the matter, Loulou?" says Phil, who has always been the quickest on the uptake when it comes to Loulou and her bad moods. Not that Loulou goes in for fine tuning.

"Nothing *you* can fix," says Loulou rudely. She takes off her sweater-coat and sticks out her chest. *Marmoreal*, she thinks. So much for the female poets, who are flat-chested as well as everything else.

"Hey Loulou, how about a little nictitation?" says one of the poets.

"Up your nose," says Loulou.

"She thinks it's something dirty," says a second one. "She's confusing it with micturition."

"All it means is winking, Loulou," says the first one.

"He got it out of Trivial Pursuit," says a third.

Loulou takes one loaf out of the oven, turns it out, taps the bottom, puts it back into the pan and into the oven. They can go on like that for hours. It's enough to drive you right out of your tree, if you pay any attention to them at all.

"Why do you put up with us, Loulou?" Phil asked her once. Loulou sometimes wonders, but she doesn't know. She knows why they put up with her though, apart from the fact that she pays the mortgage: she's solid, she's predictable, she's always there, she makes them feel safe. But lately she's been wondering: who is there to make her feel safe?

It's another day, and Loulou is on her way to seduce her accountant. She's wearing purple boots, several years old and with watermarks on them from the slush, a cherry-coloured dirndl she made out of curtain material when she was at art school, and a Peruvian wedding shirt dyed mauve; this is the closest she ever comes to getting dressed up. Because of the section of the city she's going to, which is mostly middle-European shops, bakeries and clothing stores with yellowing embroidered blouses in the windows and places where you can buy hand-painted wooden Easter eggs and chess sets with the pawns as Cossacks, she's draped a black wool shawl over her head. This, she thinks, will make her look more ethnic and therefore more inconspicuous: she's feeling a little furtive. One of the poets has said that Loulou is to *subdued* as Las Vegas at night is to a sixty-watt light bulb, but in fact, with her long off-black hair and her large dark eyes and the strong planes of her face, she does have a kind of peasant look. This is enhanced by the two plastic shopping bags she carries, one in either hand. These do not contain groceries, however, but her receipts and cheque stubs for the two previous years. Loulou is behind on her income tax, which is why she got the accountant in the first place. She doesn't see why she shouldn't kill two birds with one stone.

Loulou is behind on her income tax because of her fear of money. When she was married to Bob, neither of them had any money anyway, so the income tax wasn't a problem. Phil, the man she lived with after that, was good with numbers, and although he had no income and therefore no income tax, he treated hers as a game, a kind of superior Scrabble. But her present husband, Calvin, considers money boring. It's all right to have some—as Loulou does, increasingly—but talking about it is sordid and a waste of time. Calvin claims that those who can actually read income-tax forms, let alone understand them, have already done severe and permanent damage to their brains. Loulou has taken to sending out her invoices and toting up her earnings in the coachhouse, instead of at the kitchen table as she used to, and adding and subtracting are acquiring overtones of forbidden sex. Perhaps this is what has led her to the step she is now about to take. You may as well be hung, thinks Loulou, for a sheep as a lamb.

In addition, Loulou has recently been feeling a wistful desire to be taken care of. It comes and goes, especially on cloudy days, and mostly Loulou pays scant attention to it. Nevertheless it's there. Everyone depends on her, but when she needs help, with her income tax for instance, nobody's within call. She could ask Phil to do it again, but Calvin might make a fuss about it. She wants to be able to turn her two plastic shopping bags over to some man, some quiet methodical man with inner strength, and not too ugly, who could make sense of their contents and tell her she has nothing to worry about and, hopefully, nothing to pay.

Before Loulou found this particular accountant, she

spent several afternoons window-shopping for one down
at King and Bay. When it came right down to it,
however, she was so intimidated by the hermetically
sealed glass towers and the thought of receptionists with
hair-dos and nail polish that she didn't even go in
through the doors at any of the addresses she'd looked
up in the Yellow Pages. Instead, she stood at street
corners as if waiting for the light to change, watching the
businessmen hurry past, sometimes in overcoats of the
kind the poets never wear, solid-looking and beige or
navy blue but slit provocatively up the back, or in three-
piece suits, challengingly done up with hundreds of
buttons and zippers, their tight tennis-playing butts
concealed under layers of expensive wool blend, their
ties waving enticingly under their chins like the loose
ends of macramé wall hangings: one pull and the whole
thing would unravel. The poets, in their track suits or
jeans, seem easier of access, but they are hedged with
paradox and often moody. The businessmen would be
simple and unspoiled, primary reds and blues rather
than puce and lilac, potatoes rather than, like the poets,
slightly over-ripe avocadoes.

The sight of them filled Loulou with unspecific lust,
though she found them touching also. She was like a
middle-aged banker surrounded by sixteen-year-old vir-
gins: she longed to be the first, though the first of what
she wasn't sure. But she knew she knew lots of things
they were unlikely to know: the poets, on their good
days, have been nothing if not inventive.

Loulou doesn't think of the accountant she has now as
a real one, by which she means a frightening one. He is
not in a glass tower, he has no polished receptionist,
though he does have a certificate on the wall and even a
three-piece suit (though, Loulou suspects, only one).
She discovered him by accident when she was down on
Queen Street buying fresh chicken from A. Stork, the
best place for it in her opinion, especially when you need
a lot, as she did that day because all of the poets were

coming for dinner. Heading for the streetcar stop with her sackful of tender flesh, Loulou saw a hand-lettered sign in the window of a dry-goods store: INCOME TAX, and underneath it some foreign language. It was the hand-lettered sign that did it for Loulou: badly lettered at that, she could do much better. On impulse she'd pushed open the door and gone in.

There was a tiny bald-headed man behind the counter, barricaded in with bolts of maroon cloth, a rack of cheesy-looking buttons on the wall behind him, but he turned out not to be the accountant. The accountant was in a separate room at the back, with nothing in it except a wooden desk of the sort Loulou associated with her grade-school teachers, and one other chair and a filing cabinet. He stood up when Loulou came in and offered to take her sack of chicken and put it somewhere for her. "No thanks," said Loulou, because she could see there was nowhere for him to put it—there was a fern on the filing cabinet, obviously on its last legs—and that he would merely get more flustered than he already was if she said yes; so she went through their first interview with a bag of still-warm cut-up chicken in her lap.

She's seen him twice since then. He takes more time with her than he really needs to, maybe because he's not what you would call all that busy. He also talks to her more than he needs to. By now, Loulou knows quite a lot about him. Getting started is harder than it used to be, he's told her. The dry-goods store belongs to his father, who gives him the office rent-free, in return for doing the accounts. The father is first-generation Czech, and he himself knows two other languages besides English. In this district—he spread his hands in a kind of resigned shrug while saying this—it helps. He does a couple of local bakeries and a hardware store and a second-hand jeweller's and a few of his father's old friends. Maybe when the recession is over things will pick up. He has volunteered, too, that his hobby is weight-lifting. Loulou has not asked whether or not he's married; she sus-

pects not. If he were married, his fern would be in better
shape.

While he talks, Loulou nods and smiles. She isn't sure
how old he is. Young, she thinks, though he tries to make
himself look older by wearing silver-rimmed glasses. She
thinks he has nice hands, not like an accountant's at all,
not spindly. The second time, he went out into the main
store and came back with cups of tea, which Loulou
found thoughtful. Then he asked her advice about a
carpet. Already she felt sorry for him. He hardly even
goes out for lunch, she's discovered; mostly he just gets
take-out from the deli across the street. She's considered
bringing him some muffins.

These topics—carpets, weight-lifting, food—are easy
for Loulou. What is more difficult is that he's decided
she's not just a potter but an artist, and his idea of an
artist does not at all accord with Loulou's view of herself.
He wants her to be wispy and fey, impractical, unearthly
almost; he talks, embarrassingly, about "the creative
impulse." This is far too close to the poets for Loulou.
She's tried to explain that she works with clay, which is
hardly ethereal. "It's like mud pies," she said, but he
didn't want to hear that. Nor could she find the words to
make him understand what she meant: that when she's
throwing a pot she feels exhilaration, exactly the same
kind she felt as a child while making a terrible mess of
her mother's back porch. If he could see her the way she
really is when she's working, guck all over her hands,
he'd know she's not exactly essence of roses.

The second time she saw him, the accountant said he
envied her freedom. He would like to do something
more creative himself, he said, but you have to make a
living. Loulou refrained from pointing out that she
seems to be doing a sight better at it than he is. She's
much more tactful with him than she's ever been with
the poets. The fact is that she's starting to enjoy his
version of her. Sometimes she even believes it, and
thinks she might be on the verge of learning something

new about herself. She's beginning to find herself mysterious. It's partly for this reason she wants to sleep with the accountant; she thinks it will change her.

The poets would laugh if they knew, but then she's not about to tell them. She did announce his advent though, that first night, while the poets were all sitting around the table eating chicken and discussing something they called "the language." They do this frequently these days and Loulou is getting bored with it. "The lauguage" is different from just words: it has this mystical aura around it, like religion, she can tell by the way their voices drop reverently whenever they mention it. That night they had all just finished reading a new book. "I'm really getting into the language," one said, and the others chewed in silent communion.

"I've got myself an accountant," Loulou said loudly, to break the spell.

"You've *got* him, but have you *had* him yet?" Bob said. The others laughed, all except Calvin, and began discussing the accountant's chances of escape from Loulou, which they rated at nil. They went on to detail the positions and locations in which Loulou could be expected to finally entrap him—under the desk, on top of the filing cabinet—and the injuries he would sustain. They pictured him fending her off with pens.

Loulou gnawled grimly at a chicken leg. They didn't believe any of this would happen, of course. They were too conceited: having known them, how could she stoop so low? Little did they know.

Loulou approaches the door of the dry-goods store, whistling Mozart between her teeth. Partly she's thinking about the accountant and what his body might be like under his suit, but partly she's thinking about tomorrow, when she has to start work on an order of twelve slab planters for one of her good customers. Either way, it's a question of the right placement of the feet. Like a Judo expert, which she is not, Loulou is always conscious of the position of her feet in relation to the rest of her.

The accountant is waiting for her, shadowy behind the dust-filmed glass of the door. It's after six and the store is closed. Loulou said, slyly, that she couldn't make it any earlier. She didn't want the little bald-headed man lurking around.

The accountant unlocks the door and lets her in. They go back through the smell of wool and freshly torn cotton into his office, and Loulou dumps out her bag of receipts (done up in bundles, with elastic bands: she's not without a sense of decency), all over his desk. He looks pleased, and says they certainly do have a lot of things to catch up on.

He brings in some cups of tea, sits down, picks up a newly sharpened pencil, and asks her how much of her living space can be written off as working space. Loulou explains about the coach-house. She doesn't use any of the actual house herself, she says, not for working, because the poets are always using it. Sometimes they live there too, though it depends.

"On what?" says the accountant, frowning a little.

"On whether they're living anywhere else," says Loulou.

When he hears that they don't pay rent, the accountant makes a tut-tutting sound and tells Loulou that she should not let things go on like this. Loulou says that the poets never have any money, except sometimes from grants. The accountant gets out of his chair and paces around the room, which is difficult for him because Loulou is taking up a lot of space in it. He says that Loulou is allowing herself to be imposed upon and she should get herself out of this situation, which is doing her no good at all.

Loulou may have felt this herself from time to time, but hearing the accountant say it right out in the open air disturbs her. Where would the poets go? Who would take care of them? She doesn't wish to dwell on this right now, it's far too complicated, and perhaps even painful. Instead she stands up, plants her feet firmly apart, intercepts the accountant as he strides past, and, with a tug here and a little pressure there, ends up with his arms more or less around her. She backs herself up against the desk for balance, puts one hand behind her, and upsets his cup of tea into the wastepaper basket. He doesn't notice a thing; luckily it isn't hot.

After a short time the accountant takes off his silver-rimmed glasses, and after another short time he says, in a voice half an octave lower than his normal one, "I wasn't expecting this." Loulou says nothing—she lies only when absolutely necessary—and starts undoing his vest buttons. When she's down to the shirt he lifts his head, glances around the room, and murmurs, "Not here." Which is just as well, because he hasn't got his carpet yet and the floor is painted concrete.

He leads her into the darkened dry-goods store and begins sorting through the bolts of cloth. Loulou can't figure out what he's doing until he selects a roll of dark-pink velvet, unfurls it, and lays it out on the floor behind the counter, with a little flourish, like a cloak over a mud puddle. Loulou admires the way he does this; he's too deft not to have done it before. She lies down on the pink velvet, reaches up for him, and after a few minutes of shaky-fingered fumbling with the clothes they make love, somewhat rapidly. This floor is concrete too and the pink velvet isn't very thick. Loulou worries about his knees.

"Well," says the accountant. Then he sits up and starts putting on his clothes. He does this very skillfully. Loulou wishes he would wait a few minutes—it would be friendlier—but already he's doing up his buttons. Maybe he's afraid someone will come in. He rolls up the pink velvet and inserts the bolt back into its proper slot on the shelf. They go back to his office and he locates his glasses and puts them on, and tells her he'll have some figures for her in maybe two weeks. He doesn't say anything

about seeing her in the meantime: perhaps his image of
her as a delicate artistic flower has been shaken. He
kisses her good-bye, though. The last thing he says to
her is, "You shouldn't let people take advantage of you."
Loulou knows he thinks he's just done this very thing
himself. He's like the poets: he thinks she can't see
through him.

Loulou decides to walk back to her house, which is at
least a mile away, instead of taking the streetcar. She
needs time to calm down. On the one hand she's elated,
as she always is when she accomplishes something she's
set out to do, but on the other hand she's disoriented. Is
she different now, or not? Apart from the actual sex,
which Loulou would never knock, and it was fine though
a little on the swift side, what has it all boiled down to?
She doesn't feel more known, more understood. Instead
she feels less understood. She feels nameless. It's as if all
those words which the poets have attached to her over
the years have come undone and floated off into the sky,
like balloons. If she were one of the poets, she would get
something out of this: this is exactly the sort of thing they
like to write about. A non-event, says Phil, is better to
write about than an event, because with a non-event you
can make up the meaning yourself, it means whatever
you say it means. For the poets nothing is wasted,
because even if it is, they can write about the waste.
What she ought to do is throw them all out on their ears.

Loulou reaches her three-storey red-brick house and
notes, as she always does, the mangy state of the lawn.
The poets are divided on the subject of the lawn: some of
them think lawns are bourgeois, others think that to say
lawns are bourgeois is outdated. Loulou says she'll be
damned if she'll cut it herself. The lawn is a stand-off.
She goes up the front walk, not whistling, and unlocks
her front door. In the hallway the familiar smell of the
house envelops her, but it's like a smell from childhood.
It's the smell of something left behind.

The poets are in the kitchen, sitting around the table,

which is littered with papers and coffee cups and plates
with crumbs and smears of butter on them. Loulou looks
from one poet to another as if they are figures in a
painting, as if she's never seen them before. She could
walk out of this room, right this minute, and never come
back, and fifty years later they would all still be in there,
with the same plates, the same cups, the same crumby
butter. Only she doesn't know where she would go.

"We're out of muffins," says Bob.

Loulou stares at him. "Piss on the muffins," she says at
last, but without conviction. He looks tired, she thinks.
He is showing signs of age, they all are. This is the first
time she's noticed it. They won't go on forever.

"Where've you been?" says Calvin. "It's past seven-
thirty." This is his way of saying they want their dinner.

"My God, you're helpless," says Loulou. "Why didn't
you just phone out for some pizza?" To her knowledge
they have never phoned out for pizza. They've never had
to.

She sits down heavily at the table. The life she's led up
to now seems to her entirely crazed. How did she end up
in this madhouse? By putting one foot in front of the
other and never taking her eyes off her feet. You could
end up anywhere that way. It isn't that the accountant is
normal, any more than the poets are; nor is he a possible
alternative. She won't even sleep with him again, not on
purpose anyway. But he is other, he is another. She too
could be other. But which other? What, underneath it
all, is Loulou really like? How can she tell? Maybe she is
what the poets say she is, after all; maybe she has only
their word, their words, for herself.

"*Pizza*," Bob is beginning, in an injured tone. "Pig of a
dog. . . ." But the others shut him up. They can see
that something is wrong, and they very much don't want
to know what.

"Reify the pizza," says Calvin to Phil. "You use phone.
Is modern western invention of technology." Now
they're pretending to be foreigners of some kind. This is

a game they play more frequently when there is tension
in the air than when there isn't.

"Insert finger in possible small hole," says Calvin.
"Twist wrist."

"With anchovies then," says Bob, not joining in.
Loulou hears their voices coming to her across space, as
if they're in another room. What she sees is the grain of
the wood in the table right by her hand.

"Loulou thinks *to reify* means *to make real*," says Phil
to everyone, when he's hung up the phone. They're
always talking about her in the third person like that,
telling each other what she thinks. The truth is that she's
never heard the word before in her life.

"So what is it, smartass?" says Loulou with an effort,
squeezing out a little belligerence to set them at ease.

"If Loulou didn't exist, God would have to invent her,"
says Bob.

"God, hell," says Phil. "*We* would. We did it the first
time, right?"

This is going too far for Loulou. Nobody invented her,
thank you very much. They make things up about her,
but that's a whole other story. "Up your nose," says
Loulou.

"To reify is to make into a thing," says Phil, "which, as
I'm sure most of us will agree, is hardly the same."

Loulou looks around the room. They are all in place,
they're all watching her, to see what she will say next.
She sticks out her chin at them. "Why not?" she says.
"What's the big difference?" and they relax, they laugh,
they give each other little punches on the shoulder as if
they're part of a team and they've just scored a point.
That, they tell each other, is just like Loulou, and
suddenly she sees that this is what they require of her,
possibly all they require: that she should be *just like
Loulou*. No more, but certainly no less. Maybe it's not
so bad.

Uglypuss

Joel hates November. As far as he's concerned they could drop it down the chute and he wouldn't complain. Drizzle and chill, everyone depressed, and then the winter to go through afterwards. The landlord has turned down the heat again, which means Joel has to either let his buns solidify and break off or use the electric heater, which means more money, because the electricity's extra. The landlord does this to spite him, Joel, personally. Just for that, Joel refuses to move. He tells other people he likes the building, which he does: it's a golden oldie, a mansion that's seen better days, with an arched entrance-way and stained glass. But also he won't give the old rent-gouger the satisfaction. Becka could handle him, when she was still living here. All she'd had to do was lean over the banister while the old bugger was standing below, and use her good voice, the furry one, and up went the temperature; a trick that's not possible for Joel.

He'd like to be someplace warm, but who can afford it? Too bad they made grants taxable, not that he's likely to get another one the ways things are going.

Things are not going too well. He's beginning to think street theatre should stay in California: up here you can only do it three months of the year, and some of that is too hot, they steam inside those outsize masks. Even directing is no picnic. Last summer he got a sunburn, on the top of his head, where he's beginning to go bald. It was right after this that Becka caught him in the bathroom, standing with his back to the mirror, looking at his head from behind with a plastic violet-framed hand mirror, hers. She wouldn't let up on that for weeks. "Checked out your manly beauty this morning?" "Thought about Hair-Weeve?" "You'd look cute as a blonde. It would go with the skull." "Chest wigs yet?" "You could cut off some of your beard and glue it on the top, right?" Maybe he had it coming; he remembered getting onto her about spending twenty-five dollars at the hairdresser's once, soon after she'd moved in with him. It was her twenty-five dollars, but they were supposed to be sharing expenses. He'd called it an indulgence. She remembered that he remembered, of course. She has a memory like a rat-trap: full of rats.

Joel's fingers are cold. The apartment is like a football game in the rain. He puts down the black Bic ball-point with which he hasn't written anything for the past half hour, stretches, scratches his head. He recalls, for an instant and with irritation, the Italian calligraphy pen Becka affected for a while: an affectation that has gone the way of all the others. Then he turns back to square one.

The piece they're working on is for two weeks from now: the Crucifixion according to Solemate Sox, with management as Judas. They're going to do it right beside the picket lines, which will cheer the picketers up, or that was the general idea. Joel isn't too sure about this piece, and there's been a certain amount of debate about it within the group. The concept was Becka's: she justified it by saying they should pick symbolism the workers can tune into, and most of these workers are Portuguese, they'll know all about Judas, you only have to look at the statues on their lawns, all those bleeding plaster Jesuses and Virgin Marys with their creepy-looking babies. Though for the same reason some of the others felt that Christ as a large knitted sock, in red and white stripes, might turn out to be too much for them. There could be a communications breakdown. Joel himself had been uneasy, but he'd voted on Becka's side, because they'd still been trying to work it out then and he knew what hell there would be to pay if he'd come out against her. Just another example, she would have said, of how he would never let her express herself.

He hopes it won't rain: if it does, the giant sock will get waterlogged, among other things. Maybe they should scrap it, try for another approach. Whatever they do, though, they'll probably have the assistant manager and the old boy himself coming outside and accusing them of anti-Semitism. This happens to Joel a lot; it's escalated after the piece on Lebanon and arms sales to South Africa they did outside the Beth Tzedec on Yom Kippur. Possibly the portable canvas mass grave, filled with baby dolls and splashed with red paint, had been going too far. A couple of the troupe members had wondered whether it was in bad taste, but Joel had said that bad taste was just an internalized establishment enforcer.

Joel doesn't believe in pulling punches. And if you punch, they punch back. It's getting so he can hardly go to parties anymore. Though it's not all parties he should avoid, only certain kinds, the kinds where he will find his own second cousins and men he went to *shul* with, who are now dentists or have gone into business. Even before the Lebanon piece, they were none too polite. At the last party, a woman he didn't know at all, an older woman, came up to him and said, "Instead of shaking your hand I should kick you in the stomach."

"What for?" said Joel.

"You know what for," the woman said. "You've got a nerve. Eating our food. Better you should choke."

"Don't you think there should be an open discussion of the situation?" said Joel. "Like they do in Israel?"

"Goys have no right," said the woman.

"So who's a goy?" said Joel.

"You," said the woman. "You're not a real Jew."

"All of a sudden you're some kind of self-appointed committee on racial purity?" said Joel. "Anyway, read the Torah. They used to stone the prophets."

"Shmuck," said the woman.

Joel tries not to let it get to him: he's got his

credentials ready. You want murdered relatives? he'll tell
them. I've got.

Then how can you betray them? they'll say. Spitting
on the dead.

You think they'd agree with what's happening? he'll
say. Two wrongs don't make a right.

Then there's a silence in him, because that's a thing no
one will ever know.

Joel's head hurts. He gets up from his desk, sits down in
the chair he thinks in, which is like the one at home that
his father used to lie in to read the paper, a Lay-Zee-Boy
recliner, covered in black naugahyde. Joel bought his at
least third-hand from the Goodwill, out of nostalgia and a
wish for comfort; though Becka said he did it to affront
her. She could never stand any of his furniture, especially the Ping-Pong table; she was always lobbying for a
real dining-room table, though, as Joel would point out
with great reasonableness, it wouldn't have a double
function.

"You're always talking about bourgeoise," she'd say,
which wasn't true. "But that chair is the essence. Eau de
bourgeoise." She pronounced it in three syllables: *boor-
joo-ice*. Maybe she did this on purpose, to get at him
by mutilating the word, though the only time he'd cor-
rected her (the *only* time, he's sure of that), she'd said,
"Well, excuse me for living." Could he help it if he'd
spent a year in Montreal? And she hadn't. He couldn't
help any of the things that he had and she hadn't.

Early on, he thought they'd been engaging in a
dialogue, out of which, sooner or later, a consensus
would emerge. He thought they'd been involved in a
process of mutual adjustment and counter-adjustment.
But viewed from here and now, it was never a dialogue.
It was merely a degrading squabble.

Joel decides not to brood any more about boring
personal shit. There are more important things in the

world. He picks up this morning's paper, from where it lies in segments on the floor, in which he knows he will read distorted and censored versions of some of them; but just as he's settling down to the purblind and moronic "Letters to the Editor" section, the phone rings. Joel hesitates before answering it: maybe it will be Becka, and he never knows which angle she'll be coming at him from. But curiosity wins, as it often does where Becka is concerned.

It isn't Becka though. "I'm going to cut your nuts off," says a male voice, almost sensuously, into his ear.

"To whom do you wish to speak?" says Joel, doing his best imitation of an English butler from a thirties film. Joel watches a lot of late movies.

This isn't the first phone call like this he's had. Sometimes they're anti-Semites, wanting to cut his Jewish nuts off; sometimes they're Jews, wanting to cut his nuts off because they don't think he's Jewish enough. In either case the message is the same: his nuts must go. Maybe he should introduce the two sides and they could cut each other's nuts off; that seems to be their shtick. He likes his where they are.

Joel's elocution throws the guy and he mumbles something about dirty Commie bastards. Joel tells him that Mr. Murgatroyd is not home at the moment; would he care to leave his name and number? The coward hangs up, and so does Joel. He's sweating all over. He didn't when this first started happening, but the ones at two A.M. have been getting to him.

Joel doesn't want to turn into one of those paranoids who dive under the sofa every time there's a knock at the door. No Gestapo here, he tells himself. What he needs is some food. He goes out to the kitchen and rummages through the refrigerator, finding not much. Of the two of them, it was Becka who'd done most of the shopping. Without her, he's reverted to his old habits: pizza, Kentucky Fried, doughnuts from the Dunkin' Dough-nuts. He knows it's unhealthy, but he indulges in unhealth as a kind of perverse rebellion against her. He used to justify his tastes by saying that this was what the average worker eats, but he knew even at the time that he was using ideology to cover for addiction. He must be getting middle-aged though, because he's still taking the vitamin pills Becka used to foist on him, threatening him with beri-beri, constipation, and scurvy if he dodged. He recalls with some pain her roughage phase.

The truth is that even Becka's normal cooking, good though it was, made him nervous. He always felt he was in the wrong house, not his, since he'd never associated home with edible food. His mother had been such a terrible cook that he'd left the dinner table hungry more evenings than not. At midnight he would prowl through his mother's apartment, stomach growling so loud you'd have thought it would wake her up, on bare criminal feet into the kitchen. Then followed the hunt for the only remotely digestible objects in the place, which were always baked goods from stores like Hunt's or Woman's Bakery, apple turnovers, muffins, cupcakes, cookies. She used to hide them on him; they'd never be in the refrigerator or the breadbox, not once she'd figured out that it was him who'd been eating them at night. Carefully, like a safe-cracker turning a sensitive combination lock, he'd dismantle the kitchen, moving one pot at a time, one stack of dishes. Sometimes she'd go so far as to stash them in the living room; once, even in the bathroom, under the sink. That was stooping pretty low. He remembers the sense of challenge, the mounting excitement, the triumph when he would finally uncover those familiar sweet oily brown-paper bags with their tightly screwed tops and their odour, faintly stale. He has an image of himself, in his pyjamas, crouching beside the cache he's just dragged out from under the easy chair, cramming in the Chelsea buns, gloating. Next day she'd never mention it. Once or twice he failed, but only once or twice. She never mentioned that, either.

Now, prodding the shambles in his own refrigerator,

Joel can't find anything to eat. There's half a pint of yoghurt, but it's left over from Becka and, by now, questionable. He decides to go out. He locates his jacket finally, which is in the nest of clothing at the bottom of the hall closet. Things somehow don't stay hung up when he hangs them. The jacket has *Bluejays* across the back and is ravelling at the cuffs; it has grease on it from where he crawled under the car, years ago, trying to prove to someone or other that he knew why it was leaking; a futile exercise. The car had been completely irrational; there was never a plausible explanation for any of the things it did, any of the parts that fell off it. Joel felt that driving it was like thumbing your nose at the car establishment, at car snobbery, at the Platonic idea of cars; he refused to trade it in. This was the car that finally got stolen. "They were doing us all a favour," said Becka.

Becka once threatened to burn his Bluejays jacket. She said if he had to wear a stupid macho label, at least he could pick a winner; which goes to show how much she knows about it. Expos she could live with. By that time he'd started ignoring her; the text anyway, not the subtext. In so far as that was possible.

As he's doing up the zipper the phone rings. Joel thinks it may be another nut-cutter; he should get a telephone-answering machine, the kind you can listen in on. But this time it really is Becka. The small sad voice tonight, the one he never trusts. She's more believable when she's being loud.

"Hi, Becka," he says, carefully neutral. "How are things going?" She was the one who walked out, though "walked" is too mild a description of it, so if there's conciliation to be done she can do it. "You want something?" he adds.

"Don't be like that," she says, after a short evaluating pause.

"Like what?" he says. "What am I being like that's so terrible?"

She sighs. He's familiar with these sighs of hers: she

sighs over the phone better than any woman he's ever
known. If he hadn't been sighed at by her so often, if he
didn't know the hidden costs, he'd fall for it. She dodges
his question, though; once she'd have met it head-on. "I
thought maybe I could come over," she says. "So we
could talk about it."

"Sure," says Joel, sliding into an old habit: he's never
refused an offer to talk about it. But also he knows where
talking about it leads. He pictures Becka's body, which
she always holds back as the clincher; which is what he
calls lush and she calls fat. Some of their first arguments
were over this difference of opinion. "I'll be here," he
says. If it's an offer, why turn it down?

But after he puts down the phone he regrets his easy
acquiescence. So they go to bed. So what? What's it
expected to prove? Is she working up to another move,
back in? He's not sure he feels like going through the
whole wash and spin cycle once again. Anyway, he's
hungry. He types out a note—writing would be too
intimate—saying he's been called out suddenly, to an
important meeting, and he'll talk to her later. He doesn't
say *see*. He opens the back door, which is the one she'll
use, and tapes the note to it, noticing as he does so that
someone has thrown an egg at his door: the remains are
oozing down the paintwork, partly solidified, the broken
shell is on the sidewalk.

Joel goes back in, closes the door. It's dark out there.
Someone has taken a lot of trouble, going around to the
back like that; someone who knows exactly who lives
behind his door. It wasn't just a random shot, someone
who happened to be passing by with an egg in his hand
and got a sudden urge to hurl it. He has choices: maybe
it's one of the nut-slicers, an idea he doesn't relish.
Maybe it's the landlord: that's what he thought last week,
when he found a nail hammered through the back tire of
his bicycle. He doesn't think it's anyone official. He's

suspected the RCMP of bugging his phone, more than once, he knows that squeaky-clean sound on the line, and no doubt he's on their list, most people who do anything at all in this country are. But eggs they wouldn't bother with.

Or maybe it's Becka. Throwing an egg at his door, then phoning him to make up because she feels guilty about something she'll never confess to him she's done, that's her style. "What egg?" she'll say to him if he asks, making her innocent chipmunk eyes, and how will he ever know? Once, when they were at a party together, they heard a gossipy story about a woman who'd recently split up with a man they both knew. She'd gone to the post office and filled out a change-of-address card in his name, redirecting all his mail to a town somewhere in the middle of Africa. At the time, and because he didn't like the guy much, Joel had found this hilarious. Becka hadn't, though she'd listened to the story more carefully than he had, and had asked questions. It strikes him now that she'd been filing it away for future reference. Now he tries to remember the rest of the story, the other things the woman had done: intercepting the man's shirts on the way back from the laundry and cutting off all the buttons, sending funeral wreaths to his new girl friend. Joel is safe on both counts: no laundered shirts, no new girl friend. It's just the mail he'll have to watch.

Now he's wondering whether going out is such a good idea. Becka still has a key, which he'll have to do something about pretty soon. Maybe she'll be in his apartment, waiting for him, when he gets back. He decides to take his chances. When she finds he isn't there, she can stay or she can go, it's up to her. (Leaving it up to her has always been one of his best tactics. It drives her mad.) Either way, he's made his move. He's shown her he's not eager. Any effort put out this time around is going to be hers.

As he searches for his wallet in the jumble of paperbacks, papers, and socks beside the bed, Uglypuss brushes against his legs, purring. He scratches her between the ears and pulls her up slowly by the tail, which he's convinced cats like. ("Cut that out, you'll break its spine," Becka would protest. But Uglypuss was his goddamn cat, to begin with.)

"Uglypuss," he says. He's had her almost as long as he's had his Lay-Zee-Boy recliner and his Ping-Pong table: she's been through a lot with him. She turns her odd face up at him, half orange, half black, divided down the nose, a Yin and Yang cat, as Becka used to say during her organic-cereal and body-mind-energy phase.

She follows him to the door, the front one this time; he'll leave through the communal vestibule, walk down the steps, where there are street lights. She meows, but he doesn't want her going out, not at night. Even though she's spayed, she wanders, and sometimes gets into fights. Maybe the toms can't tell she's a girl; or maybe they think she is, but she disagrees. He used to make pointed analyses of Uglypuss's sexual hang-ups, to Becka, over breakfast. Whatever the reason, she gets herself messed up: her ears are nicked, and he's had it with the antibiotic ointment, which she licks off anyway. He thinks of distracting her with food, but he's out of cat kibble, which is one more reason for going out. He takes the container of dubious yoghurt out of the refrigerator and leaves it on the floor, opened for her.

Joel wipes his mouth, pushes the plate away. He's stuffed down everything: weiner schnitzel, home fries, the lot. Now he's full and lazy. The back room of the Blue Danube used to be one of his favourite places to eat, before he moved in with Becka, or rather, she moved in with him. It's inexpensive and you get a lot for your money, good quality too. It has another advantage: other people who want cheap food come here, art students, in pairs or singly, out-of-work actors or actresses, those on the prowl but not desperate or rich or impervious enough to go to singles bars. Joel wouldn't want to pick up the kind of girl who would go to singles bars.

Becka never liked this place, so he gradually eased out of the habit of coming here. The last time they ate together it was here, though: a sure sign, for both of them, that the tide had turned.

Becka had come back from the washroom and plunked herself down opposite him, as though she'd just made an earth-shattering discovery. "Guess what's written in the women's can?" she'd asked.

"I'll bite," said Joel.

"Women make love. Men make war," she said.

"So?" Joel said. "Is the lipstick pink or red?"

"So it's true."

"That's supposed to be an insight?" said Joel. "It's not *men* that make war. It's *some* men. You think those young working-class guys want to march off and be slaughtered? It's the generals, it's the. . . ."

"But it's not women, is it?" said Becka.

"That's got nothing to do with anything," Joel said, exasperated.

"That's what I mean about you," said Becka. "It's only your goddamned point of view that's valid, right?"

"Bullshit," he said. "We aren't talking about points of view. We're talking about *history*."

As he said this, the futility of what he was trying to do swept over him, as it sometimes does: what's the point of continuing, in a society like this one, where it's always two steps forward and two back? The frustration, the lack of money, the indifference, and on top of that the incessant puerile bickering on the left over who's more pure. If there was a real fight (he thinks "guns" but not "war"), if it was out in the open, things would be clearer; but this too can be seen as a temptation, the impulse to romanticize other people's struggles. It's hard to decide what form of action is valid. Do you have to be dead to be authentic, as the purists seem to believe? Though he hasn't noticed any of them actually lining up for the firing

squads. Maybe he's chosen the wrong mode; maybe
street theatre doesn't fit in up here, where the streets are
so neat and clean and nobody lives on them, in shacks or
storm sewers or laid out on mats along the sidewalks.
Sometimes he thinks maybe they're all just play-acting,
indulging in a game of adult dress-ups that accomplishes
nothing in the end.

But these moods of his seldom last long. "Wars are
fought so those in power can stay there," he said to
Becka, trying to be patient.

"You don't think you're ever going to *win*, do you?"
Becka said softly. She can read his mind, but only at bad
times.

"It's not about winning," Joel said. "I know whose side
I'd rather be on, that's all."

"How about being on mine?" Becka said. "For a
change."

"What the shit are you talking about?" said Joel.

"I'm not hungry," said Becka. "Let's go home."

It's the word *home* that echoes in the air here for Joel
now, plaintively, in a minor key. Home isn't a place,
Becka said once, it's a feeling. Maybe that's what's the
matter with it, Joel answered. For him, when he was
growing up, home was the absence of a thing that should
have been there. Going home was going into noth-
ingness. He'd rather be out.

He looks around the room, which is smoke-filled,
bare-walled, his gaze passing over couples, resting
longer on women by themselves. Why not admit it? He's
come out tonight because he's looking for it, as so many
times before: someone to go home with, to her home,
not his, in the hope that this unknown place, yet another
unknown place, will finally contain something he wants
to have. It's Becka's phone call that's done it: she has that
effect on him. Every move to encircle him, pin him
down, force him into a corner, only makes him more
desperate to escape. She never came right out and said
so, but what she wanted was permanence, commitment,

monogamy, the works. Forty years of the same thing night after night was a long time to contemplate.

He sees a girl he knows slightly, remembers from the summer, when they were doing the Cannibal Monster Tomato play down near Leamington, for the itinerant harvesters. (Cold-water shacks. Insecticides in the lungs. No medical protection. Intimidation. It was a good piece.) The girl was a minor player, someone who carried a sign. As he recalls, she was getting laid by one of the troupe; that was the only explanation he could think of at the time for her presence among them. He hopes he was right, he hopes she's not too political. Becka wasn't political when he first met her. In those days she was doing art therapy at one of the nuthouses, helping the loonies to express themselves with wet newspaper and glue. She'd had a calmness, a patience that he's since realized was only a professional veneer, but at the time he'd settled into it like a hammock. He'd enjoyed trying to educate her, and she'd gotten into it to parrot him or please him. What a mistake.

In recent years, he's come to realize that the kind of women that ought to turn him on—left-leaning intellectual women who can hold up their end of a debate, who believe in fifty-fifty, who can be good pals—aren't the kind that actually do. He's not ashamed of this discovery, as he would have been once. He prefers women who are soft-spoken and who don't live all the time in their heads, who don't take everything with deadly seriousness. What he needs is someone who won't argue about whether he's too macho, whether he should or shouldn't encourage the capitalists by using under-arm deodorant, whether the personal is political or the political is personal. whether he's anti-Semitic, anti-female, anti-anything. Someone who won't argue.

He pushes back his chair and walks over, ready for rejection. They can always tell him to go away. He doesn't mind that much, he never tries to force the issue. There's no sense in being obnoxious, and he doesn't want to be with anyone who doesn't want to be with him. He's never seen the point of rape.

This girl has reddish hair, parted in the middle and drawn back. She's crouched over her noodles, pretending to be absorbed in a large but paperbacked book that's propped open beside her plate. Joel goes through the openers: "Hi, good to see you again. Mind if I join you?"

She glances up, with that little frown he's seen on their faces so often, that coming-out-of-the-trance face, *Oh, you startled me*, as if she hasn't been aware of his approach. She's been aware. She recognizes him, hesitates, deciding; then she smiles. She's grateful, he sees, for the company: it must be all over with what's-his-name. Relieved, he sits down. Even though he knows no one is really watching him, it still makes him feel like an idiot to be sent away, like a puppy that's made a mess.

Now for the book: that's always a good way in. He turns it so he can see the title. *Quilt-Making Through History*. That's a hard one: he knows nothing and cares less about quilt-making. He guesses that she's the kind of girl who would read about it but would never actually do it; though opening up with a statement to this effect would be far too aggressive. It's a mistake to begin by putting them down.

"Like a beer," he says, "or are you a vegetarian?"

"As a matter of fact I am," she says, with that superior tight mini-smile they give you. She hasn't got the joke. Joel sighs; they're off to a roaring start.

"Then I guess you mind if I smoke?" he says.

She relents; evidently she doesn't want to drive him away. "You go ahead," she says. "It's a big room." She doesn't add that it's full of smoke already, and he likes her better.

He thinks of saying, "Live around here?" but he can't, not again. "Tell me about yourself" is out too. Instead he finds himself shifting almost immediately, much sooner than he usually does, into social realism. "This day has been total shit," he says. He feels this, it's not fake, the

day *has* been total shit; but on another level he's aware
it's a useful ploy: if they feel sorry for you, how can they
turn you down?

Becka used to accuse him of having a detachable prick.
In her version, he unscrewed it, put it on a leash, and
took it out for walks, like a dachshund without legs or a
kind of truffle-hunting pig (her metaphor). According to
her, it would stick itself into any hole or crevice it could
find, anything vaguely funnel-shaped, remotely female.
In her more surrealistic inventions (when she was still
trying to live with what she called this habit of his,
before she switched to *compulsion*, when she was still
trying to be humorous about it), he'd find himself stuck
somewhere, in a mouse-hole or a dead tree or an outside
faucet, unable to get loose, because his prick had made a
mistake. What could you expect, she said, from a
primitive animal with no eyes?

"If I got you a sheep and a pair of rubber boots, would
you stay home more?" she said. "We could keep it in the
garage. If we had a garage. If it wasn't too boor-joo-ice to
have a garage."

But she was wrong, it isn't the sex he's after. It isn't
only the sex. Sometimes he thinks, in the middle of it,
that really he'd rather be jogging around the block or
watching a movie or playing Ping-Pong. Sex is merely a
social preliminary, the way a handshake used to be; it's
the first step in getting to know someone. Once it's out of
the way, you can concentrate on the real things; though
without it, somehow you can't. He likes women, he likes
just talking with them sometimes. The ones he likes
talking with, having a laugh with, these are the ones that
become what he refers to privately as "repeaters."

"How come I'm not enough for you?" Becka said, soon
after the first two or three, when she'd figured it out. He
wasn't a very good liar; he resented having to conceal
things.

"It's not important," he said, trying to comfort her; she
was crying. He still loved her in a simple way then. "It's

no more important than sneezing. It's not an emotional
commitment. You're an emotional commitment."

"If it's not important, why do you do it?" she said.

He wasn't able to answer that. "This is just the way I
am," he said finally. "It's part of me. Can't you accept it?"

"But this is just the way *I* am," she said, crying even
more. "You make me feel like nothing. You make me feel
I'm worth nothing to you. I'm not even worth any more
than a sneeze."

"That's blackmail," he said, pulling away. He couldn't
stand to have love and fidelity extracted from him, like
orange juice or teeth. No squeezers. No pliers. She
should have known she was the central relationship: he'd
told her often enough.

This girl's name, which he's forgotten but which he
digs out of her by pretending to almost remember it, is
Amelia. She works, of course, in a bookstore. Looking
more closely, he can see she's not quite as young as he
first thought. There are tiny shrivellings beginning
around her eyes, a line forming from the nostril to the
corner of her mouth; later it will extend down to her
chin, which is small and pointed, and she will develop
that peevish, starved look. Redheads have delicate skin,
they age early. She has a chain around her neck, with a
glass pendant on it containing dried flowers. He guesses
she'll be the kind of girl who has prisms hanging in her
window and a poster of a whale over the bed, and when
they get to her place, she does.

Amelia turns out to be one of the vocal kind, which he
likes: it's a tribute, in a way. He's surprised, too: you
couldn't have told it by looking at her, that almost prissy
restraint and decorum, the way she tightened her little
bum, moved it away when he put his hand on it as she
was unlocking the door. Joel doesn't know why he always
expects girls with pierced ears and miniature gold stars
in them, high cheekbones and frail rib cages, to be quiet

in bed. It's some antiquated notion he has about good taste, though he should know by now that the thin ones have more nerve-endings per square inch.

Afterwards she goes back to being subdued, as if she's faintly ashamed of herself for those groans, for having clutched him like that, as if he's not a semi-stranger after all. He wonders how many times she's gone home with someone she barely knows; he's curious, he'd like to ask, "You do this often?" But he knows from past experience they're likely to find this insulting, some kind of obscure slur on their moral standards; even if, like himself, they do. Sometimes, especially when they're younger, he feels he ought to tell them they shouldn't behave like this. Not all men are good risks, even the ones who eat at the Blue Danube. They could be violent, into whips or safety pins, perverts, murderers; not like him. But any interference from him could be interpreted as patriarchal paternalism: he knows that from experience too. It's their own lookout; anyway, why should he complain?

Amelia lies against him, head on his biceps, red hair spilling across his arm, her mouth relaxed; he's grateful for her simple physical presence, the animal warmth. Women don't like the term "muff," he knows that; but for him it's both descriptive and affectionate: something furry that keeps you warm. This is the kind of thing he needs to get him through November. She's even being friendly, in a detached sort of way. He can't always depend on them to be friendly afterwards. They've been known to hold it against him, as if it's something he's done all by himself, to them instead of with them; as if they've had nothing to do with it.

He likes this one well enough to suggest that maybe they could watch the late show on TV, which isn't an experience he'd want to share with just anyone. Sex yes, late movies no. He wonders if she's got any food in the house, some cake maybe, which they could eat right off the

plate while watching, licking the icing from each other's
fingers. He's hungry again, but more than that, he wants
the feeling of comfort this would bring. There's something about lemon icing in a dark room. But when she
says without any undertones that, no, she'd like some
sleep, she needs to get up early to go to her fitness class
before work, that's all right with him too. He puts on his
clothes, lighthearted; this whole thing has cheered him
up a lot. He has that secret feeling of having gotten away
with it again, in the bedroom window and out again
without being caught: no sticky flypaper here. He
remembers, briefly, the day he figured out his mother
was hiding the cookies, not so he wouldn't find them, but
so he would, and how enraged, how betrayed he'd been.
He'd seen the edge of her green chenille bathrobe
whisking back around the corner; she'd been standing in
the hall outside the kitchen, listening to him eat. She
must have known what a rotten cook she was, and this
was her backhanded way of making sure he got at least
some food into him. That's what he thinks now, but at the
time he merely felt he'd been controlled, manipulated
by her all along. Maybe that was when he started to have
his first doubts about free will.

Amelia has turned on her side and is almost asleep.
He kisses her, says he'll let himself out. He wonders if he
likes her well enough to see her again, decides he
probably doesn't. Nevertheless he makes a note of her
phone number, memorizing it off the bedside phone;
he'll jot it down later, out in the kitchen, where she won't
notice. He never knows when a thing like that will come
in handy. Any port in a storm, and when he's at a low
point, a trough in the graph, he needs to be with
someone and it doesn't much matter who, within limits.

He pisses into her toilet, flushes it, noting the anti-
nuke sticker on the mirror, the pots of herbs struggling
for existence on the windowsill. Then he goes into the
kitchenette and turns on the light, taking a quick peek
into the refrigerator in passing, on the off-chance she's

got something unhealthy and delicious in there. But she's a tofu girl, and reluctantly he's out the door.

He's not thinking about Becka. He doesn't remember her till his key's in the lock, when he has a sudden image of her, waiting on the other side, black hair falling around her face like something in a Lorca play, large wounded eyes regarding him, some deadly instrument in her hand: a corkscrew, a potato peeler, or, more historically, an ice-pick, though he doesn't own one. Cautiously he opens the door, eases through, is relieved when nothing happens. Maybe it's finally over, after all. It occurs to him that he's forgotten to buy cat food.

His relief lasts until he hits the living room. She's been here, all right. He gazes at the innards of his Lay-Zee-Boy, strewn across the floor, its wiry guts protruding from what's left of the frame, at the hunks of soft foam from the sofa washing against the fireplace as if it's a shore, as if Becka has been a storm, a hurricane. In another corner he finds all his Ping-Pong balls, lined up in a row and stomped on; they look like hatched-out turtle eggs. Some of his underwear is lying in the fireplace, charred around the edges, still smouldering.

He shrugs. Histrionic bitch, he thinks. So he'll replace it: there's nothing here that can't be duplicated. She won't get to him that easily. She hasn't touched the typewriter, though: she knows exactly how far she can go.

Then he sees the note. *Want Uglypuss back? It's in a garbage can. Start looking.* The note is pinned to the big orange art-shop candle on the mantelpiece, one of the first things she gave him. It's as if he's finally had a visit from Santa Claus, who has turned out to be the monster his mother was always warning him against when he showed symptoms of wanting a Christmas like some of the other kids on the block. *Santa Claus brings you lumps of coal and rotten potatoes. What do you need it for?*

But this was no Santa Claus, it was Becka, who knows

just where to slide in the knife. Dead or alive, she doesn't say. She's never exactly loved Uglypuss, but surely she wouldn't murder. He fears the worst, but he can't assume it. He'll have to go and see. He hears the claws scrabbling on metal, the plaintive wails, the mounting panic, as he does up his zipper again. Finally he knows she'll stop at nothing.

He walks in a widening circle through the streets around his house, opening every can, digging through the bags, listening for faint meows. He shouldn't be spending time on something this trivial, this personal; he should be conserving his energy for the important things. What he needs is perspective. This is Becka controlling him again. Maybe she was lying, maybe Uglypuss is safe and sound at her new place, purring beside the hot-air register. Maybe Becka is making him go through all this for nothing, hoping he'll arrive on her doorstep and she can torture him or reward him, whichever she feels like at the moment.

"Uglypuss!" he calls. He tells himself he's in a state of shock, it will hit him tomorrow, when the full implication of a future without Uglypuss will sink in. At the moment though he's thinking: *Why did I have to give it that dumb name?*

Becka walks along the street. She has often walked along this particular street. She tells herself there is nothing unusual about it.

Both of her hands are bare, and there's blood on the right one and four thin lines of it across her cheek. In her right hand she's carrying an axe. Actually it's smaller than an axe, it's a hatchet, the one Joel keeps beside the fireplace to split the kindling when he lights the fire. Once she liked to make love with him on the rug in front of the fireplace, in the orange glow from the candle. That was until he said there was always a draft and he'd rather be in bed, where it was warmer. After a while she figured out that he didn't really like being looked at; he had an odd sort of modesty, as if he felt his body belonged to him alone. Once she tried flattering him about it, but this was a bad move, you weren't supposed to compare. So then it was under the covers, like a married couple. Before that she used to bug him about keeping the axe in the living room, she wanted him to leave it on the back porch and split the kindling out there instead; she told him she didn't like getting splinters.

It was looking at the axe that finally did it. Joel was gone when he said he'd be there. She didn't know exactly where he'd gone but she knew in general. He was always doing that to her. She waited for an hour and a half, pacing, reading his magazines, surrounded by a space that used to be hers and still felt like it. The heat was off, which meant Joel had been antagonizing the landlord again. She thought about lighting a fire. Uglypuss came and rubbed against her legs and complained, and when she went into the kitchen to put out some food, there was the yoghurt she'd bought herself, opened on the floor.

She asked herself how long she was going to wait. Even if he came back soon, he'd have that smug look and the smell of it still on him. She'd have the choice of ignoring it, in which case he won, or saying something, in which case he won also, because then he could accuse her of intruding on his privacy. It would be just another example, he'd say, of why things couldn't work out. That would make her angry—they could, they could work out if he'd only try—and then he would criticize her for being angry. Her anger would be a demonstration of the power he still holds over her. She knows it, but she can't control it. This time was once too often. It was always once too often.

Becka walks quickly, head a little down and forward, as if she has to push to make her way through the air. Her hair blows back in the wind. It's beginning to drizzle. In her left hand she's carrying a green plastic garbage bag, screwed shut and knotted at the top. The street she's on is Spadina, a street she remembers from childhood as the place where she would be taken by her grandfather when he wanted to pay visits to some of his old cronies. She'd be shown off by him, and given things to eat. That was before the Chinese mostly took over. It's well enough lighted, even at this time of night, bamboo furniture, wholesale clothing, restaurants, ethnic as they say; but she's not buying or eating, she's just looking, thanks, for a garbage can, someplace to dump the bag. An ordinary garbage can is all she asks; why can't she find one?

She can't believe she's done what she's just done. What horrifies her is that she enjoyed it, the axe biting into the black naugahyde of that ratty chair of his, into the sofa, the stuffing she'd pulled out and thrown around, it might as well have been Joel. Though if he'd been there he would have stopped her. Just by being there, by looking at her as if to say, *You mean you really can't think of anything more important to do?*

This is what he's turned me into, she thinks. I was never this mean before, I used to be a nice person, a nice girl. Didn't I?

Today, before calling him, she'd been sick of the taste of the inside of her own mouth. She'd had enough of solitude, enough freedom. A woman without a man is like a fish without a bicycle. Brave words, she'd said them once herself. That was before she figured out she wasn't a fish. Today she thought she still loved him, and love conquers all, doesn't it? Where there's love there's hope. Maybe they could get back, together. Now, she doesn't know.

She thinks about stuffing the garbage bag into a mailbox, the parcel kind, or a newspaper stand. She could put in the quarter, open the box, take out the newspaper, leave the bag. Someone would find it quicker that way. She is not heartless.

But suddenly there's a garbage can, not a plastic one

but old-style metal, in front of a Chinese fruit-and-vegetable store. She goes over to it, leans the hatchet against it, sets down the bag, tries to lift the lid. Either it's stuck or her hands are numb. She bangs it against a telephone pole; several people look at her. At last the lid comes loose. Luckily the can is half empty. She drops the bag in. Not a sound: she sprayed in some boot water-proofer, which was about the only thing she could think of: breathing the fumes makes you dizzy. Kids at high school used to get high on it. The stupid cat clawed its way through the first two garbage bags, before she thought of tying it up in one of Joel's shirts and spraying it with boot water-proofer to quiet it down. She doesn't know if it went unconscious; maybe it just couldn't get through Joel's shirt and decided not to fight a losing battle. Maybe it's catatonic. To coin a phrase. She hopes she hasn't killed it. She pokes the bag a little: there's a wiggle. She's relieved, but she doesn't relent and let it loose. Why should she have all the grief? Let him have some, for a change.

This is what will really get to him, she knows: this theft. His kidnapped child, the one he wouldn't let her have. *We're not ready yet* and all that crap. Crap! He'd always thought more of the cat than he did of her. It used to make her sick, to watch the way he'd pick it up by the tail and run it through his hands, like sand, and the cat loved it, like the nauseating masochist it was. It was the kind of cat that drooled when you stroked it. It fawned all over him. Maybe the real reason she couldn't stand it was that it was a grotesque and stunted furry little parody of herself. Maybe this was what she looked like, to other people, when she was with him. Maybe this was what she looked like to him. She thinks of herself lying with her eyes closed and her mouth slack and open. Did he remember what she looked like at those moments, when he was with others?

She doesn't close the lid on the garbage can. She leaves the hatchet where it is, walks away. She feels smaller, diminished, as if something's been sucking on her neck. Anger is supposed to be liberating, so goes the mythology, but her anger has not freed her in any way that she can see. It's only made her emptier, flowing out of her like this. She doesn't want to be angry; she wants to be comforted. She wants a truce.

She can remember, just barely, having had confidence in herself. She can't recall where she got it from. Go through life with your mouth open, that used to be her motto. Live in the now. Encounter experience fully. Hold out your arms in welcome. She once thought she could handle anything.

Tonight she feels dingy, old. Soon she will start getting into the firming cream; she will start worrying about her eyelids. Beginning again is supposed to be exciting, a challenge. Beginning again is fine as an idea, but what with? She's used it all up; she's used up.

Still, she would like to be able to love someone; she would like to feel inhabited again. This time she wouldn't be so picky, she'd settle for a man maybe a little worn around the edges, a second, with a few hairline cracks, a few pulled threads, something from a fire sale, someone a little damaged. Like those ads for adoptable children in the *Star*: "Today's Child." Today's lover. A man in a state of shock, a battered male. She'd take a divorced one, an older one, someone who could only get it up for kinky sex, anything, as long as he'd be grateful. That's what she wants, when it comes right down to it: a gratitude equal to her own. But even in this she's deluding herself. Why should such a man be any different from the rest? They're all a little damaged. Anyway, she'd be clutching at a straw, and who wants to be a straw?

She should never have called him. She should know by now that over is over, that when it says *The End* at the end of a book it means there isn't any more; which she can never quite believe. The problem is that she's invested so much suffering in him, and she can't shake the notion that so much suffering has to be worth something. Maybe unhappiness is a drug, like any other: you could develop a tolerance to it, and then you'd want more.

People came to the end of what they had to say to one another, Joel told her once, during one of their many sessions about whether they should stay together or not; the time he was trying for wisdom. After that point, he said, it was only repetition. But Becka protested; Becka hadn't come to the end of what she had to say, or so she thought. That was the trouble: she never came to the end of what she had to say. He'd push her too far and she'd blurt things out, things she couldn't retrieve, she would make clumsy mistakes of a kind she never made with other people, the landlord for instance, with whom she was a miracle of tact. But with Joel, the irrevocable is always happening.

He once told her he wanted to share his life with her. He said he'd never asked anyone that before. How she melted over that, how she lapped it up! But he never said he wanted her to share her life with him, which, when it happened, turned out to be a very different thing.

What now, now that she's done it? Time will go on. She'll walk back to the row house in Cabbagetown she shares with two other women. This is about all she can afford; at least she has her own room. She hardly ever sees the other two women; she know them mostly by their smells, burnt toast in the mornings, incense (from one of them, the one with the lay-over boyfriend) at night. The situation reeks of impermanence. She got the place by answering an ad in the paper, *Third woman needed, share kitchen, no drugs or freaks,* after moving out of the apartment she still thinks of as her own, and after a miserable week with her mother, who thought but did not say that it served her right for not insisting on marriage. What did she expect anyway, from a man like that? Not a real job. Not a real Jew. Not real.

When she gets to the house she'll be worn out, her adrenaline high gone, replaced by a flat grey fatigue. She'll put on her most penitential nightgown, blue-flowered flannelette, the one Joel hates because it reminds him of landladies. She'll fix herself a hot-water bottle and climb into a bed which does not yet smell like hers and feel sorry for herself. Maybe she should go out hunting, sit in a bar, something she's never done, though there's always a first time. But she needs her sleep. Tomorrow she has to go to work, at her new job, her old job, mixing poster paints for the emotionally disturbed, a category that right now includes her. It doesn't pay well and there are hazards, but these days she's lucky to have it.

She couldn't stay with the troupe, even though she'd done such a good job of the headless corpses for the El Salvador piece in the spring, even though it was her who'd come up with Christ as a knitted sock. It would be disruptive for the troupe, they both agreed on that, to have her there; the tension, the uneven balance of conflicting egos. Or words to that effect. He was so good at that bullshit, the end result of which was that she'd been out of a job and he hadn't, and for a while she'd even felt noble about it.

Becka's four blocks away from the garbage can now, and it's raining in earnest. She stands under an awning, waiting for the rain to slow down, trying to decide whether or not to give in and take the streetcar. She wants to walk all the way back, to get rid of this furious energy.

It's time for Joel to be coming home. She pictures him opening the door, throwing his jacket on the floor; she sees what he will find. Now she feels as if she's committed a sacrilege. Why should she feel that way? Because for at least two years she thought he was God.

He isn't God. She can see him, in his oily Bluejays jacket, running through the streets, panting because he'll be out of breath, he'll have eaten too much for dinner, with whatever slut he'd picked up, plunging his hands into chilly garbage, calling like a fool: *Uglypuss!* People will think he's crazy. But he will only be mad with grief.

Like her, leaning her forehead against the cold shop window, staring through the dark glass, yellowed by those plastic things they put there to keep the sun from fading the colours, at the fur-coated woman inside, tears oozing down her cheeks. She can't even remember now which garbage can she put the damn thing in, she couldn't find it again if she looked. She should have taken it home with her. It was her cat too, more or less, once. It purred and drooled for her, too. It kept her company. How could she have done that to it? Maybe the boot spray will make it feeble-minded. That's all he'll need, a feeble-minded cat. Not that anyone will be able to tell the difference.

In her either, if she goes on like this. She wipes her nose and eyes on her damp sleeve, straightens. When she gets home she'll do some Yogic breathing and concentrate on the void for a while, trying once more for serenity, and take a bath. *My heart does not bleed,* she tells herself. But it does.

Betty

When I was seven we moved again, to a tiny wooden cottage on the Saint Marys River, upstream from Sault Sainte Marie. We were only renting the cottage for the summer, but for the time being it was our house, since we had no other. It was dim and mousy-smelling and very cramped, stuffed with all the things from the place before that were not in storage. My sister and I preferred to spend most of our time outside it.

There was a short beach, behind which the cottages, with their contrasting trim—green against white, maroon against robin's-egg blue, brown against yellow— were lined up like little shoe-boxes, each with its matching outhouse at an unsanitary distance behind. But we were forbidden to swim in the water, because of the strong current. There were stories of children who had been swept away, down toward the rapids and the locks and the Algoma Steel fires of the Soo which we could sometimes see from our bedroom window on overcast nights, glowing dull red against the clouds. We were allowed to wade though, no further than the knee, and we would stand in the water, strands of loose weed tangling against our ankles, and wave at the lake freighters as they slid past, so close we could see not only the flags and sea gulls at their sterns but the hands of the sailors and the ovals of their faces as they waved back to us. Then the waves would come, washing over our thighs up to the waists of our bloomered and skirted seersucker bathing suits, and we would scream with delight.

Our mother, who was usually on the shore, reading or

talking to someone but not quite watching us, would sometimes mistake the screams for drowning. Or she would say later, "You've been in over your knees," but my sister would explain that it was only the boat waves. My mother would look at me to see if this was the truth. Unlike my sister, I was a clumsy liar.

The freighters were huge, cumbersome, with rust staining the holes for their anchor chains and enormous chimneys from which the smoke spurted in grey burps. When they blew their horns, as they always did when approaching the locks, the windows in our cottage rattled. For us, they were magical. Sometimes things would drop or be thrown from them, and we would watch these floating objects eagerly, running along the beach to be there when they landed, wading out to fish them in. Usually these treasures turned out to be only empty cardboard boxes or punctured oil cans, oozing dark brown grease and good for nothing. Several times we got orange crates, which we used as cupboards or stools in our hide-outs.

We liked the cottage partly because we had places to make these hide-outs. There had never been room before, since we had always lived in cities. Just before this it was Ottawa, the ground floor of an old three-tiered red-brick apartment building. On the floor above us lived a newly married couple, the wife English and Protestant, the husband French and Catholic. He was in the air force, and was away a lot, but when he came back on leave he used to beat up his wife. It was always about eleven o'clock at night. She would flee downstairs to my mother for protection, and they would sit in the kitchen with cups of tea. The wife would cry, though quietly, so as not to wake us—my mother insisted on that, being a believer in twelve hours of sleep for children—display her bruised eye or cheek, and whisper about his drinking. After an hour or so there would be a discreet knock on the door, and the airman, in full uniform, would ask my mother politely if he could have his wife back upstairs where she belonged. It was a religious

dispute, he would say. Besides, he'd given her fifteen
dollars to spend on food and she had served him fried
Kam. After being away a month, a man expected a good
roast, pork or beef, didn't my mother agree? "I kept my
mouth shut and my eyes open," my mother would say.
He never seemed that drunk to her, but with the polite
kind you couldn't tell what they would do.

I wasn't supposed to know about any of this. I was
considered either too young or too good; but my sister,
who was four years older, was given hints, which she
passed along to me with whatever she thought fit to add.
I saw the wife a number of times, going up or down the
stairs outside our door, and once she did have a black
eye. I never saw the man, but by the time we left Ottawa
I was convinced he was a murderer.

This might have explained my father's warning when
my mother told him she had met the young couple who
lived in the right-hand cottage. "Don't get too involved,"
he said. "I don't want her running over here at all hours
of the night." He had little patience with my mother's
talents as a sympathetic listener, even when she teased
him by saying, "But I listen to *you*, dear." She attracted
people he called "sponges."

He didn't seem to have anything to worry about. This
couple was very different from the other one. Fred and
Betty insisted on being called Fred and Betty, right
away. My sister and I, who had been drilled to call
people Mr. and Mrs., had to call them Fred and Betty
also, and we could go over to their house whenever we
wanted to. "I don't want you to take that at face value,"
our mother said. Times were hard but our mother had
been properly brought up, and we were going to be, too.
Nevertheless, at first we went to Fred and Betty's as
often as we could.

Their cottage was exactly the same size as ours, but
since there was less furniture in it it seemed bigger. Ours
had Ten-Test walls between the rooms, painted lime
green, with lighter squares on the paint where other

people had once hung pictures. Betty had replaced her walls with real plywood and painted the inside bright yellow, and she'd made yellow-and-white curtains for the kitchen, a print of chickens coming out of eggshells. She'd sewed herself a matching apron from the left-over material. They owned their cottage rather than renting it; as my mother said, you didn't mind doing the work then. Betty called the tiny kitchen a kitchenette. There was a round ironwork table tucked into one corner, with two scrolled ironwork chairs, painted white, one for Betty and one for Fred. Betty called this corner the breakfast nook.

There was more to do at Fred and Betty's than at our house. They had a bird made of hollow coloured glass that perched on the edge of a tumbler of water, teetering back and forth until it would finally dip its head into the water and take a drink. They had a front-door knocker in the shape of a woodpecker: you pulled a string, and the woodpecker pecked at the door. They also had a whistle in the shape of a bird that you could fill with water and blow in to and it would warble, "like a canary," Betty said. And they took the Saturday coloured funnies. Our parents didn't, and they didn't like us reading trash, as they called it. But Fred and Betty were so friendly and kind to us, what, as my mother said, could they do?

Beyond all these attractions there was Fred. We both fell in love with Fred. My sister would climb into his lap and announce that he was her boyfriend and she was going to marry him when she grew up. She would then make him read the funnies to her and tease him by trying to take the pipe out of his mouth or by tying his shoelaces together. I felt the same way, but I knew it was no good saying so. My sister had staked her claim: when she said she was going to do a thing she usually did it. And she hated my being what she called a copy-cat. So I would sit in the breakfast nook on one of the scrolled ironwork chairs while Betty made coffee, watching my sister and Fred on the living-room couch.

There was something about Fred that attracted people. My mother, who was not a flirtatious woman—she went in for wisdom, instead—was livelier when he was around. Even my father liked him, and would sometimes have a beer with him when he got back from the city. They would sit on the porch of Fred's cottage in Betty's yellow wicker chairs, swatting at the sand flies and discussing baseball scores. They seldom mentioned their jobs. I'm not sure what Fred did, but it was in an office. My father was "in wallpaper," my mother said, but I was never very clear about what that meant. It was more exciting when they talked about the war. My father's bad back had kept him out of it, much to his disgust, but Fred had been in the navy. He never said too much about it, though my father was always prompting him; but we knew from Betty that they were engaged just before Fred left and married right after he came back. Betty had written letters to him every single night and mailed them once a week. She did not say how often Fred had written to her. My father didn't like many people, but he said that Fred wasn't a fool.

Fred didn't seem to make any efforts to be nice to people. I don't think he was even especially handsome. The difficulty is that though I can remember Betty down to the last hair and freckle, I can't remember what Fred looked like. He had dark hair and a pipe, and he used to sing to us if we pestered him enough. "Sioux City Sue," he would sing, "Your hair is red, your eyes are blue, I'd swap my horse and dog for you . . ." Or he would sing "Beautiful Brown Eyes" to my sister, whose eyes were brown as compared with my own watery blue. This hurt my feelings, as the song contained the line, "I'll never love blue eyes again." It seemed so final, a whole lifetime of being unloved by Fred. Once I cried, which was made worse by the fact that I couldn't explain to anyone what was wrong; and I had to undergo the humiliation of Fred's jocular concern and my sister's scorn, and the worse humiliation of being comforted by

Betty in the kitchenette. It was a humiliation because it was obvious even to me that Betty didn't grasp things very well. "Don't pay any attention to *him*," she said, having guessed that my tears had something to do with Fred. But that was the one piece of advice I couldn't take.

Fred, like a cat, wouldn't go two steps out of his way for you really, as my mother said later. So it was unfair that everyone was in love with Fred, but no one, despite her kindness, was in love with Betty. It was Betty who always greeted us at the door, asked us in, and talked to us while Fred slouched on the couch reading the paper. She fed us cookies and milk-shakes and let us lick out the bowls when she was baking. Betty was such a nice person; everyone said so, but no one would have called Fred exactly that. Fred, for instance, did not laugh much, and he only smiled when he was making rude remarks, mostly to my sister. "Stuffing your face again?" he would say. "Hey, baggy-pants." Whereas Betty never said things like that, and she was always either smiling or laughing.

She laughed a lot when Fred called her Betty Grable, which he did at least once a day. I couldn't see why she laughed. It was supposed to be a compliment, I thought. Betty Grable was a famous movie star; there was a picture of her thumbtacked to the wall in Fred and Betty's outhouse. Both my sister and I preferred Fred and Betty's outhouse to our own. Theirs had curtains on the window, unlike ours, and it had a little wooden box and a matching wooden scoop for the lye. We only had a cardboard box and an old trowel.

Betty didn't really look like Betty Grable, who was blonde and not as plump as our Betty. Still, they were both beautiful, I thought. I didn't realize until much later that the remark was cruel; for Betty Grable was renowned for her legs, whereas our Betty had legs that started at her waist and continued downwards without a curve or a pause until they reached her feet. At the time

they seemed like ordinary legs. Sitting in the kitchenette, I saw a lot of Betty's legs, for she wore halter tops
and shorts, with her yellow apron over them. Somehow
Betty could never get her legs to tan despite the hours
she spent crocheting in her wicker chair, the top part of
her in the shade of the porch but her legs sticking out
into the sun.

My father said that Betty had no sense of humour. I
couldn't understand this at all. If you told her a joke she
would always laugh, even if you got it mixed up, and she
told jokes of her own, too. She would print the word
"BED," making the E smaller and thicker than the B and
the D. "What's this?" she would say. "It's the little dark E
in BED." I didn't get this joke the first time she told it
and she had to explain it to me. "Little darkie," she said,
her slightly protruding teeth shining with good humour.
We had never been to the United States, even though
we could see it across the river, a strip of green trees that
faded west into the blue of Lake Superior, and the only
black people I had seen were the characters in the
comics. There was L'il 8-Ball, and the Africans in Tarzan,
and Lothar in Mandrake the Magician, who wore a lion
skin. I couldn't see what any of them had to do with the
word *bed*.

My father also said that Betty had no sex appeal. This
didn't seem to bother my mother in the least. "She's a
very nice girl," she would answer complacently, or, "She
has very nice colouring." My mother and Betty were
soon collaborating on a scheme for making the preserv-
ing easier. Most people still had Victory gardens, though
the war was over, and the months of July and August
were supposed to be spent putting up as many jars of
fruit and vegetables as you could. My mother's garden
was half-hearted, like most of her housekeeping efforts.
It was a small patch beside the outhouse where squash
vines rambled over a thicket of overgrown tomato plants
and a few uneven lines of dwarfed carrots and beets. My
mother's talent, we had heard her say, was for people.

Betty and Fred didn't have a garden at all. Fred wouldn't have worked in it, and when I think of Betty now I realize that a garden would have been too uncontained for her. But she had Fred buy dozens of six-quart baskets of strawberries, peaches, beans, tomatoes, and Concord grapes, on his trips into the city; and she persuaded my mother to give up on her own garden and join her in her mammoth canning sessions.

My mother's wood stove was unbearably hot for such an operation, and Betty's little electric range was too small; so Betty got "the boys," as she called Fred and my father, to set up the derelict wood stove that until then had been rusting behind Betty's outhouse. They put it in our back yard, and my mother and Betty would sit at our kitchen table, which had been carried outside, peeling, slicing, and talking, Betty with her round pin-cushion cheeks flushed redder than usual by the heat and my mother with an old bandanna wrapped around her head, making her look like a gipsy. Behind them the canning kettles bubbled and steamed, and on one side of the table the growing ranks of Crown jars, inverted on layers of newspapers, cooled and sometimes leaked or cracked. My sister and I hung around the edges, not wanting to be obvious enough to be put to work, but coveting the empty six-quart baskets. We could use them in our hide-out, we felt; we were never sure what for, but they fitted neatly into the orange crates.

I learned a lot about Fred during Betty's canning sessions: how he liked his eggs, what size socks he took (Betty was a knitter), how well he was doing at the office, what he refused to eat for dinner. Fred was a picky eater, Betty said joyfully. Betty had almost nothing else to talk about, and even my mother, veteran of many confidences, began to talk less and smoke more than usual when Betty was around. It was easier to listen to disasters than to Betty's inexhaustible and trivial cheer. I began to think that I might not want to be married to Fred after all. He unrolled from Betty's mouth like a long ribbon of soggy newspaper printed from end to end with nothing but the weather. Neither my sister nor I was interested in sock sizes, and Betty's random, unexciting details diminished Fred in our eyes. We began to spend less of our playtime at Fred and Betty's and more in our hide-out, which was in a patch of scrubby oak on a vacant lot along the shore. There we played complicated games of Mandrake the Magician and his faithful servant Lothar, with our dolls as easily hypnotized villains. My sister was always Mandrake. When we tired of this, we would put on our bathing suits and go wading along the shore, watching for freighters and throwing acorns into the river to see how quickly they would be carried away by the current.

It was on one of these wading expeditions that we met Nan. She lived ten lots down, in a white cottage with red trim. Unlike many of the other cottages, Nan's had a real dock, built out into the river and anchored around the posts with piles of rocks. She was sitting on this dock when we first saw her, chewing gum and flipping through a stack of airplane cards from Wings cigarettes. Everyone knew that only boys collected these. Her hair and her face were light brown, and she had a sleek plump sheen, like caramel pudding.

"What're you doing with *those*?" were my sister's first words. Nan only smiled.

That same afternoon Nan was allowed into our hide-out, and after a cursory game of Mandrake, during which I was demoted to the lowly position of Narda, the two of them sat on our orange crates and exchanged what seemed to me to be languid and pointless comments.

"You ever go to the store?" Nan asked. We never did. Nan smiled some more. She was twelve; my sister was only eleven and three-quarters.

"There's cute boys at the store," Nan said. She was wearing a peasant blouse with a frill and an elastic top that she could slide down over her shoulders if she wanted to. She stuck her airplane cards into her shorts pocket and we went to ask my mother if we could walk to the store. After that, my sister and Nan went there almost every afternoon.

The store was a mile and a half from our cottage, a hot walk along the shore past the fronts of other cottages where fat mothers basked in the sun and other, possibly hostile children paddled in the water; past rowboats hauled up on the sand, along cement breakwaters, through patches of beach grass that cut your ankles if you ran through it and beach peas that were hard and bitter-tasting. In some places we could smell the outhouses. Just before the store, there was an open space with poison ivy, which we had to wade around.

The store had no name. It was just "the store," the only store for the cottagers since it was the only one they could walk to. I was allowed to go with my sister and Nan, or rather, my mother insisted that I go. Although I hadn't said anything to her about it, she could sense my misery. It wasn't so much my sister's desertion that hurt, but her blithe unconsciousness of it. She was quite willing to play with me when Nan wasn't around.

Sometimes, when the sight of my sister and Nan conspiring twenty paces ahead of me made me too unhappy, I would double back and go to Fred and Betty's. There I would sit facing backwards on one of Betty's kitchen chairs, my two hands rigid in the air, holding a skein of sky-blue wool while Betty wound it into balls. Or, under Betty's direction, I crocheted sweaty, uneven little pink and yellow dolls' dresses for the dolls my sister was, suddenly, too old to play with.

On better days I would make it as far as the store. It was not beautiful or even clean, but we were so used to wartime drabness and grime that we didn't notice. It was a two-storey building of unpainted wood which had weathered grey. Parts of it were patched with tar paper, and it had coloured metal signs nailed around the front screen door and windows: Coca-Cola, 7-Up, Salada Tea. Inside, it had the sugary, mournful smell of old general stores, a mixture of the cones for the ice-cream cones, the packages of Oreo cookies, the open boxes of jaw-breakers and licorice whips that lined the counter, and that other smell, musky and sharp, part dry-rot and part sweat. The bottles of pop were kept in a metal cooler with a heavy lid, filled with cold water and chunks of ice melted to the smoothness of the sand-scoured pieces of glass we sometimes found on the beach.

The owner of the store and his wife lived on the second floor, but we almost never saw them. The store was run by their two daughters, who took turns behind the counter. They were both dark and they both wore shorts and polka-dot halter tops, but one was friendly and the other one, the thinner, younger one, was not. She would take our pennies and ring them into the cash register without saying a word, staring over our heads out the front window with its dangling raisin-covered fly-papers as if she was completely detached from the activity her hands were performing. She didn't dislike us; she just didn't see us. She wore her hair long and done in a sort of roll at the front, and her lipstick was purplish.

The first time we went to the store we found out why Nan collected airplane cards. There were two boys there, sitting on the grey, splintery front steps, their arms crossed over their knees. I had been told by my sister that the right thing to do with boys was to ignore them; otherwise they would pester you. But these boys knew Nan, and they spoke to her, not with the usual taunts, but with respect.

"You got anything new?" one of them said.

Nan smiled, brushed back her hair and wiggled her shoulders a little inside her peasant blouse. Then she slid her airplane cards slowly out of her shorts pocket and began riffling through them.

"You got any?" the other boy said to my sister. For once she was humbled. After that, she got my mother to switch brands and built up her own pack. I saw her in front of the mirror about a week later, practising that tantalizing slide, the cards coming out of her pocket like a magician's snake.

When I went to the store I always had to bring back a loaf of wax-papered bread for my mother, and sometimes a package of "Jiffy" Pie Crust, if they had any. My sister never had to: she had already discovered the advantages of being unreliable. As payment, and, I'm sure, as compensation for my unhappiness, my mother gave me a penny a trip, and when I had saved five of these pennies I bought my first Popsicle. Our mother had always refused to buy them for us, although she permitted ice-cream cones. She said there was something in Popsicles that was bad for you, and as I sat on the front steps of the store, licking down to the wooden stick, I kept looking for this thing. I visualized it as a sort of core, like the white fingernail-shaped part in a kernel of corn, but I couldn't find anything.

My sister and Nan were sitting beside me on the front steps. There were no boys at the store that day, so they had nothing else to do. It was even hotter than usual, and airless; there was a shimmer over the river, and the freighters wavered as they passed through it. My Popsicle was melting almost before I could eat it. I had given my sister half of it, which she had taken without the gratitude I had hoped for. She was sharing it with Nan.

Fred came around the corner of the building and headed towards the front door. This was no surprise, as we had seen him at the store several times before.

"Hi, beautiful," he said to my sister. We moved our rumps along the step to let him in the door.

After quite a long time he came out, carrying a loaf of bread. He asked us if we wanted a lift with him in his car: he was just coming back from the city, he said. Of course we said yes. There was nothing unusual about any of this, except that the daughter, the thinner, purple one, stepped outside the door and stood on the steps as we were driving off. She folded her arms across her chest in that slump-shouldered pose of women idling in doorways. She wasn't smiling. I thought she had come out to watch the Canada Steamship Lines freighter that was going past, but then I saw that she was staring at Fred. She looked as if she wanted to kill him.

Fred didn't seem to notice. He sang all the way home. "Katy, oh beautiful Katy," he sang, winking at my sister, whom he sometimes called Katy since her name was Catherine. He had the windows open, and dust from the rutted gravel road poured over us, whitening our eyebrows and turning Fred's hair grey. At every jolt my sister and Nan screamed gleefully, and after a while I forgot my feelings of exclusion and screamed too.

It seemed as if we had lived in the cottage for a long time, though it was only one summer. By August I could hardly remember the apartment in Ottawa and the man who used to beat up his wife. That had happened in a remote life; and, despite the sunshine, the water, the open space, a happier one. Before, our frequent moves and the insecurities of new schools had forced my sister to value me: I was four years younger, but I was loyal and always there. Now those years were a canyon between us, an empty stretch like a beach along which I could see her disappearing ahead of me. I longed to be just like her, but I could no longer tell what she was like.

In the third week of August the leaves started to turn, not all at once, just a single red one here and there, like a warning. That meant it would soon be time for school and another move. We didn't even know where we would be moving to this time, and when Nan asked us what school we went to, we were evasive.

"I've been to eight different schools," my sister said proudly. Because I was so much younger, I had only been to two. Nan, who had been to the same one all her life, slipped the edge of her peasant blouse over her shoulders and down to her elbows to show us that her breasts were growing. The rings around her nipples had softened and started to puff out; otherwise she was as flat as my sister.

"So what," said my sister, rolling up her jersey. This was a competition I couldn't be part of. It was about change, and, increasingly, change frightened me. I walked back along the beach to Betty's house, where my latest piece of grubby crocheting was waiting for me and where everything was always the same.

I knocked on the screen door and opened it. I meant to say, "Can I come in?" the way we always did, but I didn't say it. Betty was sitting by herself at the iron table of the breakfast nook. She had on her shorts and a striped sailor top, navy blue and white with a little anchor pin, and the apron with the yellow chickens coming out of their eggs. For once she wasn't doing anything, and there was no cup of coffee in front of her. Her face was white and uncomprehending, as if someone had just hit her for no reason.

She saw me, but she didn't smile or ask me in. "What am I going to do?" she said.

I looked around the kitchen. Everything was in its place: the percolator gleamed from the stove, the glass bird was teetering slowly down, there were no broken dishes, no water on the floor. What had happened?

"Are you sick?" I said.

"There's nothing I can do," Betty said.

She looked so strange that I was frightened. I ran out of the kitchen and across the hillocky grass to get my mother, who always knew what should be done.

"There's something wrong with Betty," I said.

My mother was mixing something in a bowl. She rubbed her hands together to get the dough off, then wiped them on her apron. She didn't look surprised or ask me what it was. "You stay here," she said. She picked up her package of cigarettes and went out the door.

That evening we had to go to bed early because my mother wanted to talk to my father. We listened, of course; it was easy through the Ten-Test walls.

"I saw it coming," my mother said. "A mile away."

"Who is it?" my father said.

"She doesn't know," said my mother. "Some girl from town."

"Betty's a fool," my father said. "She always was." Later, when husbands and wives leaving each other became more common, he often said this, but no matter which one had left it was always the woman he called the fool. His highest compliment to my mother was that she was no fool.

"That may be," said my mother. "But you'd never want to meet a nicer girl. He was her whole life."

My sister and I whispered together. My sister's theory was that Fred had run away from Betty with another woman. I couldn't believe this: I had never heard of such a thing happening. I was so upset I couldn't sleep, and for a long time after that I was anxious whenever my father was away overnight, as he frequently was. What if he never came back?

We didn't see Betty after that. We knew she was in her cottage, because every day my mother carried over samples of her tough and lumpy baking, almost as if someone had died. But we were given strict orders to stay away, and not to go peering in the windows as our mother must have known we longed to do. "She's having a nervous breakdown," our mother said, which for me called up an image of Betty lying disjointed on the floor like a car at the garage.

We didn't even see her on the day we got into my father's second-hand Studebaker, the back seat packed to the windowtops with only a little oblong space for me to crouch in, and drove out to the main highway to begin the six-hundred-mile journey south to Toronto. My father had changed jobs again; he was now in building materials, and he was sure, since the country was having a boom, that this was finally the right change. We spent September and part of October in a motel while my father looked for a house. I had my eighth birthday and my sister turned twelve. Then there was another new school, and I almost forgot about Betty.

But a month after I had turned twelve myself, Betty was suddenly there one night for dinner. We had people for dinner a lot more than we used to, and sometimes the dinners were so important that my sister and I ate first. My sister didn't care, as she had boyfriends by that time. I was still in public school and had to wear lisle stockings instead of the seamed nylons my sister was permitted. Also, I had braces. My sister had had braces at that age too, but she had somehow managed to make them seem rakish and daring, so that I had longed for a mouthful of flashing silver teeth like hers. But she no longer had them, and my own mouth in its shackles felt clumsy and muffled.

"You remember Betty," my mother said.

"Elizabeth," Betty said.

"Oh yes, of course," said my mother.

Betty had changed a lot. Before, she had been a little plump; now she was buxom. Her cheeks were as round and florid as two tomatoes, and I thought she was using too much rouge until I saw that the red was caused by masses of tiny veins under her skin. She was wearing a long black pleated skirt, a white short-sleeved angora sweater with a string of black beads, and open-toed black velvet pumps with high heels. She smelled strongly of Lily of the Valley. She had a job, my mother told my father later, a very good job. She was an executive secretary, and now called herself Miss instead of Mrs.

"She's doing very well," my mother said, "considering what happened. She's pulled herself together."

"I hope you don't start inviting her to dinner all the time," said my father, who still found Betty irritating in spite of her new look. She laughed more than ever now, and crossed her legs frequently.

"I feel I'm the only real friend she has," said my mother. She didn't say Betty was the only real friend she had, though when my father said "your friend" everyone knew who he meant. My mother had a lot of friends, and her talent for wise listening was now a business asset for my father.

"She says she'll never marry again," said my mother.

"She's a fool," my father said.

"If I ever saw anyone cut out for marriage, it was her," said my mother. This remark increased my anxiety about my own future. If all Betty's accomplishments had not been enough for Fred, what hope was there for me? I did not have my sister's natural flair, but I had thought there would be some tricks I could learn, dutifully, painstakingly. We were taking Home Economics at school and the teacher kept saying that the way to a man's heart was through his stomach. I knew this wasn't true—my mother was still a slapdash cook, and when she gave the best dinners she had a woman in to help—but I laboured over my blancmange and Harvard beets as if I believed it.

My mother started inviting Betty to dinner with men who were not married. Betty smiled and laughed and several of the men seemed interested, but nothing came of it.

"After the way she was hurt, I'm not surprised," my mother said. I was now old enough to be told things, and besides, my sister was never around. "I heard it was a secretary at his company he ran off with. They even got married, after the divorce." There was something else about Betty, she told me, although I must never mention it as Betty found it very distressing. Fred's brother, who was a dentist, had killed his wife because he got involved—my mother said "involved" richly, as if it was a kind of dessert—with his dental technician. He had put his wife into the car and run a tube in from the exhaust pipe, and then tried to pretend it was suicide. The police had found out though, and he was in jail.

This made Betty much more interesting in my eyes. It was in Fred's blood, then, this tendency towards involvement. In fact it could just as easily have been Betty herself who had been murdered. I now came to see Betty's laugh as the mask of a stricken and martyred woman. She was not just a wife who had been deserted. Even I could see that this was not a tragic position, it was a ridiculous and humiliating one. She was much more than that: she was a woman who had narrowly escaped death. That Betty herself saw it this way I soon had no doubt. There was something smug and even pious about the way she kept mother's single men at a polite distance, something faintly nun-like. A lurid aura of sacrificial blood surrounded her. Betty had been there, she had passed through it, she had come out alive, and now she was dedicating herself to, well, to something else.

But it was hard for me to sustain this version of Betty for long. My mother soon ran out of single men and Betty, when she came to dinner, came alone. She talked as incessantly about the details surrounding the other women at her office as she had about Fred. We soon knew how they all took their coffee, which ones lived with their mothers, where they had their hair done, and what their apartments looked like. Betty herself had a darling apartment on Avenue Road, and she had re-done it all herself and even made the slipcovers. Betty was as devoted to her boss as she had once been to Fred. She did all his Christmas shopping, and each year we heard what he had given to his employees, what to his wife and children, and what each item had cost. Betty seemed, in a way, quite happy.

We saw a lot of Betty around Christmas; my mother said she felt sorry for her because she had no family. Betty was in the habit of giving us Christmas presents that made it obvious she thought we were younger than we were. She favoured Parcheesi sets and angora mittens a size too small. I lost interest in her. Even her unending cheerfulness came to seem like a perversion, or a defect almost like idiocy. I was fifteen now and in the throes of adolescent depression. My sister was away at

Queen's; sometimes she gave me clothes she no longer wanted. She was not exactly beautiful—both her eyes and her mouth were too large—but everyone called her vivacious. They called me nice. My braces had come off, but it didn't seem to make any difference. What right had Betty to be cheerful? When she came to dinner, I excused myself early and went to my room.

One afternoon, in the spring of grade eleven, I came home from school to find my mother sitting at the dining-room table. She was crying, which was so rare that my immediate fear was that something had happened to my father. I didn't think he had left her; that particular anxiety was past. But perhaps he had been killed in a car crash.

"Mum, what is it?" I said.

"Bring me a glass of water," she said. She drank some of it and pushed back her hair. "I'm all right now," she said. "I just had a call from Betty. It was very upsetting; she said horrible things to me."

"Why?" I said. "What did you do?"

"She accused me of . . . horrible things." My mother swabbed at her eyes. "She was screaming. I've never heard Betty scream in my life before. After all that time I spent with her. She said she never wanted to speak to me again. Where would she get such an idea?"

"What idea?" I said. I was just as mystified as my mother was. My mother was a bad cook, but she was a good woman. I could not imagine her doing anything that would make anyone want to scream at her.

My mother held back slightly. "Things about Fred," she said. "She must be crazy. I hadn't seen her for a couple of months, and then suddenly, just like that."

"There must be something wrong with her," my father said at dinner that night. Of course he was right. Betty had an undetected brain tumour, which was discovered when her strange behaviour was noticed at the office. She died in the hospital two months later, but my mother didn't hear about it till afterwards. She was contrite; she felt she should have visited her friend in the hospital, despite the abusive phone call.

"I ought to have known it was something like that," she said. "Personality change, that's one of the clues." In the course of her listening, my mother had picked up a great deal of information about terminal illnesses.

But for me, this explanation wasn't good enough. For years after that, Betty followed me around, waiting for me to finish her off in some way more satisfactory to both of us. When I first heard about her death I felt doomed. This, then, was the punishment for being devoted and obliging, this was what happened to girls such as (I felt) myself. When I opened the high-school yearbook and my own face, in pageboy haircut and tentative, appeasing smile, stared back at me, it was Betty's eyes I superimposed on mine. She had been kind to me when I was a child, and with the callousness of children towards those who are kind but not enchanting, I had preferred Fred. In my future I saw myself being abandoned by a succession of Freds who were running down the beach after a crowd of vivacious girls, all of whom looked remarkably like my sister. As for Betty's final screams of hatred and rage, they were screams of protest against the unfairness of life. That anger, I knew, was my own, the dark side of that terrible and deforming niceness that had marked Betty like the aftermath of some crippling disease.

People change, though, especially after they are dead. As I passed beyond the age of melodrama I came to see that if I did not want to be Betty, I would have to be someone else. Furthermore, I was already quite different from Betty. In a way, she had absolved me from making the demanded choices by having made them so thoroughly herself. People stopped calling me a nice girl and started calling me a clever one, and after a while I enjoyed this. Betty herself, baking oatmeal cookies in the ephemeral sunlight of fifteen years before, slid back into three dimensions. She was an ordinary woman who had died too young of an incurable disease. Was that it, was that all?

From time to time I would like to have Betty back, if only for an hour's conversation. I would like her to forgive me for my rejection of her angora mittens, for my secret betrayals of her, for my adolescent contempt. I would like to show her this story I have told about her and ask her if any of it is true. But I can think of nothing I want to ask her that I could phrase in a way that she would care to understand. She would only laugh in her accepting, uncomprehending way and offer me something, a chocolate brownie, a ball of wool.

Fred, on the other hand, no longer intrigues me. The Freds of this world make themselves explicit by what they do and choose. It is the Bettys who are mysterious.

Bluebeard's Egg

❧

Sally stands at the kitchen window, waiting for the sauce she's reducing to come to a simmer, looking out. Past the garage the lot sweeps downwards, into the ravine; it's a wilderness there, of bushes and branches and what Sally thinks of as vines. It was her idea to have a kind of terrace, built of old railroad ties, with wild flowers growing between them, but Edward says he likes it the way it is. There's a playhouse down at the bottom, near the fence; from here she can just see the roof. It has nothing to do with Edward's kids, in their earlier incarnations, before Sally's time; it's more ancient than that, and falling apart. Sally would like it cleared away. She thinks drunks sleep in it, the men who live under the bridges down there, who occasionally wander over the fence (which is broken down, from where they step on it) and up the hill, to emerge squinting like moles into the light of Sally's well-kept back lawn.

Off to the left is Ed, in his windbreaker; it's officially spring, Sally's blue scylla is in flower, but it's chilly for this time of year. Ed's windbreaker is an old one he won't throw out; it still says WILDCATS, relic of some team he was on in high school, an era so prehistoric Sally can barely imagine it; though picturing Ed at high school is not all that difficult. Girls would have had crushes on him, he would have been unconscious of it; things like that don't change. He's puttering around the rock garden now; some of the rocks stick out too far and are in danger of grazing the side of Sally's Peugeot, on its way to the garage, and he's moving them around. He likes doing things like that, puttering, humming to himself. He won't wear work gloves, though she keeps telling him he could squash his fingers.

Watching his bent back with its frayed, poignant lettering, Sally dissolves; which is not infrequent with her. *My darling Edward*, she thinks. *Edward Bear, of little brain. How I love you*. At times like this she feels very protective of him.

Sally knows for a fact that dumb blondes were loved, not because they were blondes, but because they were dumb. It was their helplessness and confusion that were so sexually attractive, once; not their hair. It wasn't false, the rush of tenderness men must have felt for such women. Sally understands it.

For it must be admitted: Sally is in love with Ed because of his stupidity, his monumental and almost energetic stupidity: energetic, because Ed's stupidity is not passive. He's no mere blockhead; you'd have to be working at it to be that stupid. Does it make Sally feel smug, or smarter than he is, or even smarter than she really is herself? No; on the contrary, it makes her humble. It fills her with wonder that the world can contain such marvels as Ed's colossal and endearing thickness. He is just so *stupid*. Every time he gives her another piece of evidence, another tile that she can glue into place in the vast mosaic of his stupidity she's continually piecing together, she wants to hug him, and often does; and he is so stupid he can never figure out what for.

Because Ed is so stupid he doesn't even know he's stupid. He's a child of luck, a third son who, armed with nothing but a certain feeble-minded amiability, manages to make it through the forest with all its witches and traps and pitfalls and end up with the princess, who is Sally, of course. It helps that he's handsome.

On good days she sees his stupidity as innocence, lamb-like, shining with the light of (for instance) green daisied meadows in the sun. (When Sally starts thinking this way about Ed, in terms of the calendar art from the service-station washrooms of her childhood, dredging up images of a boy with curly golden hair, his arm thrown around the neck of an Irish setter—a notorious brainless beast, she reminds herself—she knows she is sliding over the edge, into a ghastly kind of sentimentality, and that she must stop at once, or Ed will vanish, to be replaced by a stuffed facsimile, useful for little else but an umbrella stand. Ed is a real person, with a lot more to him than these simplistic renditions allow for; which sometimes worries her.) On bad days though, she sees his stupidity as wilfulness, a stubborn determination to shut things out. His obtuseness is a wall, within which he can go about his business, humming to himself, while Sally, locked outside, must hack her way through the brambles with hardly so much as a transparent raincoat between them and her skin.

Why did she choose him (or, to be precise, as she tries to be with herself and sometimes is even out loud, *hunt him down*), when it's clear to everyone she had other options? To Marylynn, who is her best though most recent friend, she's explained it by saying she was spoiled when young by reading too many Agatha Christie murder mysteries, of the kind in which the clever and witty heroine passes over the equally clever and witty first-lead male, who's helped solve the crime, in order to marry the second-lead male, the stupid one, the one who would have been arrested and condemned and executed if it hadn't been for her cleverness. Maybe this is how she sees Ed: if it weren't for her, his blundering too-many-thumbs kindness would get him into all sorts of quagmires, all sorts of sink-holes he'd never be able to get himself out of, and then he'd be done for.

"Sink-hole" and "quagmire" are not flattering ways of speaking about other women, but this is what is at the back of Sally's mind; specifically, Ed's two previous wives. Sally didn't exactly extricate him from their clutches. She's never even met the first one, who moved to the west coast fourteen years ago and sends Christmas cards, and the second one was middle-aged and already in the act of severing herself from Ed before Sally came along. (For Sally, "middle-aged" means anyone five years older than she is. It has always meant this. She applies it only to women, however. She doesn't think of Ed as middle-aged, although the gap between them is considerably more than five years.)

Ed doesn't know what happened with these marriages, what went wrong. His protestations of ignorance, his refusal to discuss the finer points, is frustrating to Sally, because she would like to hear the whole story. But it's also cause for anxiety: if he doesn't know what happened with the other two, maybe the same thing could be happening with her and he doesn't know about that, either. Stupidity like Ed's can be a health hazard, for other people. What if he wakes up one day and decides that she isn't the true bride after all, but the false one? Then she will be put into a barrel stuck full of nails and rolled downhill, endlessly, while he is sitting in yet another bridal bed, drinking champagne. She remembers the brand name, because she bought it herself. Champagne isn't the sort of finishing touch that would occur to Ed, though he enjoyed it enough at the time.

But outwardly Sally makes a joke of all this. "He doesn't *know*," she says to Marylynn, laughing a little, and they shake their heads. If it were them, they'd know, all right. Marylynn is in fact divorced, and she can list every single thing that went wrong, item by item. After doing this, she adds that her divorce was one of the best things that ever happened to her. "I was just a nothing before," she says. "It made me pull myself together."

Sally, looking across the kitchen table at Marylynn, has to agree that she is far from being a nothing now. She started out re-doing people's closets, and has worked that up into her own interior-design firm. She does the houses of the newly rich, those who lack ancestral furniture and the confidence to be shabby, and who wish their interiors to reflect a personal taste they do not in reality possess.

"What they want are mausoleums," Marylynn says, "or hotels," and she cheerfully supplies them. "Right down to the ash-trays. Imagine having someone else pick out your ash-trays for you."

By saying this, Marylynn lets Sally know that she's not including her in that category, though Sally did in fact hire her, at the very first, to help with a few details around the house. It was Marylynn who redesigned the wall of closets in the master bedroom and who found Sally's massive Chinese mahogany table, which cost her another seven hundred dollars to have stripped. But it turned out to be perfect, as Marylynn said it would. Now she's dug up a nineteenth-century keyhole desk, which both she and Sally know will be exactly right for the bay-windowed alcove off the living room. "Why do you need it?" Ed said in his puzzled way. "I thought you worked in your study." Sally admitted this, but said they could keep the telephone bills in it, which appeared to satisfy him. She knows exactly what she needs it for: she needs it to sit at, in something flowing, backlit by the morning sunlight, gracefully dashing off notes. She saw a 1940's advertisement for coffee like this once, and the husband was standing behind the chair, leaning over, with a worshipful expression on his face.

Marylynn is the kind of friend Sally does not have to explain any of this to, because it's assumed between them. Her intelligence is the kind Sally respects.

Marylynn is tall and elegant, and makes anything she is wearing seem fashionable. Her hair is prematurely grey and she leaves it that way. She goes in for loose blouses in cream-coloured silk, and eccentric scarves gathered from interesting shops and odd corners of the world, thrown carelessly around her neck and over one shoulder. (Sally has tried this toss in the mirror, but it doesn't work.) Marylynn has a large collection of unusual shoes; she says they're unusual because her feet are so big, but Sally knows better. Sally, who used to think of herself as pretty enough and now thinks of herself as doing quite well for her age, envies Marylynn her bone structure, which will serve her well when the inevitable happens.

Whenever Marylynn is coming to dinner, as she is today—she's bringing the desk, too—Sally takes especial care with her clothes and make-up. Marylynn, she knows, is her real audience for such things, since no changes she effects in herself seem to affect Ed one way or the other, or even to register with him. "You look fine to me," is all he says, no matter how she really looks. (But does she want him to see her more clearly, or not? Most likely not. If he did he would notice the incipient wrinkles, the small pouches of flesh that are not quite there yet, the network forming beneath her eyes. It's better as it is.)

Sally has repeated this remark of Ed's to Marylynn, adding that he said it the day the Jacuzzi overflowed because the smoke alarm went off, because an English muffin she was heating to eat in the bathtub got stuck in the toaster, and she had to spend an hour putting down newspaper and mopping up, and only had half an hour to dress for a dinner they were going to. "Really I looked like the wrath of God," said Sally. These days she finds herself repeating to Marylynn many of the things Ed says: the stupid things. Marylynn is the only one of Sally's friends she has confided in to this extent.

"Ed is cute as a button," Marylynn said. "In fact, he's just like a button: he's so bright and shiny. If he were mine, I'd get him bronzed and keep him on the mantelpiece."

Marylynn is even better than Sally at concocting formulations for Ed's particular brand of stupidity, which can irritate Sally: coming from herself, this sort of comment appears to her indulgent and loving, but from Marylynn it borders on the patronizing. So then she sticks up for Ed, who is by no means stupid about everything. When you narrow it down, there's only one area of life he's hopeless about. The rest of the time he's intelligent enough, some even say brilliant: otherwise, how could he be so successful?

Ed is a heart man, one of the best, and the irony of this is not lost on Sally: who could possibly know less about the workings of hearts, real hearts, the kind symbolized by red satin surrounded by lace and topped by pink bows, than Ed? Hearts with arrows in them. At the same time, the fact that he's a heart man is a large part of his allure. Women corner him on sofas, trap him in bay-windows at cocktail parties, mutter to him in confidential voices at dinner parties. They behave this way right in front of Sally, under her very nose, as if she's invisible, and Ed lets them do it. This would never happen if he were in banking or construction.

As it is, everywhere he goes he is beset by sirens. They want him to fix their hearts. Each of them seems to have a little something wrong—a murmur, a whisper. Or they faint a lot and want him to tell them why. This is always what the conversations are about, according to Ed, and Sally believes it. Once she'd wanted it herself, that mirage. What had she invented for him, in the beginning? A heavy heart, that beat too hard after meals. And he'd been so sweet, looking at her with those stunned brown eyes of his, as if her heart were the genuine topic, listening to her gravely as if he'd never heard any of this twaddle before, advising her to drink less coffee. And she'd felt such triumph, to have carried off her imposture, pried out of him that miniscule token of concern.

Thinking back on this incident makes her uneasy, now that she's seen her own performance repeated so many times, including the hand placed lightly on the heart, to call attention of course to the breasts. Some of these women have been within inches of getting Ed to put his head down on their chests, right there in Sally's living room. Watching all this out of the corners of her eyes while serving the liqueurs, Sally feels the Aztec rise within her. *Trouble with your heart? Get it removed,* she thinks. *Then you'll have no more problems.*

Sometimes Sally worries that she's a nothing, the way Marylynn was before she got a divorce and a job. But Sally isn't a nothing; therefore, she doesn't need a divorce to stop being one. And she's always had a job of some sort; in fact she has one now. Luckily Ed has no objection; he doesn't have much of an objection to anything she does.

Her job is supposed to be full-time, but in effect it's part-time, because Sally can take a lot of the work away and do it at home, and, as she says, with one arm tied behind her back. When Sally is being ornery, when she's playing the dull wife of a fascinating heart man—she does this with people she can't be bothered with—she says she works in a bank, nothing important. Then she watches their eyes dismiss her. When, on the other hand, she's trying to impress, she says she's in P.R. In reality she runs the in-house organ for a trust company, a medium-sized one. This is a thin magazine, nicely printed, which is supposed to make the employees feel that some of the boys are doing worthwhile things out there and are human beings as well. It's still the boys, though the few women in anything resembling key positions are wheeled out regularly, bloused and suited and smiling brightly, with what they hope will come across as confidence rather than aggression.

This is the latest in a string of such jobs Sally has held over the years: comfortable enough jobs that engage only half of her cogs and wheels, and that end up leading nowhere. Technically she's second-in-command: over her is a man who wasn't working out in management, but who couldn't be fired because his wife was related to the chairman of the board. He goes out for long alcoholic lunches and plays a lot of golf, and Sally runs the show.

This man gets the official credit for everything Sally does right, but the senior executives in the company take Sally aside when no one is looking and tell her what a great gal she is and what a whiz she is at holding up her end.

The real pay-off for Sally, though, is that her boss provides her with an endless supply of anecdotes. She dines out on stories about his dim-wittedness and pomposity, his lobotomized suggestions about what the two of them should cook up for the magazine; *the organ*, as she says he always calls it. "He says we need some fresh blood to perk up the organ," Sally says, and the heart men grin at her. "He actually said that?" Talking like this about her boss would be reckless—you never know what might get back to him, with the world as small as it is—if Sally were afraid of losing her job, but she isn't. There's an unspoken agreement between her and this man: they both know that if she goes, he goes, because who else would put up with him? Sally might angle for his job, if she were stupid enough to disregard his family connections, if she coveted the trappings of power. But she's just fine where she is. Jokingly, she says she's reached her level of incompetence. She says she suffers from fear of success.

Her boss is white-haired, slender, and tanned, and looks like an English gin ad. Despite his vapidity he's outwardly distinguished, she allows him that. In truth she pampers him outrageously, indulges him, covers up for him at every turn, though she stops short of behaving like a secretary: she doesn't bring him coffee. They both have a secretary who does that anyway. The one time he made a pass at her, when he came in from lunch visibly reeling, Sally was kind about it.

Occasionally, though not often, Sally has to travel in connection with her job. She's sent off to places like Edmonton, where they have a branch. She interviews the boys at the middle and senior levels; they have lunch, and the boys talk about ups and downs in oil or the slump in the real-estate market. Then she gets taken on tours of shopping plazas under construction. It's always windy, and grit blows into her face. She comes back to home base and writes a piece on the youthfulness and vitality of the West.

She teases Ed, while she packs, saying she's going off for a rendezvous with a dashing financier or two. Ed isn't threatened; he tells her to enjoy herself, and she hugs him and tells him how much she will miss him. He's so dumb it doesn't occur to him she might not be joking. In point of fact, it would have been quite possible for Sally to have had an affair, or at least a one- or two-night stand, on several of these occasions: she knows when those chalk lines are being drawn, when she's being dared to step over them. But she isn't interested in having an affair with anyone but Ed.

She doesn't eat much on the planes; she doesn't like the food. But on the return trip, she invariably saves the pre-packaged parts of the meal, the cheese in its plastic wrap, the miniature chocolate bar, the bag of pretzels. She ferrets them away in her purse. She thinks of them as supplies, that she may need if she gets stuck in a strange airport, if they have to change course because of snow or fog, for instance. All kinds of things could happen, although they never have. When she gets home she takes the things from her purse and throws them out.

Outside the window Ed straightens up and wipes his earth-smeared hands down the sides of his pants. He begins to turn, and Sally moves back from the window so he won't see that she's watching. She doesn't like it to be too obvious. She shifts her attention to the sauce: it's in the second stage of a *sauce suprême*, which will make all the difference to the chicken. When Sally was learning this sauce, her cooking instructor quoted one of the great chefs, to the effect that the chicken was merely a canvas.

He meant as in painting, but Sally, in an undertone to
the woman next to her, turned it around. "Mine's canvas
anyway, sauce or no sauce," or words to that effect.

Gourmet cooking was the third night course Sally has
taken. At the moment she's on her fifth, which is called
Forms of Narrative Fiction. It's half reading and half
writing assignments—the instructor doesn't believe you
can understand an art form without at least trying it
yourself—and Sally purports to be enjoying it. She tells
her friends she takes night courses to keep her brain
from atrophying, and her friends find this amusing:
whatever else may become of Sally's brain, they say, they
don't see atrophying as an option. Sally knows better, but
in any case there's always room for improvement. She
may have begun taking the courses in the belief that this
would make her more interesting to Ed, but she soon
gave up on that idea: she appears to be neither more nor
less interesting to Ed now than she was before.

Most of the food for tonight is already made. Sally tries
to be well organized: the overflowing Jacuzzi was an
aberration. The cold watercress soup with walnuts is
chilling in the refrigerator, the chocolate mousse ditto.
Ed, being Ed, prefers meatloaf to sweetbreads with pine
nuts, butterscotch pudding made from a package to
chestnut purée topped with whipped cream. (Sally burnt
her fingers peeling the chestnuts. She couldn't do it the
easy way and buy it tinned.) Sally says Ed's preference
for this type of food comes from being pre-programmed
by hospital cafeterias when he was younger: show him a
burned sausage and a scoop of instant mashed potatoes
and he salivates. So it's only for company that she can
unfurl her *boeuf en daube* and her salmon *en papillote*,
spread them forth to be savoured and praised.

What she likes best about these dinners though is
setting the table, deciding who will sit where and, when
she's feeling mischievous, even what they are likely to
say. Then she can sit and listen to them say it.
Occasionally she prompts a little.

Tonight will not be very challenging, since it's only the heart men and their wives, and Marylynn, whom Sally hopes will dilute them. The heart men are forbidden to talk shop at Sally's dinner table, but they do it anyway. "Not what you really want to listen to while you're eating," says Sally. "All those tubes and valves." Privately she thinks they're a conceited lot, all except Ed. She can't resist needling them from time to time.

"I mean," she said to one of the leading surgeons, "basically it's just an exalted form of dress-making, don't you think?"

"Come again?" said the surgeon, smiling. The heart men think Sally is one hell of a tease.

"It's really just cutting and sewing, isn't it?" Sally murmured. The surgeon laughed.

"There's more to it than that," Ed said, unexpectedly, solemnly.

"What more, Ed?" said the surgeon. "You could say there's a lot of embroidery, but that's in the billing." He chuckled at himself.

Sally held her breath. She could hear Ed's verbal thought processes lurching into gear. He was delectable.

"Good judgement," Ed said. His earnestness hit the table like a wet fish. The surgeon hastily downed his wine.

Sally smiled. This was supposed to be a reprimand to her, she knew, for not taking things seriously enough. *Oh, come on, Ed,* she could say. But she knows also, most of the time, when to keep her trap shut. She should have a light-up JOKE sign on her forehead, so Ed would be able to tell the difference.

The heart men do well. Most of them appear to be doing better than Ed, but that's only because they have, on the whole, more expensive tastes and fewer wives. Sally can calculate these things and she figures Ed is about par.

These days there's much talk about advanced technologies, which Sally tries to keep up on, since they interest Ed. A few years ago the heart men got themselves a new facility. Ed was so revved up that he told Sally about it, which was unusual for him. A week later Sally said she would drop by the hospital at the end of the day and pick Ed up and take him out for dinner; she didn't feel like cooking, she said. Really she wanted to check out the facility; she likes to check out anything that causes the line on Ed's excitement chart to move above level.

At first Ed said he was tired, that when the day came to an end he didn't want to prolong it. But Sally wheedled and was respectful, and finally Ed took her to see his new gizmo. It was in a cramped, darkened room with an examining table in it. The thing itself looked like a television screen hooked up to some complicated hardware. Ed said that they could wire a patient up and bounce sound waves off the heart and pick up the echoes, and they would get a picture on the screen, an actual picture, of the heart in motion. It was a thousand times better than an electrocardiogram, he said: they could see the faults, the thickenings and cloggings, much more clearly.

"Colour?" said Sally.

"Black and white," said Ed.

Then Sally was possessed by a desire to see her own heart, in motion, in black and white, on the screen. At the dentist's she always wants to see the X-rays of her teeth, too, solid and glittering in her cloudy head. "Do it," she said, "I want to see how it works," and though this was the kind of thing Ed would ordinarily evade or tell her she was being silly about, he didn't need much persuading. He was fascinated by the thing himself, and he wanted to show it off.

He checked to make sure there was nobody real booked for the room. Then he told Sally to slip out of her clothes, the top half, brassière and all. He gave her a

paper gown and turned his back modestly while she
slipped it on, as if he didn't see her body every night of
the week. He attached electrodes to her, the ankles and
one wrist, and turned a switch and fiddled with the dials.
Really a technician was supposed to do this, he told her,
but he knew how to run the machine himself. He was
good with small appliances.

Sally lay prone on the table, feeling strangely naked.
"What do I do?" she said.

"Just lie there," said Ed. He came over to her and tore
a hole in the paper gown, above her left breast. Then he
started running a probe over her skin. It was wet and
slippery and cold, and felt like the roller on a roll-on
deodorant.

"There," he said, and Sally turned her head. On the
screen was a large grey object, like a giant fig, paler in
the middle, a dark line running down the centre. The
sides moved in and out; two wings fluttered in it, like an
uncertain moth's.

"That's it?" said Sally dubiously. Her heart looked so
insubstantial, like a bag of gelatin, something that would
melt, fade, disintegrate, if you squeezed it even a little.

Ed moved the probe, and they looked at the heart
from the bottom, then the top. Then he stopped the
frame, then changed it from a positive to a negative
image. Sally began to shiver.

"That's wonderful," she said. He seemed so distant,
absorbed in his machine, taking the measure of her
heart, which was beating over there all by itself,
detached from her, exposed and under his control.

Ed unwired her and she put on her clothes again,
neutrally, as if he were actually a doctor. Nevertheless
this transaction, this whole room, was sexual in a way she
didn't quite understand; it was clearly a dangerous place.
It was like a massage parlour, only for women. Put a
batch of women in there with Ed and they would never
want to come out. They'd want to stay in there while he

ran his probe over their wet skins and pointed out to them the defects of their beating hearts.

"Thank you," said Sally.

Sally hears the back door open and close. She feels Ed approaching, coming through the passages of the house towards her, like a small wind or a ball of static electricity. The hair stands up on her arms. Sometimes he makes her so happy she thinks she's about to burst; other times she thinks she's about to burst anyway.

He comes into the kitchen, and she pretends not to notice. He puts his arms around her from behind, kisses her on the neck. She leans back, pressing herself into him. What they should do now is go into the bedroom (or even the living room, even the den) and make love, but it wouldn't occur to Ed to make love in the middle of the day. Sally often comes across articles in magazines about how to improve your sex life, which leave her feeling disappointed, or reminiscent: Ed is not Sally's first and only man. But she knows she shouldn't expect too much of Ed. If Ed were more experimental, more interested in variety, he would be a different kind of man altogether: slyer, more devious, more observant, harder to deal with.

As it is, Ed makes love in the same way, time after time, each movement following the others in an exact order. But it seems to satisfy him. Of course it satisfies him: you can always tell when men are satisfied. It's Sally who lies awake, afterwards, watching the pictures unroll across her closed eyes.

Sally steps away from Ed, smiles at him. "How did you make out with the women today?" she says.

"What women?" says Ed absently, going towards the sink. He knows what women.

"The ones out there, hiding in the forsythia," says Sally. "I counted at least ten. They were just waiting for a chance."

She teases him frequently about these troops of women, which follow him around everywhere, which are invisible to Ed but which she can see as plain as day.

"I bet they hang around outside the front door of the hospital," she will say, "just waiting till you come out. I bet they hide in the linen closets and jump out at you from behind, and then pretend to be lost so you'll take them by the short cut. It's the white coat that does it. None of those women can resist the white coats. They've been conditioned by Young Doctor Kildare."

"Don't be silly," says Ed today, with equanimity. Is he blushing, is he embarrassed? Sally examines his face closely, like a geologist with an aerial photograph, looking for telltale signs of mineral treasure: markings, bumps, hollows. Everything about Ed means something, though it's difficult at times to say what.

Now he's washing his hands at the sink, to get the earth off. In a minute he'll wipe them on the dish towel instead of using the hand towel the way he's supposed to. Is that complacency, in the back turned to her? Maybe there really are these hordes of women, even though she's made them up. Maybe they really do behave that way. His shoulders are slightly drawn up: is he shutting her out?

"I know what they want," she goes on. "They want to get into that little dark room of yours and climb up onto your table. They think you're delicious. They'll gobble you up. They'll chew you into tiny pieces. There won't be anything left of you at all, only a stethoscope and a couple of shoelaces."

Once Ed would have laughed at this, but today he doesn't. Maybe she's said it, or something like it, a few times too often. He smiles though, wipes his hands on the dish towel, peers into the fridge. He likes to snack.

"There's some cold roast beef," Sally says, baffled.

* * *

Sally takes the sauce off the stove and sets it aside for later: she'll do the last steps just before serving. It's only two-thirty. Ed has disappeared into the cellar, where Sally knows he will be safe for a while. She goes into her study, which used to be one of the kids' bedrooms, and sits down at her desk. The room has never been completely redecorated: there's still a bed in it, and a dressing table with a blue flowered flounce Sally helped pick out, long before the kids went off to university: "flew the coop," as Ed puts it.

Sally doesn't comment on the expression, though she would like to say that it wasn't the first coop they flew. Her house isn't even the real coop, since neither of the kids is hers. She'd hoped for a baby of her own when she married Ed, but she didn't want to force the issue. Ed didn't object to the idea, exactly, but he was neutral about it, and Sally got the feeling he'd had enough babies already. Anyway, the other two wives had babies, and look what happened to them. Since their actual fates have always been vague to Sally, she's free to imagine all kinds of things, from drug addiction to madness. Whatever it was resulted in Sally having to bring up their kids, at least from puberty onwards. The way it was presented by the first wife was that it was Ed's turn now. The second wife was more oblique: she said that the child wanted to spend some time with her father. Sally was left out of both these equations, as if the house wasn't a place she lived in, not really, so she couldn't be expected to have any opinion.

Considering everything, she hasn't done badly. She likes the kids and tries to be a friend to them, since she can hardly pretend to be a mother. She describes the three of them as having an easy relationship. Ed wasn't around much for the kids, but it's him they want approval from, not Sally; it's him they respect. Sally is more like a confederate, helping them get what they want from Ed.

When the kids were younger, Sally used to play

Monopoly with them, up at the summer place in
Muskoka Ed owned then but has since sold. Ed would
play too, on his vacations and on the weekends when he
could make it up. These games would all proceed along
the same lines. Sally would have an initial run of luck
and would buy up everything she had a chance at. She
didn't care whether it was classy real estate, like
Boardwalk or Park Place, or those dingy little houses on
the other side of the tracks; she would even buy train
stations, which the kids would pass over, preferring to
save their cash reserves for better investments. Ed, on
the other hand, would plod along, getting a little here, a
little there. Then, when Sally was feeling flush, she
would blow her money on next-to-useless luxuries such
as the electric light company; and when the kids started
to lose, as they invariably did, Sally would lend them
money at cheap rates or trade them things of her own, at
a loss. Why not? She could afford it.

Ed meanwhile would be hedging his bets, building up
blocks of property, sticking houses and hotels on them.
He preferred the middle range, respectable streets but
not flashy. Sally would land on his spaces and have to
shell out hard cash. Ed never offered deals, and never
accepted them. He played a lone game, and won more
often than not. Then Sally would feel thwarted. She
would say she guessed she lacked the killer instinct; or
she would say that for herself she didn't care, because
after all it was only a game, but he ought to allow the kids
to win, once in a while. Ed couldn't grasp the concept of
allowing other people to win. He said it would be
condescending towards the children, and anyway you
couldn't arrange to have a dice game turn out the way
you wanted it to, since it was partly a matter of chance. If
it was chance, Sally would think, why were the games so
similar to one another? At the end, there would be Ed,
counting up his paper cash, sorting it out into piles of
bills of varying denominations, and Sally, her vast
holdings dwindled to a few shoddy blocks on Baltic

Avenue, doomed to foreclosure: extravagant, generous, bankrupt.

On these nights, after the kids were asleep, Sally would have two or three more rye-and-gingers than were good for her. Ed would go to bed early—winning made him satisfied and drowsy—and Sally would ramble about the house or read the endings of murder mysteries she had already read once before, and finally she would slip into bed and wake Ed up and stroke him into arousal, seeking comfort.

Sally has almost forgotten these games. Right now the kids are receding, fading like old ink; Ed on the contrary looms larger and larger, the outlines around him darkening. He's constantly developing, like a Polaroid print, new colours emerging, but the result remains the same: Ed is a surface, one she has trouble getting beneath.

"Explore your inner world," said Sally's instructor in *Forms of Narrative Fiction*, a middle-aged woman of scant fame who goes in for astrology and the Tarot pack and writes short stories, which are not published in any of the magazines Sally reads. "Then there's your outer one," Sally said afterwards, to her friends. "For instance, she should really get something done about her hair." She made this trivial and mean remark because she's fed up with her inner world; she doesn't need to explore it. In her inner world is Ed, like a doll within a Russian wooden doll, and in Ed is Ed's inner world, which she can't get at.

She takes a crack at it anyway: Ed's inner world is a forest, which looks something like the bottom part of their ravine lot, but without the fence. He wanders around in there, among the trees, not heading in any special direction. Every once in a while he comes upon a strange-looking plant, a sickly plant choked with weeds and briars. Ed kneels, clears a space around it, does some pruning, a little skilful snipping and cutting, props it up. The plant revives, flushes with health, sends out a grateful red blossom. Ed continues on his way. Or it may be a conked-out squirrel, which he restores with a drop from his flask of magic elixir. At set intervals an angel appears, bringing him food. It's always meatloaf. That's fine with Ed, who hardly notices what he eats, but the angel is getting tired of being an angel. Now Sally begins thinking about the angel: why are its wings frayed and dingy grey around the edges, why is it looking so withered and frantic? This is where all Sally's attempts to explore Ed's inner world end up.

She knows she thinks about Ed too much. She knows she should stop. She knows she shouldn't ask, "Do you still love me?" in the plaintive tone that sets even her own teeth on edge. All it achieves is that Ed shakes his head, as if not understanding why she would ask this, and pats her hand. "Sally, Sally," he says, and everything proceeds as usual; except for the dread that seeps into things, the most ordinary things, such as rearranging the chairs and changing the burnt-out lightbulbs. But what is it she's afraid of? She has what they call everything: Ed, their wonderful house on a ravine lot, something she's always wanted. (But the hill is jungly, and the house is made of ice. It's held together only by Sally, who sits in the middle of it, working on a puzzle. The puzzle is Ed. If she should ever solve it, if she should ever fit the last cold splinter into place, the house will melt and flow away down the hill, and then. . . .) It's a bad habit, fooling around with her head this way. It does no good. She knows that if she could quit she'd be happier. She ought to be able to: she's given up smoking.

She needs to concentrate her attention on other things. This is the real reason for the night courses, which she picks almost at random, to coincide with the evenings Ed isn't in. He has meetings, he's on the boards of charities, he has trouble saying no. She runs the courses past herself, mediaeval history, cooking, anthropology, hoping her mind will snag on something;

she's even taken a course in geology, which was fascinating, she told her friends, all that magma. That's just it:
everything is fascinating, but nothing enters her. She's
always a star pupil, she does well on the exams and
impresses the teachers, for which she despises them.
She is familiar with her brightness, her techniques; she's
surprised other people are still taken in by them.

Forms of Narrative Fiction started out the same way.
Sally was full of good ideas, brimming with helpful
suggestions. The workshop part of it was anyway just like
a committee meeting, and Sally knew how to run those,
from behind, without seeming to run them: she'd done it
lots of times at work. Bertha, the instructor, told Sally
she had a vivid imagination and a lot of untapped
creative energy. "No wonder she never gets anywhere,
with a name like Bertha," Sally said, while having coffee
afterwards with two of the other night-coursers. "It goes
with her outfits, though." (Bertha sports the macramé
look, with health-food sandals and bulky-knit sweaters
and hand-weave skirts that don't do a thing for her
square figure, and too many Mexican rings on her hands,
which she doesn't wash often enough.) Bertha goes in for
assignments, which she calls learning by doing. Sally
likes assignments: she likes things that can be completed
and then discarded, and for which she gets marks.

The first thing Bertha assigned was The Epic. They
read *The Odyssey* (selected passages, in translation, with
a plot summary of the rest); then they poked around in
James Joyce's *Ulysses*, to see how Joyce had adapted the
epic form to the modern-day novel. Bertha had them
keep a Toronto notebook, in which they had to pick out
various spots around town as the ports of call in *The
Odyssey*, and say why they had chosen them. The
notebooks were read out loud in class, and it was a
scream to see who had chosen what for Hades. (The
Mount Pleasant Cemetery, McDonald's, where, if you
eat the forbidden food, you never get back to the land of
the living, the University Club with its dead ancestral

souls, and so forth.) Sally's was the hospital, of course; she had no difficulty with the trench filled with blood, and she put the ghosts in wheelchairs.

After that they did The Ballad, and read gruesome accounts of murders and betrayed love. Bertha played them tapes of wheezy old men singing traditionally, in the Doric mode, and assigned a newspaper scrapbook, in which you had to clip and paste up-to-the-minute equivalents. The *Sun* was the best newspaper for these. The fiction that turned out to go with this kind of plot was the kind Sally liked anyway, and she had no difficulty concocting a five-page murder mystery, complete with revenge.

But now they are on Folk Tales and the Oral Tradition, and Sally is having trouble. This time, Bertha wouldn't let them read anything. Instead she read to them, in a voice, Sally said, that was like a gravel truck and was not conducive to reverie. Since it was the Oral Tradition, they weren't even allowed to take notes; Bertha said the original hearers of these stories couldn't read, so the stories were memorized. "To recreate the atmosphere," said Bertha, "I should turn out the lights. These stories were always told at night." "To make them creepier?" someone offered. "No," said Bertha. "In the days, they worked." She didn't do that, though she did make them sit in a circle.

"You should have seen us,". Sally said afterwards to Ed, "sitting in a circle, listening to fairy stories. It was just like kindergarten. Some of them even had their mouths open. I kept expecting her to say, 'If you need to go, put up your hand.'" She was meaning to be funny, to amuse Ed with this account of Bertha's eccentricity and the foolish appearance of the students, most of them middle-aged, sitting in a circle as if they had never grown up at all. She was also intending to belittle the course, just slightly. She always did this with her night courses, so Ed wouldn't get the idea there was anything in her life that was even remotely as important as he was.

But Ed didn't seem to need this amusement or this belittlement. He took her information earnestly, gravely, as if Bertha's behaviour was, after all, only the procedure of a specialist. No one knew better than he did that the procedures of specialists often looked bizarre or incomprehensible to onlookers. "She probably has her reasons," was all he would say.

The first stories Bertha read them, for warm-ups ("No memorizing for *her*," said Sally), were about princes who got amnesia and forgot about their true loves and married girls their mothers had picked out for them. Then they had to be rescued, with the aid of magic. The stories didn't say what happened to the women the princes had already married, though Sally wondered about it. Then Bertha read them another story, and this time they were supposed to remember the features that stood out for them and write a five-page transposition, set in the present and cast in the realistic mode. ("In other words," said Bertha, "no real magic.") They couldn't use the Universal Narrator, however: they had done that in their Ballad assignment. This time they had to choose a point of view. It could be the point of view of anyone or anything in the story, but they were limited to one only. The story she was about to read, she said, was a variant of the Bluebeard motif, much earlier than Perrault's sentimental rewriting of it. In Perrault, said Bertha, the girl has to be rescued by her brothers; but in the earlier version things were quite otherwise.

This is what Bertha read, as far as Sally can remember:

There were once three young sisters. One day a beggar with a large basket on his back came to the door and asked for some bread. The eldest sister brought him some, but no sooner had she touched him than she was compelled to jump into his basket, for the beggar was really a wizard in disguise. ("So much for United Appeal," Sally murmured. "She should have said, 'I gave

at the office.'") The wizard carried her away to his house
in the forest, which was large and richly furnished.
"Here you will be happy with me, my darling," said the
wizard, "for you will have everything your heart could
desire."

This lasted for a few days. Then the wizard gave the
girl an egg and a bunch of keys. "I must go away on a
journey," he said, "and I am leaving the house in your
charge. Preserve this egg for me, and carry it about with
you everywhere; for a great misfortune will follow from
its loss. The keys open every room in the house. You may
go into each of them and enjoy what you find there, but
do not go into the small room at the top of the house, on
pain of death." The girl promised, and the wizard
disappeared.

At first the girl contented herself with exploring the
rooms, which contained many treasures. But finally her
curiosity would not let her alone. She sought out the
smallest key, and, with beating heart, opened the little
door at the top of the house. Inside it was a large basin
full of blood, within which were the bodies of many
women, which had been cut to pieces; nearby were a
chopping block and an axe. In her horror, she let go of
the egg, which fell into the basin of blood. In vain did
she try to wipe away the stain: every time she succeeded
in removing it, back it would come.

The wizard returned, and in a stern voice asked for the
egg and the keys. When he saw the egg, he knew at once
she had disobeyed him and gone into the forbidden
room. "Since you have gone into the room against my
will," he said, "you shall go back into it against your
own." Despite her pleas he threw her down, dragged
her by the hair into the little room, hacked her into
pieces and threw her body into the basin with the
others.

Then he went for the second girl, who fared no better
than her sister. But the third was clever and wily. As
soon as the wizard had gone, she set the egg on a shelf,

out of harm's way, and then went immediately and
opened the forbidden door. Imagine her distress when
she saw the cut-up bodies of her two beloved sisters; but
she set the parts in order, and they joined together and
her sisters stood up and moved, and were living and
well. They embraced each other, and the third sister hid
the other two in a cupboard.

When the wizard returned he at once asked for the
egg. This time it was spotless. "You have passed the
test," he said to the third sister. "You shall be my bride."
("And second prize," said Sally, to herself this time, "is
two weeks in Niagara Falls.") The wizard no longer had
any power over her, and had to do whatever she asked.
There was more, about how the wizard met his come-
uppance and was burned to death, but Sally already
knew which features stood out for her.

At first she thought the most important thing in the story
was the forbidden room. What would she put in the
forbidden room, in her present-day realistic version?
Certainly not chopped-up women. It wasn't that they
were too unrealistic, but they were certainly too sick, as
well as being too obvious. She wanted to do something
more clever. She thought it might be a good idea to have
the curious woman open the door and find nothing there
at all, but after mulling it over she set this notion aside.
It would leave her with the problem of why the wizard
would have a forbidden room in which he kept nothing.

That was the way she was thinking right after she got
the assignment, which was a full two weeks ago. So far
she's written nothing. The great temptation is to cast
herself in the role of the cunning heroine, but again it's
too predictable. And Ed certainly isn't the wizard; he's
nowhere near sinister enough. If Ed were the wizard,
the room would contain a forest, some ailing plants and
feeble squirrels, and Ed himself, fixing them up; but

then, if it were Ed the room wouldn't even be locked, and there would be no story.

Now, as she sits at her desk, fiddling with her felt-tip pen, it comes to Sally that the intriguing thing about the story, the thing she should fasten on, is the egg. Why an egg? From the night course in Comparative Folklore she took four years ago, she remembers that the egg can be a fertility symbol, or a necessary object in African spells, or something the world hatched out of. Maybe in this story it's a symbol of virginity, and that is why the wizard requires it unbloodied. Women with dirty eggs get murdered, those with clean ones get married.

But this isn't useful either. The concept is so outmoded. Sally doesn't see how she can transpose it into real life without making it ridiculous, unless she sets the story in, for instance, an immigrant Portuguese family, and what would she know about that?

Sally opens the drawer of her desk and hunts around in it for her nail file. As she's doing this, she gets the brilliant idea of writing the story from the point of view of the egg. Other people will do the other things: the clever girl, the wizard, the two blundering sisters, who weren't smart enough to lie, and who will have problems afterwards, because of the thin red lines running all over their bodies, from where their parts joined together. But no one will think of the egg. How does it feel, to be the innocent and passive cause of so much misfortune?

(Ed isn't the Bluebeard: Ed is the egg. Ed Egg, blank and pristine and lovely. Stupid, too. Boiled, probably. Sally smiles fondly.)

But how can there be a story from the egg's point of view, if the egg is so closed and unaware? Sally ponders this, doodling on her pad of lined paper. Then she resumes the search for her nail file. Already it's time to begin getting ready for her dinner party. She can sleep on the problem of the egg and finish the assignment tomorrow, which is Sunday. It's due on Monday, but

Sally's mother used to say she was a whiz at getting things done at the last minute.

After painting her nails with *Nuit Magique*, Sally takes a bath, eating her habitual toasted English muffin while she lies in the tub. She begins to dress, dawdling; she has plenty of time. She hears Ed coming up out of the cellar; then she hears him in the bathroom, which he has entered from the hall door. Sally goes in through the other door, still in her slip. Ed is standing at the sink with his shirt off, shaving. On the weekends he leaves it until necessary, or until Sally tells him he's too scratchy.

Sally slides her hands around his waist, nuzzling against his naked back. He has very smooth skin, for a man. Sally smiles to herself: she can't stop thinking of him as an egg.

"Mmm," says Ed. It could be appreciation, or the answer to a question Sally hasn't asked and he hasn't heard, or just an acknowledgement that she's there.

"Don't you ever wonder what I think about?" Sally says. She's said this more than once, in bed or at the dinner table, after dessert. She stands behind him, watching the swaths the razor cuts in the white of his face, looking at her own face reflected in the mirror, just the eyes visible above his naked shoulder. Ed, lathered, is Assyrian, sterner than usual; or a frost-covered Arctic explorer; or demi-human, a white-bearded forest mutant. He scrapes away at himself, methodically destroying the illusion.

"But I already know what you think about," says Ed.

"How?" Sally says, taken aback.

"You're always telling me," Ed says, with what might be resignation or sadness; or maybe this is only a simple statement of fact.

Sally is relieved. If that's all he's going on, she's safe.

Marylynn arrives half an hour early, her pearl-coloured Porsche leading two men in a delivery truck up the driveway. The men install the keyhole desk, while Marylynn supervises: it looks, in the alcove, exactly as Marylynn has said it would, and Sally is delighted. She sits at it to write the cheque. Then she and Marylynn go into the kitchen, where Sally is finishing up her sauce, and Sally pours them each a Kir. She's glad Marylynn is here: it will keep her from dithering, as she tends to do just before people arrive. Though it's only the heart men, she's still a bit nervous. Ed is more likely to notice when things are wrong than when they're exactly right.

Marylynn sits at the kitchen table, one arm draped over the chairback, her chin on the other hand; she's in soft grey, which makes her hair look silver, and Sally feels once again how banal it is to have ordinary dark hair like her own, however well-cut, however shiny. It's the confidence she envies, the negligence. Marylynn doesn't seem to be trying at all, ever.

"Guess what Ed said today?" Sally says.

Marylynn leans further forward. "What?" she says, with the eagerness of one joining in a familiar game.

"He said, 'Some of these femininists go too far,'" Sally reports. "'*Femininists.*' Isn't that sweet?"

Marylynn holds the pause too long, and Sally has a sudden awful thought: maybe Marylynn thinks she's showing off, about Ed. Marylynn has always said she's not ready for another marriage yet; still, Sally should watch herself, not rub her nose in it. But then Marylynn laughs indulgently, and Sally, relieved, joins in.

"Ed is unbelievable," says Marylynn. "You should pin his mittens to his sleeves when he goes out in the morning."

"He shouldn't be let out alone," says Sally.

"You should get him a seeing-eye dog," says Marylynn, "to bark at women."

"Why?" says Sally, still laughing but alert now, the cold beginning at the ends of her fingers. Maybe Marylynn knows something she doesn't; maybe the house is beginning to crumble, after all.

"Because he can't see them coming," says Marylynn. "That's what you're always telling me."

She sips her Kir; Sally stirs the sauce. "I bet he thinks I'm a femininist," says Marylynn.

"You?" says Sally. "Never." She would like to add that Ed has given no indication of thinking anything at all about Marylynn, but she doesn't. She doesn't want to take the risk of hurting her feelings.

The wives of the heart men admire Sally's sauce; the heart men talk shop, all expect Walter Morly, who is good at by-passes. He's sitting beside Marylynn, and paying far too much attention to her for Sally's comfort. Mrs. Morly is at the other end of the table, not saying much of anything, which Marylynn appears not to notice. She keeps on talking to Walter about St. Lucia, where they've both been.

So after dinner, when Sally has herded them all into the living room for coffee and liqueurs, she takes Marylynn by the elbow. "Ed hasn't seen our desk yet," she says, "not up close. Take him away and give him your lecture on nineteenth-century antiques. Show him all the pigeon-holes. Ed loves pigeon-holes." Ed appears not to get this.

Marylynn knows exactly what Sally is up to. "Don't worry," she says, "I won't rape Dr. Morly; the poor creature would never survive the shock," but she allows herself to be shunted off to the side with Ed.

Sally moves from guest to guest, smiling, making sure everything is in order. Although she never looks directly, she's always conscious of Ed's presence in the room, any room; she perceives him as a shadow, a shape seen dimly at the edge of her field of vision, recognizable by the outline. She likes to know where he is, that's all. Some people are on their second cup of coffee. She walks towards the alcove: they must have finished with the desk by now.

But they haven't, they're still in there. Marylynn is bending forward, one hand on the veneer. Ed is standing too close to her, and as Sally comes up behind them she sees his left arm, held close to his side, the back of it pressed against Marylynn, her shimmering upper thigh, her ass to be exact. Marylynn does not move away.

It's a split second, and then Ed sees Sally and the hand is gone; there it is, on top of the desk, reaching for a liqueur glass.

"Marylynn needs more Tia Maria," he says. "I just told her that people who drink a little now and again live longer." His voice is even, his face is as level as ever, a flat plain with no signposts.

Marylynn laughs. "I once had a dentist who I swear drilled tiny holes in my teeth, so he could fix them later," she says.

Sally sees Ed's hand outstretched towards her, holding the empty glass. She takes it, smiling, and turns away. There's a roaring sound at the back of her head; blackness appears around the edges of the picture she is seeing, like a television screen going dead. She walks into the kitchen and puts her cheek against the refrigerator and her arms around it; as far as they will go. She remains that way, hugging it; it hums steadily, with a sound like comfort. After a while she lets go of it and touches her hair, and walks back into the living room with the filled glass.

Marylynn is over by the french doors, talking with Walter Morly. Ed is standing by himself, in front of the fireplace, one arm on the mantelpiece, his left hand out of sight in his pocket.

Sally goes to Marylynn, hands her the glass. "Is that enough?" she says.

Marylynn is unchanged. "Thanks, Sally," she says, and goes on listening to Walter, who has dragged out his usual piece of mischief: some day, when they've perfected it, he says, all hearts will be plastic, and this will be a vast improvement on the current model. It's an

obscure form of flirtation. Marylynn winks at Sally, to
show that she knows he's tedious. Sally, after a pause,
winks back.

She looks over at Ed, who is staring off into space, like
a robot which has been parked and switched off. Now
she isn't sure whether she really saw what she thought
she saw. Even if she did, what does it mean? Maybe it's
just that Ed, in a wayward intoxicated moment, put his
hand on the nearest buttock, and Marylynn refrained
from a shriek or a flinch out of good breeding or the
desire not to offend him. Things like this have happened
to Sally.

Or it could mean something more sinister: a familiari-
ty between them, an understanding. If this is it, Sally
has been wrong about Ed, for years, forever. Her version
of Ed is not something she's perceived but something
that's been perpetrated on her, by Ed himself, for
reasons of his own. Possibly Ed is not stupid. Possibly
he's enormously clever. She thinks of moment after
moment when this cleverness, this cunning, would have
shown itself if it were there, but didn't. She has watched
him so carefully. She remembers playing Pick Up Sticks,
with the kids, Ed's kids, years ago: how if you moved one
stick in the tangle, even slightly, everything else moved
also.

She won't say anything to him. She can't say anything:
she can't afford to be wrong, or to be right either. She
goes back into the kitchen and begins to scrape the
plates. This is unlike her—usually she sticks right with
the party until it's over—and after a while Ed wanders
out. He stands silently, watching her. Sally concentrates
on the scraping: dollops of *sauce suprême* slide into the
plastic bag, shreds of lettuce, rice, congealed and lumpy.
What is left of her afternoon.

"What are you doing out here?" Ed asks at last.

"Scraping the plates," Sally says, cheerful, neutral. "I
just thought I'd get a head start on tidying up."

"Leave it," says Ed. "The woman can do that in the

morning." That's how he refers to Mrs. Rudge, although she's been with them for three years now: *the woman*. And Mrs. Bird before her, as though they are inter-changeable. This has never bothered Sally before. "Go on out there and have a good time."

Sally puts down the spatula, wipes her hands on the hand towel, puts her arms around him, holds on tighter than she should. Ed pats her shoulder. "What's up?" he says; then, "Sally, Sally." If she looks up, she will see him shaking his head a little, as if he doesn't know what to do about her. She doesn't look up.

Ed has gone to bed. Sally roams the house, fidgeting with the debris left by the party. She collects empty glasses, picks up peanuts from the rug. After a while she realizes that she's down on her knees, looking under a chair, and she's forgotten what for. She goes upstairs, creams off her make-up, does her teeth, undresses in the darkened bedroom and slides into bed beside Ed, who is breathing deeply as if asleep. *As if*.

Sally lies in bed with her eyes closed. What she sees is her own heart, in black and white, beating with that insubstantial moth-like flutter, a ghostly heart, torn out of her and floating in space, an animated valentine with no colour. It will go on and on forever; she has no control over it. But now she's seeing the egg, which is not small and cold and white and inert but larger than a real egg and golden pink, resting in a nest of brambles, glowing softly as though there's something red and hot inside it. It's almost pulsing; Sally is afraid of it. As she looks it darkens: rose-red, crimson. This is something the story left out, Sally thinks: the egg is alive, and one day it will hatch. But what will come out of it?

Spring Song of the Frogs

Women's lips are paler again. They wax and wane, from season to season. They haven't been this pale for years; not for fifteen or twenty years at least. Will can't remember when it was, when he last saw those shades of rich vanilla, of melting orange sherbet, of faded pink satin, on women's mouths. Some time before he started really noticing. All this past winter the lips were dark instead, mulberry, maroon, so that the mouths looked like the mouths of old-fashioned dolls, sharply defined against the china white of the skin. Now the skins are creamier, except on the ones who had ignored whatever wordless decree has gone out and have begun to tan.

This woman, whose name is Robyn, has a mouth the colour of a fingernail, the wan half-moon at the base. Her own fingernails are painted to match: someone has decided that they should no longer look as if they've been dipped in blood. She has on a loose cool dress, cotton in a pink so faint it's like something that's run in the wash, with buttons down the front, the top three undone. By the way she's glanced down once or twice, she's wondering if she's gone too far.

Will smiles at her, looking into her eyes, which are possibly blue; he can't tell in this light. She smiles back. She won't be able to keep staring him in the eye for long. After she blinks and shifts, she'll have three choices. The menu, on grey paper with offset handwriting, French style, which she's already studied; the view off to the side, towards the door, but it's too early for that; or the wall behind him. Will knows what's on it: a framed poster advertising a surrealist art show of several years back,

147

with a drawing on it, fleshy pink with pinky-grey
shadows, which suggests a part of the body, though it's
difficult to say which part. Something about to grow hair,
become sexual in a disagreeable way. Either she'll react
to it or she won't see it all. Instead she'll glance at her
own reflection in the glass, checking herself out as if she's
a stranger she might consider picking up: a deep look,
brief but sincere.

The waitress arrives, a thin girl in a red brushcut, with
a purple feather earring dangling from one ear. She
stands as though her head is fixed on a hook and the rest
of her body is drooping down from it, with no tendons.
She's wearing what could be tuxedo pants. The restaurant is in a district of second-hand clothing stores, where
foreign-looking women with stumpy legs and black hair
pulled back into buns come to shuffle through the racks,
and also where girls like this one get their outlandish
costumes. The belt is wide red plastic, and could be
either twenty-five years old or brand new; the shirt is a
man's dress shirt, with pleats, the sleeves rolled to the
elbow. The girl's arms, bone-skinny and white, come out
of the puffs of cloth like the stems of peonies that have
been grown in darkness.

Her thighs will be much the same. Will can remember
the thighs in the ancient men's magazines, the ones that
were passed around when he was at school, black-and-
white photos on cheap paper, with no air-brushing, the
plump women posed in motel rooms, the way the garters
would sink into the flesh of thighs and rump. Now there's
no flesh, the thighs have shrivelled up, they're all muscle
and bone. Even the *Playboy* centrefolds look as if they're
made of solid gristle. It's supposed to be sexy to show
them in leg warmers.

Will asks Robyn if she'd like something to drink.

"A Perrier with a twist," says Robyn, looking up,
giving the waitress the same smile she's just given Will.

Will orders a Bloody Mary and wonders if he's made a
mistake. Possibly this waitress is a man. He's been here

several times before, never without a slight but enjoyable sense of entering forbidden territory. Any place with checked tablecloths gives him this feeling, which is left over from when he was a student and thought he would end up being something other than what he has become. In those days he drew illustrations for the campus newspaper, and designed sets. For a while he kept up the drawing, as a hobby, or that's what his ex-wife called it. Maybe later he'll go back to it, when he has the time. Some days he wanders into the galleries down here, to see what the young kids are up to. The owners approach him with cynical deference, as if all he has to offer, to them or anyone else, is his money. He never buys anything.

The waitress returns with the drinks, and Will, in view of the two slight bumps visible on her ribcage, decides that she really is a woman after all.

"I thought for a minute she was a man," he says to Robyn.

"Really?" Robyn says. She glances at the waitress, now at the next table. "Oh no," she says, as if it's a mistake she herself would never have made. "No. Definitely a woman."

"Some bread?" Will says. The bread here is placed in tiny baskets, suspended over the tables by a sort of rope-and-pulley arrangement. To get to the bread you have to either stand up or lower the basket by unhitching the rope from where it's fastened on the wall; which is awkward, but Will enjoys doing it. Maybe the theory is that your food will appeal to you more if you're allowed to participate in it, or maybe the baskets are just some designer's fiasco. He always has bread here.

"Pardon?" says Robyn, as if *bread* is a word she's never heard before. "Oh. No thanks." She gives a little shudder, as if the thought of it is slightly repulsive. Will is annoyed, but determined to have bread anyway. It's good bread, thick, brown, and warm. He turns to the wall, undoes the rope, and the basket creaks downwards.

"Oh, that's very cute," says Robyn. He catches it then, the look she's giving herself in the glass behind him. Now they are going to have to make their way through the rest of the lunch somehow. Why does he keep on, what's he looking for that's so hard to find? She has generous breasts, that's what impelled him: the hope of generosity.

The waitress comes back and Robyn, pursing her pastel-coloured lips, orders a spinach salad without the dressing. Will is beginning to sweat; he's feeling claustrophobic and is anxious to be gone. He tries to think about running his hand up her leg and around her thigh, which might be full and soft, but it's no good. She wouldn't enjoy it.

Cynthia is white on white. Her hair is nearly blonde, helped out, Will suspects: her eyebrows and eyelashes are darker. Her skin is so pale it looks powdered. She's not wearing the hospital gown but a white nightgown with ruffles, childish, Victorian, reminiscent of lacey drawers and Kate Greenaway greeting cards. Under the cloth, Will thinks, she must be translucent; you would be able to see her veins and intestines, like a guppy's. She draws the sheet up to her chest, backing away from him, against the headboard of the bed, a position that reminds him of a sickly Rosetti madonna, cringing against the wall while the angel of the Annunciation threatens her with fullness.

Will smiles with what he hopes is affability. "How are you doing, Cynthia?" he says. There's a basket on the night table, with oranges and an apple; also some flowers.

"Okay," she says. She smiles, a limp smile that denies the message. Her eyes are anxious and cunning. She wants him to believe her and go away.

"Your mum and dad asked me to drop by," Will says. Cynthia is his niece.

"I figured," says Cynthia. Maybe she means that he wouldn't have come otherwise, or maybe she means that they have sent him as a substitute for themselves. She is probably right on both counts. It's a family myth that Will is Cynthia's favourite uncle. Like many myths, it had some basis in truth, once, when—just after his own marriage broke up—he was reaching for a sense of family, and would read Cynthia stories and tickle her under the arms. But that was years ago.

Last night, over the phone, his sister used this past as leverage. "You're the only one who can talk to her. She's cut us off." Her voice was angry rather than despairing.

"Well, I don't know," Will said dubiously. He has no great faith in his powers as a mediator, a confidant, even a strong shoulder. He used to have Cynthia up to the farm, when his own sons were younger and Cynthia was twelve or so. She was tanned then, a tomboy; she liked to wander over the property by herself, picking wild apples. At night she would wolf down the dinners Will would cook for the four of them, five if he had a woman up—plates of noodles Alfredo, roast beef with Yorkshire pudding, fried chicken, steaks, sometimes a goose which he'd bought from the people across the way.

There was nothing wrong with Cynthia then; she wore her hair loose, her skin was golden, and Will felt a disturbing sexual pull towards her which he certainly doesn't feel now. The boys felt it too, and would tease and provoke her, but she stood up to them. She said there was nothing they could do she couldn't do too, and she was almost right. Then they got into their motor-cycle-and-car phase, and Cynthia changed. All of a sudden she didn't like getting grease on her hands; she began painting her nails. Will sees this now as the beginning of the end.

"It's an epidemic," his sister said over the phone. "It's some kind of a fad. You know what she actually said? She actually said a lot of the girls at school were doing it. She's so goddamned competitive."

"I'll go in," Will said. "Is there anything I should take? Some cheese maybe?" His sister is married to a man whose eyebrows are so faint they're invisible. Will, who doesn't like him, thinks of him as an albino.

"How about a good slap on the backside," said his sister. "Not that she's got one left."

Then she began to cry, and Will said she shouldn't worry, he was sure it would all turn out fine in the end.

At the moment he doesn't believe it. He looks around the room, searching for a chair. There is one, but Cynthia's sky-blue dressing-gown is across it. Just as well: if he sits down, he'll have to stay longer.

"Just okay?" he says.

"I gained a pound," she says. This is intended to placate him. He'll have to check with the doctor, as his sister wants a full report, and Cynthia, she claims, is not accurate on the subject of her weight.

"That's wonderful," he says. Maybe it's true, since she's so unhappy about it.

"I hardly ate anything," she says, plaintively but also boasting.

"You're trying though," says Will. "That's good." Now that he's here, he wishes to be helpful. "Maybe tomorrow you'll eat more."

"But if I hardly ate anything and I gained a pound," she says, "what's going to happen? I'll get fat."

Will doesn't know what to say. Reason, he knows, doesn't work; it's been tried. It would do no good to tell her she's a wraith, that if she doesn't eat she'll digest herself, that her heart is a muscle like any other muscle and if it isn't fed it will atrophy.

Suddenly Will is hungry. He's conscious of the oranges and the apple, right beside him on the night table, round and brightly coloured and filled with sweet juice. He wants to take something, but would that be depriving her?

"Those look good," he says.

Cynthia is scornful, as if this is some crude ploy of his to coax her to eat. "Have some," she says. "Have it all. As long as I don't have to watch. You can put it in your pocket." She speaks of the fruit as if it were an undifferentiated mass, like cold porridge.

"That's all right," says Will. "I'll leave it here for you."

"Have the flowers then," says Cynthia. This gesture too is contemptuous: he has needs, she doesn't. She is beyond needs.

Will casts around for anything: some hook, some handhold. "You should get better," he says, "so you can come up to the farm. You like it there." To himself he sounds falsely genial, wheedling.

"I'd be in the way," Cynthia says, looking away from him, out the window. Will looks too. There's nothing out there but the windows of another hospital building. "Sometimes I can see them doing operations," she says.

"I'd enjoy it," Will says, not knowing whether he's lying. "I get lonely up there on the weekends." This is true enough, but as soon as he's said it it sounds like whining.

Cynthia looks at him briefly. "You," she says, as if she has a monopoly, and who is he to talk? "Anyway, you don't have to go there if you don't want to. Nobody's making you."

Will feels shabby, like an out-of-work man begging for handouts on the street. He has seen such men and turned away from them, thinking about how embarrassed he would be if he were in their place, shuffling like that. Now he sees that what counts for them is not his feeling of embarrassment but the money. He stands foolishly beside Cynthia's bed, his offering rejected.

Cynthia has a short attention span. She's looking at her hands, spread out on the sheet now. The nails are peach-coloured, newly polished. "I used to be pretty, when I was younger," she says.

Will wants to shake her. She's barely eighteen, she

doesn't know a thing about age or time. He could say, "You're pretty now," or he could say, "You'd be pretty if you'd put on some weight," but either one of these would be playing by her rules, so he says neither. Instead he says good-bye, pecks her on the cheek, and leaves, feeling as defeated as she wants him to feel. He hasn't made any difference.

Will parks his silver BMW in the parking space, takes the key out of the ignition, puts it carefully into his pocket. Then he remembers that he should keep the key handy to lock the car from the outside. This is one of the advantages of the BMW: you can never lock yourself out. He drove a Porsche for a while, after his marriage broke up. It made him feel single and ready for anything, but he doesn't feel like that anymore. His moustache went about the same time as that car.

The parking space is off to the left of the farmhouse, demarcated by railroad ties and covered with white crushed gravel. It was like that when he bought the place, but that's what he probably would have done anyway. He keeps meaning to plant some flowers, zinnias perhaps, behind the railroad ties, but so far he hasn't got around to it.

He gets out, goes to the trunk for the groceries. Halfway to the house he realizes he's forgotten to lock the car, and goes back to do it. It's not as safe around here as it used to be. Last year he had a break-in, some kids from the town, out joy-riding. They broke plates and spread peanut butter on the walls, drank his liquor and smashed the bottles, and, as far as he could tell, screwed in all the beds. They were caught because they pinched the television set and tried to sell it. Everything was insured, but Will felt humiliated. Now he has bolt locks, and bars on the cellar windows, but anyone could break in if they really wanted to. He's thinking of getting a dog.

The air inside the house smells dead, as if it has heated

and then cooled, absorbing the smells of furniture, old wood, paint, dust. He hasn't been here for several weeks. He sets the bags down on the kitchen table, opens a few windows. In the living room there's a vase with wizened daffodils, the water stagnant and foul. He sets the vase out on the patio; he'll empty it later.

Will bought this place after his marriage broke up, so he and the boys would have somewhere they could spend time together in a regular way. Also, his wife made it clear that she'd like some weekends off. The house was renovated by the people who lived here before; just as well, since Will never would have had the time to supervise, though he frequently sketches out plans for his ideal house. Not everything here is the way he would have done it, but he likes the board-and-batten exterior and the big opened-up kitchen. Despite some jumpiness lingering from the break-in, he feels good here, better than he does in his apartment in the city.

His former house is his wife's now; he doesn't like going there. Sometimes there are younger men, referred to by their first names only. Now that the boys are almost grown up, this doesn't bother him as much as it used to: she might as well be having a good time, though the turnover rate is high. When they were married she didn't enjoy anything much, including him, including sex. She never told him what was expected of him, and he never asked.

Will unpacks the groceries, stows away the food. He likes doing this, slotting the eggs into their egg-shaped holes in the refrigerator, filing the spinach in the crisper, stashing the butter in the compartment marked BUTTER, pouring the coffee beans into the jar labelled COFFEE. It makes him feel that some things at least are in their right places. He leaves the steaks on the counter, uncorks the wine, hunts for some candles. Of the pair he finds, one has been chewed by mice. Hardened droppings are scattered about the drawer. Mice are a new development. There must be a hole somewhere. Will is

standing with the chewed candle in his hand, pondering
remedies, when he hears a car outside.

He looks out the kitchen window. Since the break-in,
he's less willing to open the door without knowing who's
outside. But it's Diane, in a car he hasn't seen before, a
cream-coloured Subaru. She always keeps her cars very
clean. For some reason she's chosen to back up the
driveway, in memory, perhaps, of the time she got stuck
in the snow and he told her it would have been easier to
get out if she'd been pointing down.

He puts the candle on the counter and goes into the
downstairs bathroom. He smiles at himself, checking to
see if there's anything caught between his teeth. He
doesn't look bad. Then he goes out to welcome Diane.
He realizes he hasn't been sure until now that she would
really turn up. It could be he doesn't deserve it.

She slides out of the car, stands up, gives him a hug
and a peck on the cheek. She has big sunglasses on, with
silly palm trees over the eyebrows. This is the kind of
extravagance Will has always liked about her. He hugs
her back, but she doesn't want to be held too long. "I
brought you something," she says, and searches inside
the car.

Will watches her while she's bending over. She has a
wide cotton skirt on, pulled tight around the waist; she's
lost a lot of weight. He used to think of her as a hefty
woman, well-fleshed and athletic, but now she's almost
spindly. In his arms she felt frail, diminished.

She straightens and turns, thrusting a bottle of wine at
him, and a round of Greek bread, fresh and spongy. Will
is reassured. He puts his arm around her waist and hugs
her again, trying to make it companionable so she won't
feel pressured. "I'm glad to see you," he says.

Diane sits at the kitchen table and they drink wine;
Will fools with the steaks, rubbing them with garlic,
massaging them with pepper and a pinch or two of dried
mustard. She used to help him with the cooking, she
knows where everything's kept. But tonight she's acting
more like a guest.

"Heard any good jokes lately?" she says. This in itself is a joke, since it was Diane who told the jokes, not Will. Diane was the one Will was with when his marriage stopped creaking and groaning and finally just fell apart. She wasn't the reason though, as he made a point of telling her. He said it could have been anyone; he didn't want her to feel responsible. He's not sure what happened after that, why they stopped seeing one another. It wasn't the sex: with her he was a good lover. He knows she liked him, and she got on well with the boys. But one day she said, "Well, I guess that's that," and Will didn't have the presence of mind to ask her what she meant.

"That's your department," Will says.

"Only because you were so sad then," says Diane. "I was trying to cheer you up. You were dragging around like you had a thyroid deficiency or something." She fiddles with her sunglasses, which are on the table. "Now it's your turn."

"You know I'm no good at it," Will says.

Diane nods. "Bad timing," she says. She stands up, reaches past Will to the counter. "What's this?" she says, picking up the chewed candle. "Something fall off?"

They eat at the round oak table they bought together at a country auction, one of the local farmers closing up and selling out. Diane has dug out the white linen table napkins she gave him one year, and has lit both candles, the chewed and the unchewed. "I believe in festivity," she said.

Now there are silences, which they both attempt to fill. Diane says she wants to talk about money. It's the right time in her life for her to become interested in money, and isn't Will an authority? She makes quite a lot, but it's hard for her to save. She wants Will to explain inflation.

Will doesn't want to talk about money, but he does it

anyway, to please her. Pleasing her is what he would like
to do, but she doesn't seem too pleased. Her face is
thinner and more lined, which makes her look more
elegant but less accessible. She's less talkative than she
used to be, as well. He remembers her voice as louder,
more insistent; she would tease him, pull him up short.
He found it amusing and it took his mind off himself. He
thinks women in general are becoming more silent: it
goes with their new pale lips. They're turning back to
secrecy, concealment. It's as if they're afraid of something, but Will can't imagine what.

Half of Diane's steak lies on her plate, untouched. "So
tell me about gold," she says.

"You're not hungry?" Will asks her.

"I was ravenous," she says. "But I'm full." Her hair has
changed too. It's longer, with light streaks. Altogether
she is more artful.

"I like being with you," Will says. "I always did."

"But not quite enough," Diane says, and then, to
make it light, "you should put an ad in the paper, Will.
The personals, *NOW* magazine. 'Nice man, executive,
with good income, no encumbrances, desires to
meet . . .'"

"I guess I'm not very good at relationships," Will says.
In his head, he's trying to complete Diane's ad. Desires
to meet what? A woman who would not look at herself in
the glass of the picture behind him. A woman who would
like what he cooks.

"Bullshit," Diane says, with a return to her old
belligerence. "What makes you think you're that much
worse at it than anyone else?"

Will looks at her throat, where it's visible at the V-neck
of her blouse. He hasn't seen an overnight case, but
maybe it's in the car. He said no strings attached.

"There's a full moon," he says. "We should go out onto
the patio."

"Not quite," says Diane, squinting up through the
glass. "And it's freezing out there, I bet."

Will goes upstairs for a plaid blanket from the boys' room to wrap around her. What he has in mind is a couple of brandies on the patio, and then they will see. As he's coming back down the stairs, he hears her in the bathroom: it sounds as if she's throwing up. Will pours the brandies, carries them outside. He wonders if he should go in, knock on the bathroom door. What if it's food poisoning? He knows he should feel compassion; instead he feels betrayed by her.

But when she comes out to stand beside him, she seems all right, and Will decides not to ask her about it. He wraps the blanket around her and keeps his arm there, and Diane leans against him.

"We could sit down," he says, in case she doesn't like the position.

"Hey," she says, "you got me flowers." She's spotted the withered daffodils. "Always so thoughtful. I bet they smell nice, too."

"I wanted you to hear the frogs," Will says. "We're just at the end of the frog season." The frogs live in the pond, down beyond the slope of the lawn. Or maybe they're toads, he's never been sure. For Will they've come to mean spring and the beginning of summer: possibilities, newness. Their silvery voices are filling the air around them now, like crickets but more prolonged, sweeter.

"What a man," Diane says. "For some it's nightingales, for some it's frogs. Next I get a box of chocolate-covered slugs, right?"

Will would like to kiss her, but the timing is wrong. She's shivering a little; against his arm she feels angular, awkward, as if she's withholding her body from him, though not quite. They stand there looking at the moon, which is cold and lopsided, and listening to the trilling of the frogs. This doesn't have the effect on Will he has hoped it would. The voices coming from the darkness below the curve of the hill sound thin and ill. There aren't as many frogs as there used to be, either.

Scarlet Ibis

Some years ago now, Christine went with Don to Trinidad. They took Lilian, their youngest child, who was four then. The others, who were in school, stayed with their grandmother.

Christine and Don sat beside the hotel pool in the damp heat, drinking rum punch and eating strange-tasting hamburgers. Lilian wanted to be in the pool all the time—she could already swim a little—but Christine didn't think it was a good idea, because of the sun. Christine rubbed sun block on her nose, and on the noses of Lilian and Don. She felt that her legs were too white and that people were looking at her and finding her faintly ridiculous, because of her pinky-white skin and the large hat she wore. More than likely, the young black waiters who brought the rum punch and the hamburgers, who walked easily through the sun without paying any attention to it, who joked among themselves but were solemn when they set down the glasses and plates, had put her in a category; one that included fat, although she was not fat exactly. She suggested to Don that perhaps he was tipping too much. Don said he felt tired.

"You felt tired before," Christine said. "That's why we came, remember? So you could get some rest."

Don took afternoon naps, sprawled on his back on one of the twin beds in the room—Lilian had a fold-out cot—his mouth slightly open, the skin of his face pushed by gravity back down towards his ears, so that he looked tauter, thinner, and more aquiline in this position than he did when awake. Deader, thought Christine, taking a

160

closer look. People lying on their backs in coffins usually—in her limited experience—seemed to have lost weight. This image, of Don encoffined, was one that had been drifting through her mind too often for comfort lately.

It was hopeless expecting Lilian to have an afternoon nap too, so Christine took her down to the pool or tried to keep her quiet by drawing with her, using Magic Markers. At that age Lilian drew nothing but women or girls, wearing very fancy dresses, full-skirted, with a lot of decoration. They were always smiling, with red, curvy mouths, and had abnormally long thick eyelashes. They did not stand on any ground—Lilian was not yet putting the ground into her pictures—but floated on the page as if it were a pond they were spread out on, arms outstretched, feet at the opposite sides of their skirts, their elaborate hair billowing around their heads. Sometimes Lilian put in some birds or the sun, which gave these women the appearance of giant airborne balloons, as if the wind had caught them under their skirts and carried them off, light as feathers, away from everything. Yet, if she were asked, Lilian would say these women were walking.

After a few days of all this, when they ought to have adjusted to the heat, Christine felt they should get out of the hotel and do something. She did not want to go shopping by herself, although Don suggested it; she felt that nothing she tried on helped her look any better, or, to be more precise, that it didn't much matter how she looked. She tried to think of some other distraction, mostly for the sake of Don. Don was not noticeably more rested, although he had a sunburn—which, instead of giving him a glow of health, made him seem angry—and he'd started drumming his fingers on tabletops again. He said he was having trouble sleeping: bad dreams, which he could not remember. Also the air-conditioning was clogging up his nose. He had been under a lot of pressure lately, he said.

Christine didn't need to be told. She could feel the
pressure he was under, like a clenched mass of something, tissue, congealed blood, at the back of her own
head. She thought of Don as being encased in a sort of
metal carapace, like the shell of a crab, that was slowly
tightening on him, on all parts of him at once, so that
something was sure to burst, like a thumb closed slowly
in a car door. The metal skin was his entire body, and
Christine didn't know how to unlock it for him and let
him out. She felt as if all her ministrations—the cold
washcloths for his headaches, the trips to the drugstore
for this or that bottle of pills, the hours of tiptoeing
around, intercepting the phone, keeping Lilian quiet,
above all the mere act of witnessing him, which was so
draining—were noticed by him hardly at all: moths
beating on the outside of a lit window, behind which
someone important was thinking about something of
major significance that had nothing to do with moths.
This vacation, for instance, had been her idea, but Don
was only getting redder and redder.

Unfortunately, it was not carnival season. There were
restaurants, but Lilian hated sitting still in them, and
one thing Don did not need was more food and
especially more drink. Christine wished Don had a
sport, but considering the way he was, he would
probably overdo it and break something.

"I had an uncle who took up hooking rugs," she'd said
to him one evening after dinner. "When he retired. He
got them in kits. He said he found it very restful." The
aunt that went with that uncle used to say, "I said for
better or for worse, but I never said for lunch."

"Oh, for God's sake, Christine," was all Don had to say
to that. He'd never thought much of her relatives. His
view was that Christine was still on the raw side of being
raw material. Christine did not look forward to the time,
twenty years away at least, when he would be home all
day, pacing, drumming his fingers, wanting whatever it
was that she could never identify and never provide.

In the morning, while the other two were beginning breakfast, Christine went bravely to the hotel's reception desk. There was a thin, elegant brown girl behind it, in lime green, Rasta beads, and *Vogue* make-up, coiled like spaghetti around the phone. Christine, feeling hot and porous, asked if there was any material on things to do. The girl, sliding her eyes over and past Christine as if she were a minor architectural feature, selected and fanned an assortment of brochures, continuing to laugh lightly into the phone.

Christine took the brochures into the ladies' room to preview them. Not the beach, she decided, because of the sun. Not the boutiques, not the night clubs, not the memories of Old Spain.

She examined her face, added lipstick to her lips, which were getting thin and pinched together. She really needed to do something about herself, before it was too late. She made her way back to the breakfast table. Lilian was saying that the pancakes weren't the same as the ones at home. Don said she had to eat them because she had ordered them, and if she was old enough to order for herself she was old enough to know that they cost money and couldn't be wasted like that. Christine wondered silently if it was a bad pattern, making a child eat everything on her plate, whether she liked the food or not; perhaps Lilian would become fat, later on.

Don was having bacon and eggs. Christine had asked Don to order yoghurt and fresh fruit for her, but there was nothing at her place.

"They didn't have it," Don said.

"Did you order anything else?" said Christine, who was now hungry.

"How was I supposed to know what you want?" said Don.

"We're going to see the Scarlet Ibis," Christine announced brightly to Lilian. She would ask them to bring back the menu, so she could order.

"What?" said Don. Christine handed him the bro-

chure, which showed some red birds with long curved
bills sitting in a tree; there was another picture of one
close up, in profile, one demented-looking eye staring
out from its red feathers like a target.

"They're very rare," said Christine, looking around for
a waiter. "It's a preservation."

"You mean a preserve," said Don, reading the brochure. "In a swamp? Probably crawling with mosquitoes."

"I don't want to go," said Lilian, pushing scraps of a
pancake around in a pool of watery syrup. This was her
other complaint, that it wasn't the right kind of syrup.

"Imitation maple flavouring," Don said, reading the
label.

"You don't even know what it is," said Christine.
"We'll take some fly dope. Anyway, they wouldn't let
tourists go there if there were that many mosquitoes. It's
a *mangrove* swamp; that isn't the same as our kind."

"I'm going to get a paper," said Don. He stood up and
walked away. His legs, coming out of the bottoms of his
Bermuda shorts, were still very white, with an overglaze
of pink down the backs. His body, once muscular, was
losing tone, sliding down towards his waist and buttocks.
He was beginning to slope. From the back, he had the
lax, demoralized look of a man who has been confined in
an institution, though from the front he was brisk
enough.

Watching him go, Christine felt the sickness in the pit
of her stomach that was becoming familiar to her these
days. Maybe the pressure he was under was her. Maybe
she was a weight. Maybe he wanted her to lift up, blow
away somewhere, like a kite, the children hanging on
behind her in a long string. She didn't know when she
had first noticed this feeling; probably after it had been
there some time, like a knocking on the front door when
you're asleep. There had been a shifting of forces,
unseen, unheard, underground, the sliding against each

other of giant stones; some tremendous damage had occurred between them, but who could tell when?

"Eat your pancakes," she said to Lillian, "or your father will be annoyed." He would be annoyed anyway: she annoyed him. Even when they made love, which was not frequently anymore, it was perfunctory, as if he were listening for something else, a phone call, a footfall. He was like a man scratching himself. She was like his hand.

Christine had a scenario she ran through often, the way she used to run through scenarios of courtship, back in high school: flirtation, pursuit, joyful acquiescence. This was an adult scenario, however. One evening she would say to Don as he was getting up from the table after dinner, "Stay there." He would be so surprised by her tone of voice that he would stay.

"I just want you to sit there and look at me," she would say.

He would not say, "For God's sake, Christine." He would know this was serious.

"I'm not asking much from you," she would say, lying.

"What's going on?" he would say.

"I want you to see what I really look like," she would say. "I'm tired of being invisible." Maybe he would, maybe he wouldn't. Maybe he would say he was coming on with a headache. Maybe she would find herself walking on nothing, because maybe there was nothing there. So far she hadn't even come close to beginning, to giving the initial command: "Stay," as if he were a trained dog. But that was what she wanted him to do, wasn't it? "Come back" was more like it. He hadn't always been under pressure.

Once Lilian was old enough, Christine thought, she could go back to work full time. She could brush up her typing and shorthand, find something. That would be good for her; she wouldn't concentrate so much on Don, she would have a reason to look better, she would either find new scenarios or act out the one that was preoccupy-

ing her. Maybe she was making things up, about Don. It
might be a form of laziness.

Christine's preparations for the afternoon were careful.
She bought some mosquito repellant at a drugstore, and
a chocolate bar. She took two scarves, one for herself,
one for Lilian, in case it was sunny. The big hat would
blow off, she thought, as they were going to be in a boat.
After a short argument with one of the waiters, who said
she could only have drinks by the glass, she succeeded in
buying three cans of Pepsi, not chilled. All these things
she packed into her bag; Lilian's bag, actually, which was
striped in orange and yellow and blue and had a picture
of Mickey Mouse on it. They'd used it for the toys Lilian
brought with her on the plane.

After lunch they took a taxi, first through the hot
streets of the town, where the sidewalks were too narrow
or nonexistent and the people crowded onto the road
and there was a lot of honking, then out through the cane
fields, the road becoming bumpier, the driver increasing
speed. He drove with the car radio on, the left-hand
window open, and his elbow out, a pink jockey cap
tipped back on his head. Christine had shown him the
brochure and asked him if he knew where the swamp
was; he'd grinned at her and said everybody knew. He
said he could take them, but it was too far to go out and
back so he would wait there for them. Christine knew it
meant extra money, but did not argue.

They passed a man riding a donkey, and two cows
wandering around by the roadside, anchored by ropes
around their necks which were tied to dragging stones.
Christine pointed these out to Lilian. The little houses
among the tall cane were made of cement blocks,
painted light green or pink or light blue; they were built
up on open-work foundations, almost as if they were on
stilts. The women who sat on the steps turned their
heads, unsmiling, to watch their taxi as it went by.

Lilian asked Christine if she had any gum. Christine didn't. Lilian began chewing on her nails, which she'd taken up since Don had been under pressure. Christine told her to stop. Then Lilian said she wanted to go for a swim. Don looked out the window. "How long did you say?" he asked. It was a reproach, not a question.

Christine hadn't said how long because she didn't know; she didn't know because she'd forgotten to ask. Finally they turned off the main road onto a smaller, muddier one, and parked beside some other cars in a rutted space that had once been part of a field.

"I meet you here," said the driver. He got out of the car, stretched, turned up the car radio. There were other drivers hanging around, some of them in cars, others sitting on the ground drinking from a bottle they were passing around, one asleep.

Christine took Lilian's hand. She didn't want to appear stupid by having to ask where they were supposed to go next. She didn't see anything that looked like a ticket office.

"It must be that shack," Don said, so they walked towards it, a long shed with a tin roof; on the other side of it was a steep bank and the beginning of the water. There were wooden steps leading down to a wharf, which was the same brown as the water itself. Several boats were tied up to it, all of similar design: long and thin, almost like barges, with rows of bench-like seats. Each boat had a small outboard motor at the back. The names painted on the boats looked East Indian.

Christine took the scarves out of her bag and tied one on her own head and one on Lilian's. Although it was beginning to cloud over, the sun was still very bright, and she knew about rays coming through overcast, especially in the tropics. She put sun block on their noses, and thought that the chocolate bar had been a silly idea. Soon it would be a brown puddle at the bottom of her bag, which luckily was waterproof. Don paced behind them as Christine knelt.

An odd smell was coming up from the water: a swamp smell, but with something else mixed in. Christine wondered about sewage disposal. She was glad she'd made Lilian go to the bathroom before they'd left.

There didn't seem to be anyone in charge, anyone to buy the tickets from, although there were several people beside the shed, waiting, probably: two plumpish, middle-aged men in T-shirts and baseball caps turned around backwards, an athletic couple in shorts with outside pockets, who were loaded down with cameras and binoculars, a trim grey-haired woman in a tailored pink summer suit that must have been far too hot. There was another woman off to the side, a somewhat large woman in a floral print dress. She'd spread a Mexican-looking shawl on the weedy grass near the shed and was sitting down on it, drinking a pint carton of orange juice through a straw. The others looked wilted and dispirited, but not this woman. For her, waiting seemed to be an activity, not something imposed: she gazed around her, at the bank, the brown water, the line of sullen mangrove trees beyond, as if she were enjoying every minute.

This woman seemed the easiest to approach, so Christine went over to her. "Are we in the right place?" she said. "For the birds."

The woman smiled at her and said they were. She had a broad face, with high, almost Slavic cheekbones and round red cheeks like those of an old-fashioned wooden doll, except that they were not painted on. Her taffy-coloured hair was done in waves and rolls, and reminded Christine of the pictures on the Toni home-permanent boxes of several decades before.

"We will leave soon," said the woman. "Have you seen these birds before? They come back only at sunset. The rest of the time they are away, fishing." She smiled again, and Christine thought to herself that it was a pity she hadn't had bands put on to even out her teeth when she was young.

This was the woman's second visit to the Scarlet Ibis preserve, she told Christine. The first was three years ago, when she stopped over here on her way to South America with her husband and children. This time her husband and children had stayed back at the hotel: they hadn't seen a swimming pool for such a long time. She and her husband were Mennonite missionaries, she said. She herself didn't seem embarrassed by this, but Christine blushed a little. She had been raised Anglican, but the only vestige of that was the kind of Christmas cards she favoured: prints of mediaeval or Renaissance old masters. Religious people of any serious kind made her nervous: they were like men in raincoats who might or might not be flashers. You would be going along with them in the ordinary way, and then there could be a swift movement and you would look down to find the coat wide open and nothing on under it but some pant legs held up by rubber bands. This had happened to Christine in a train station once.

"How many children do you have?" she said, to change the subject. Mennonite would explain the wide hips: they liked women who could have a lot of children.

The woman's crooked-toothed smile did not falter. "Four," she said, "but one of them is dead."

"Oh," said Christine. It wasn't clear whether the four included the one dead, or whether that was extra. She knew better than to say, "That's too bad." Such a comment was sure to produce something about the will of God, and she didn't want to deal with that. She looked to make sure Lilian was still there, over by Don. Much of the time Lilian was a given, but there were moments at which she was threatened, unknown to herself, with sudden disappearance. "That's my little girl, over there," Christine said, feeling immediately that this was a callous comment; but the woman continued to smile, in a way that Christine now found eerie.

A small brown man in a Hawaiian-patterned shirt came around from behind the shed and went quickly down the steps to the wharf. He climbed into one of the boats and lowered the outboard motor into the water.

"Now maybe we'll get some action," Don said. He had come up behind her, but he was talking more to himself than to her. Christine sometimes wondered whether he talked in the same way when she wasn't there at all.

A second man, East Indian, like the first, and also in a hula-dancer shirt, was standing at the top of the steps, and they understood they were to go over. He took their money and gave each of them a business card in return; on one side of it was a coloured picture of an ibis, on the other a name and a phone number. They went single file down the steps and the first man handed them into the boat. When they were all seated—Don, Christine, Lilian, and the pink-suited woman in a crowded row, the two baseball-cap men in front of them, the Mennonite woman and the couple with the cameras at the very front—the second man cast off and hopped lightly into the bow. After a few tries the first man got the motor started, and they putt-putted slowly towards an opening in the trees, leaving a wispy trail of smoke behind them.

It was cloudier now, and not so hot. Christine talked with the pink-suited woman, who had blonde hair elegantly done up in a French roll. She was from Vienna, she said; her husband was here on business. This was the first time she had been on this side of the Atlantic Ocean. The beaches were beautiful, much finer than those of the Mediterranean. Christine complimented her on her good English, and the woman smiled and told her what a beautiful little girl she had, and Christine said Lilian would get conceited, a word that the woman had not yet added to her vocabulary. Lilian was quiet; she had caught sight of the woman's bracelet, which was silver and lavishly engraved. The woman showed it to her. Christine began to enjoy herself, despite the fact that the two men in front of her were talking too loudly. They were drinking beer, from cans they'd brought with them

in a paper bag. She opened a Pepsi and shared some
with Lilian. Don didn't want any.

They were in a channel now; she looked at the trees on
either side, which were all the same, dark-leaved, rising
up out of the water, on masses of spindly roots. She
didn't know how long they'd been going.

It began to rain, not a downpour but heavily enough,
large cold drops. The Viennese woman said, "It's raining," her eyes open in a parody of surprise, holding out
her hand and looking up at the sky like someone in a
child's picture book. This was for the benefit of Lilian.
"We will get wet," she said. She took a white embroidered handkerchief out of her purse and spread it on
the top of her head. Lilian was enchanted with the
handkerchief and asked Christine if she could have one,
too. Don said they should have known, since it always
rained in the afternoons here.

The men in baseball caps hunched their shoulders,
and one of them said to the Indian in the bow, "Hey,
we're getting wet!"

The Indian's timid but closed expression did not
change; with apparent reluctance he pulled a rolled-up
sheet of plastic out from somewhere under the front seat
and handed it to the men. They spent some time
unrolling it and getting it straightened out, and then
everyone helped to hold the plastic overhead like a roof,
while the boat glided on at its unvarying pace, through
the mangroves and the steam or mist that was now rising
around them.

"Isn't this an adventure?" Christine said, aiming it at
Lilian. Lilian was biting her nails. The rain pattered
down. Don said he wished he'd brought a paper. The
men in baseball caps began to sing, sounding oddly like
boys at a summer camp who had gone to sleep one day
and awakened thirty years later, unaware of the sinister
changes that had taken place in them, the growth and
recession of hair and flesh, the exchange of their once-
clear voices for the murky ones that were now singing
off-key, out of time:

"They say that in the army,
the girls are rather fine,
They promise Betty Grable,
they give you Frankenstein . . ."

They had not yet run out of beer. One of them finished a can and tossed it overboard, and it bobbed beside the boat for a moment before falling behind, a bright red dot in the borderless expanse of dull green and dull grey. Christine felt virtuous: she'd put her Pepsi can carefully into her bag, for disposal later.

Then the rain stopped, and after some debate about whether it was going to start again or not, the two baseball-cap men began to roll up the plastic sheet. While they were doing this there was a jarring thud. The boat rocked violently, and the one man who was standing up almost pitched overboard, then sat down with a jerk.

"What the hell?" he said.

The Indian at the back reversed the motor.

"We hit something," said the Viennese woman. She clasped her hands, another classic gesture.

"Obviously," Don said in an undertone. Christine smiled at Lilian, who was looking anxious. The boat started forward again.

"Probably a mangrove root," said the man with the cameras, turning half round. "They grow out under the water." He was the kind who would know.

"Or an alligator," said one of the men in baseball caps. The other man laughed.

"He's joking, darling," Christine said to Lilian.

"But we are sinking," said the Viennese woman, pointing with one outstretched hand, one dramatic finger.

Then they all saw what they had not noticed before. There was a hole in the boat, near the front, right above the platform of loose boards that served as a floor. It was the size of a small fist. Whatever they'd hit had punched right through the wood, as if it were cardboard. Water was pouring through.

"This tub must be completely rotten," Don muttered, directly to Christine this time. This was a role she was sometimes given when they were among people Don didn't know: the listener. "They get like that in the tropics."

"Hey," said one of the men in baseball caps. "You up front. There's a hole in the goddamned boat."

The Indian glanced over his shoulder at the hole. He shrugged, looked away, began fishing in the breast pocket of his sports shirt for a cigarette.

"Hey. Turn this thing around," said the man with the camera.

"Couldn't we get it fixed, and then start again?" said Christine, intending to conciliate. She glanced at the Mennonite woman, hoping for support, but the woman's broad flowered back was towards her.

"If we go back," the Indian said patiently—he could understand English after all—"you miss the birds. It will be too dark."

"Yeah, but if we go forward we sink."

"You will not sink," said the Indian. He had found a cigarette, already half-smoked, and was lighting it.

"He's done it before," said the largest baseball cap. "Every week he gets a hole in the goddamned boat. Nothing to it."

The brown water continued to come in. The boat went forward.

"Right," Don said, loudly, to everyone this time. "He thinks if we don't see the birds, we won't pay him."

That made sense to Christine. For the Indians, it was a lot of money. They probably couldn't afford the gas if they lost the fares. "If you go back, we'll pay you anyway," she called to the Indian. Ordinarily she would have made this suggestion to Don, but she was getting frightened.

Either the Indian didn't hear her or he didn't trust

them, or it wasn't his idea of a fair bargain. He didn't smile or reply.

For a few minutes they all sat there, waiting for the problem to be solved. The trees went past. Finally Don said, "We'd better bail. At this rate we'll be in serious trouble in about half an hour."

"I should not have come," said the Viennese woman, in a tone of tragic despair.

"What with?" said the man with the cameras. The men in baseball caps had turned to look at Don, as if he were worthy of attention.

"Mummy, are we going to sink?" said Lilian.

"Of course not, darling," said Christine. "Daddy won't let us."

"Anything there is," said the largest baseball-cap man. He poured the rest of his beer over the side. "You got a jack-knife?" he said.

Don didn't, but the man with the cameras did. They watched while he cut the top out of the can, knelt down, moved a loose platform board so he could get at the water, scooped, dumped brown water over the side. Then the other men started taking the tops off their own beer cans, including the full ones, which they emptied out. Christine produced the Pepsi can from her bag. The Mennonite woman had her pint juice carton.

"No mosquitoes, at any rate," Don said, almost cheerfully.

They'd lost a lot of time, and the water was almost up to the floor platform. It seemed to Christine that the boat was becoming heavier, moving more slowly through the water, that the water itself was thicker. They could not empty much water at a time with such small containers, but maybe, with so many of them doing it, it would work.

"This really *is* an adventure," she said to Lilian, who was white-faced and forlorn. "Isn't this fun?"

The Viennese woman was not bailing; she had no container. She was making visible efforts to calm herself.

She had taken out a tangerine, which she was peeling, over the embroidered handkerchief which she'd spread out on her lap. Now she produced a beautiful little penknife with a mother-of-pearl handle. To Lilian she said, "You are hungry? Look, I will cut in pieces, one piece for you, then one for me, *ja*?" The knife was not really needed, of course. It was to distract Lilian, and Christine was grateful.

There was an audible rhythm in the boat: scrape, dump; scrape, dump. The men in baseball caps, rowdy earlier, were not at all drunk now. Don appeared to be enjoying himself, for the first time on the trip.

But despite their efforts, the level of the water was rising.

"This is ridiculous," Christine said to Don. She stopped bailing with her Pepsi can. She was discouraged and also frightened. She told herself that the Indians wouldn't keep going if they thought there was any real danger, but she wasn't convinced. Maybe they didn't care if everybody drowned; maybe they thought it was Karma. Through the hole the brown water poured, with a steady flow, like a cut vein. It was up to the level of the loose floor boards now.

Then the Mennonite woman stood up. Balancing herself, she removed her shoes, placing them carefully side by side under the seat. Christine had once watched a man do this in a subway station; he'd put the shoes under the bench where she was sitting, and a few minutes later had thrown himself in front of the oncoming train. The two shoes had remained on the neat yellow-tiled floor, like bones on a plate after a meal. It flashed through Christine's head that maybe the woman had become unhinged and was going to leap overboard; this was plausible, because of the dead child. The woman's perpetual smile was a fraud then, as Christine's would have been in her place.

But the woman did not jump over the side of the boat. Instead she bent over and moved the platform boards.

Then she turned around and lowered her large flowered rump onto the hole. Her face was towards Christine now; she continued to smile, gazing over the side of the boat at the mangroves and their monotonous roots and leaves as if they were the most interesting scenery she had seen in a long time. The water was above her ankles; her skirt was wet. Did she look a little smug, a little clever or self-consciously heroic? Possibly, thought Christine, though from that round face it was hard to tell.

"Hey," said one of the men in baseball caps, "now you're cooking with gas!" The Indian in the bow looked at the woman; his white teeth appeared briefly.

The others continued to bail, and after a moment Christine began to scoop and pour with the Pepsi can again. Despite herself, the woman impressed her. The water probably wasn't that cold but it was certainly filthy, and who could tell what might be on the other side of the hole? Were they far enough south for piranhas? Yet there was the Mennonite woman plugging the hole with her bottom, serene as a brooding hen, and no doubt unaware of the fact that she was more than a little ridiculous. Christine could imagine the kinds of remarks the men in baseball caps would make about the woman afterwards. "Saved by a big butt." "Hey, never knew it had more than one use." "Finger in the dike had nothing on her." That was the part that would have stopped Christine from doing such a thing, even if she'd managed to think of it.

Now they reached the long aisle of mangroves and emerged into the open; they were in a central space, like a lake, with the dark mangroves walling it around. There was a chicken-wire fence strung across it, to keep any boats from going too close to the Scarlet Ibis' roosting area: that was what the sign said, nailed to a post that was sticking at an angle out of the water. The Indian cut the motor and they drifted towards the fence; the other Indian caught hold of the fence, held on, and the boat

stopped, rocking a little. Apart from the ripples they'd
caused, the water was dead flat calm; the trees doubled
in it appeared black, and the sun, which was just above
the western rim of the real trees, was a red disk in the
hazy grey sky. The light coming from it was orangy-red
and tinted the water. For a few minutes nothing
happened. The man with the cameras looked at his
watch. Lilian was restless, squirming on the seat. She
wanted to draw; she wanted to swim in the pool. If
Christine had known the whole thing would take so long
she wouldn't have brought her.

"They coming," said the Indian in the bow.

"Birds ahoy," said one of the men in baseball caps, and
pointed, and then there were the birds all right, flying
through the reddish light, right on cue, first singly, then
in flocks of four or five, so bright, so fluorescent that they
were like painted flames. They settled into the trees,
screaming hoarsely. It was only the screams that revealed them as real birds.

The others had their binoculars up. Even the Viennese woman had a little pair of opera glasses. "Would
you look at that," said one of the men. "Wish I'd brought
my movie camera."

Don and Christine were without technology. So was
the Mennonite woman. "You could watch them forever,"
she said, to nobody in particular. Christine, afraid that
she would go on to say something embarrassing, pre-
tended not to hear her. *Forever* was loaded.

She took Lilian's hand. "See those red birds?" she said.
"You might never see one of those again in your entire
life." But she knew that for Lilian these birds were no
more special than anything else. She was too young for
them. She said, "Oh," which was what she would have
said if they had been pterodactyls or angels with wings as
red as blood. Magicians, Christine knew from Lilian's
last birthday party, were a failure with small children,
who didn't see any reason why rabbits shouldn't come
out of hats.

Don took hold of Christine's hand, a thing he had not done for some time; but Christine, watching the birds, noticed this only afterwards. She felt she was looking at a picture, of exotic flowers or of red fruit growing on trees, evenly spaced, like the fruit in the gardens of mediaeval paintings, solid, clear-edged, in primary colours. On the other side of the fence was another world, not real but at the same time more real than the one on this side, the men and women in their flimsy clothes and aging bodies, the decrepit boat. Her own body seemed fragile and empty, like blown glass.

The Mennonite woman had her face turned up to the sunset; her body was cut off at the neck by shadow, so that her head appeared to be floating in the air. For the first time she looked sad; but when she felt Christine watching her she smiled again, as if to reassure her, her face luminous and pink and round as a plum. Christine felt the two hands holding her own, mooring her, one on either side.

Weight returned to her body. The light was fading, the air chillier. Soon they would have to return in the increasing darkness, in a boat so rotten a misplaced foot would go through it. The water would be black, not brown; it would be full of roots.

"Shouldn't we go back?" she said to Don.

Lilian said, "Mummy, I'm hungry," and Christine remembered the chocolate bar and rummaged in her bag. It was down at the bottom, limp as a slab of bacon but not liquid. She brought it out and peeled off the silver paper, and gave a square to Lilian and one to Don, and ate one herself. The light was pink and dark at the same time, and it was difficult to see what she was doing.

When she told about this later, after they were safely home, Christine put in the swamp and the awful boat, and the men singing and the suspicious smell of the water. She put in Don's irritability, but only on days when he wasn't particularly irritable. (By then, there was less pressure; these things went in phases, Christine decided. She was glad she had never said anything, forced any issues.) She put in how good Lilian had been even though she hadn't wanted to go. She put in the hole in the boat, her own panic, which she made amusing, and the ridiculous bailing with the cans, and the Indians' indifference to their fate. She put in the Mennonite woman sitting on the hole like a big fat hen, making this funny, but admiring also, since the woman's solution to the problem had been so simple and obvious that no one else had thought of it. She left out the dead child.

She put in the rather hilarious trip back to the wharf, with the Indian standing up in the bow, beaming his heavy-duty flashlight at the endless, boring mangroves, and the two men in the baseball caps getting into a mickey and singing dirty songs.

She ended with the birds, which were worth every minute of it, she said. She presented them as a form of entertainment, like the Grand Canyon: something that really ought to be seen, if you liked birds, and if you should happen to be in that part of the world.

The Salt Garden

Alma turns up the heat, stirs the clear water in the red enamel pot, adds more salt, stirs, adds. She's making a supersaturated solution: re-making it. She made it already, at lunchtime, with Carol, but she didn't remember that you had to boil the water and she just used hot water from the tap. Nothing happened, though Alma had promised that a salt tree would form on the thread they hung down into the water, suspending it from a spoon laid crossways on the top of the glass.

"It takes time," Alma said. "It'll be here when you come home," and Carol went trustingly back to school, while Alma tried to figure out what she'd done wrong.

This experiment thing is new. Alma isn't sure where Carol picked it up. Surely not from school: she's only in grade two. But they're doing everything younger and younger. It upsets Alma to see them trying on her high heels and putting lipstick on their little mouths, even though she knows it's just a game. They wiggle their hips, imitating something they've seen on television. Maybe the experiments come from television too.

Alma has racked her brains, as she always does when Carol expresses interest in anything, searching for information she ought to possess but usually doesn't. These days, Alma encourages anything that will involve the two of them in an activity that will block out questions about the way they're living; about the where-abouts of Mort, for instance. She's tried trips to the zoo, sewing dolls' dresses, movies on Saturdays. They all work, but only for a short time.

When the experiments came up, she remembered

about putting vinegar into baking soda, to make it fizz; that was a success. Then other things started coming back to her. Now she can recall having been given a small chemistry set as a child, at the age of ten or so it must have been, by her father, who had theories in advance of his time. He thought girls should be brought up more like boys, possibly because he had no sons: Alma is an only child. Also he wanted her to do better than he himself had done. He had a job beneath his capabilities, in the post office, and he felt thwarted by that. He didn't want Alma to feel thwarted: that was how he'd attempted to warn Alma away from an early marriage, from leaving university to put Mort through architectural school by working as a secretary for a food-packing company. "You'll wake up one day and you'll feel thwarted," he told her. Alma sometimes wonders whether this word describes what she feels, but usually decides that it doesn't.

Long before that period, though, he'd tried to interest Alma in chess and mathematics and stamp collecting, among other things. Not much of this rubbed off on Alma, at least not to her knowledge; at the predictable age she became disappointingly obsessed with make-up and clothes, and her algebra marks took a downturn. But she does retain a clear image of the chemistry set, with its miniature test tubes and the wire holder for them, the candle for heating them, and the tiny corked bottles, so appealingly like doll's-house glassware, with the mysterious substances in them: crystals, powders, solutions, potions. Some of these things had undoubtedly been poisonous; probably you could not buy such chemistry sets for children now. Alma is glad not to have missed out on it, because it was alchemy, after all, and that was how the instruction book presented it: magic. *Astonish your friends. Turn water to milk. Turn water to blood.* She remembers terminology, too, though the meanings have grown hazy with time. *Precipitate. Sublimation.*

There was a section on how to do tricks with ordinary

household objects, such as how to make a hard-boiled egg go into a milk bottle, back in the days when there were milk bottles. (Alma thinks about them and sees the cream floating on the top, tastes the cardboard tops she used to beg to be allowed to lick off, smells the horse droppings from the wagons: she's getting old.) How to turn milk sour in an instant. How to make invisible writing with lemon juice. How to stop cut apples from turning brown. It's from this part of the instruction book (the best section, because who could resist the thought of mysterious powers hidden in the ordinary things around you?) that she's called back the supersaturated solution and the thread: *How to make a magical salt garden*. It was one of her favourites.

Alma's mother had complained about the way Alma was using up the salt, but her father said it was a cheap price to pay for the development of Alma's scientific curiosity. He thought Alma was learning about the spaces between molecules, but it was no such thing, as Alma and her mother both silently knew. Her mother was Irish, in dark contrast to her father's clipped and cheerfully bitter Englishness; she read tea-leaves for the neighbour women, which only they regarded as a harmless amusement. Maybe it's from her that Alma has inherited her bad days, her stretches of fatalism. Her mother didn't agree with her father's theories about Alma, and emptied out her experiments whenever possible. For her mother, Alma's fiddling in the kitchen was merely an excuse to avoid work, but Alma wasn't thinking even of that. She just liked the snowfall in miniature, the enclosed, protected world in the glass, the crystals forming on the thread, like the pictures of the Snow Queen's palace in the Hans Christian Andersen book at school. She can't remember ever having astonished any of her friends with tricks from the instruction book. Astonishing herself was enough.

* * *

The water in the pot is boiling again; it's still clear. Alma adds more salt, stirs while it dissolves, adds more. When salt gathers at the bottom of the pot, swirling instead of vanishing, she turns off the heat. She puts another spoon into the glass before pouring the hot water into it: otherwise the glass might break. She knows about this from having broken several of her mother's drinking glasses in this way.

She picks up the spoon with the thread tied to it and begins to lower the thread into the glass. While she is doing this, there is a sudden white flash, and the kitchen is blotted out with light. Her hand goes blank, then appears before her again, black, like an after-image on the retina. The outline of the window remains, framing her hand, which is still suspended above the glass. Then the window itself crumples inward, in fragments, like the candy-crystal of a shatter-proof windshield. The wall will be next, curving in towards her like the side of an inflating balloon. In an instant Alma will realize that the enormous sound has come and gone and burst her eardrums so that she is deaf, and then a wind will blow her away.

Alma closes her eyes. She can go on with this, or she can try to stop, hold herself upright, get the kitchen back. This isn't an unfamiliar experience. It's happened to her now on the average of once a week, for three months or more; but though she can predict the frequency she never knows when. It can be at any moment, when she's run the bathtub full of water and is about to step in, when she's sliding her arms into the sleeves of her coat, when she's making love, with Mort or Theo, it could be either of them and it has been. It's always when she's thinking about something else.

It isn't speculation: it's more like a hallucination. She's never had hallucinations before, except a long time ago when she was a student and dropped acid a couple of times. Everyone was doing it then, and she hadn't taken much. There had been moving lights and geometric

patterns, which she'd watched in a detached way.
Afterwards she'd wondered what all the talk about
cosmic profundity had been about, though she hadn't
wanted to say anything. People were very competitive
about the meaningfulness of their drug trips in those
days.

But none of it had been like this. It's occurred to her
that maybe these things are acid flashes, though why
should she be getting them now, fifteen years later, with
none in between? At first she was so badly frightened
that she'd considered going to see someone about it: a
doctor, a psychiatrist. Maybe she's borderline epileptic.
Maybe she's becoming schizophrenic or otherwise going
mad. But there don't seem to be any other symptoms:
just the flash and the sound, and being blown through
the air, and the moment when she hits and falls into
darkness.

The first time, she ended up lying on the floor. She'd
been with Mort then, having dinner in a restaurant,
during one of their interminable conversations about
how things could be arranged better. Mort loves the
word *arrange*, which is not one of Alma's favourites.
Alma is a romantic: if you love someone, what needs
arranging? And if you don't, why put in the effort? Mort,
on the other hand, has been reading books about Japan;
also he thinks they should draw up a marriage contract.
On that occasion, Alma pointed out that they were
already married. She wasn't sure where Japan fitted in: if
he wanted her to scrub his back, that was all right, but
she didn't want to be Wife Number One, not if it implied
a lot of other numbers, either in sequence or simulta-
neously.

Mort has a girl friend, or that's how Alma refers to her.
Terminology is becoming difficult these days: *mistress* is
no longer suitable, conjuring up as it does peach-
coloured negligées trimmed in fur, and mules, which
nobody wears anymore; nobody, that is, like Mort's girl
friend, who is a squarely built young woman with a

blunt-cut pageboy and freckles. And *lover* doesn't seem to go with the emotions Mort appears to feel towards this woman, whose name is Fran. Fran isn't the name of a mistress or a lover; more of a wife, but Alma is the wife. Maybe it's the name that's confusing Mort. Maybe that's why he feels, not passion or tenderness or devotion towards this woman, but a mixture of anxiety, guilt, and resentment, or this is what he tells Alma. He sneaks out on Fran to see Alma and calls Alma from telephone booths, and Fran doesn't know about it, which is the reverse of the way things used to be. Alma feels sorry for Fran, which is probably a defence.

It's not Fran that Alma objects to, as such. It's the rationalization of Fran. It's Mort proclaiming that there's a justifiable and even moral reason for doing what he does, that it falls into subsections, that men are polygamous by nature and so forth. That's what Alma can't stand. She herself does what she does because it's what she does, but she doesn't preach about it.

The dinner was more difficult for Alma than she'd anticipated, and because of this she had an extra drink. She stood up to go to the bathroom, and then it happened. She came to covered with wine and part of the tablecloth. Mort told her she'd fainted. He didn't say so, but she knew he put it down to hysteria, brought on by her problems with him, which to this day neither of them has precisely defined but which he thinks of as her problems, not his. She also knew that he thought she did it on purpose, to draw attention to herself, to collect sympathy and concern from him, to get him to listen to her. He was irritated. "If you were feeling dizzy," he said, "you should have gone outside."

Theo, on the other hand, was flattered when she passed out in his arms. He put it down to an excess of sexual passion, brought on by his technique, although again he didn't say so. He was quite pleased with her, and rubbed her hands and brought her a glass of water.

Theo is Alma's lover: no doubt about the terminology there. She met him at a party. He introduced himself by asking if she'd like another drink. (Mort, on the other hand, introduced himself by asking if she knew that if you cut the whiskers off cats they would no longer be able to walk along fences, which should have been a warning of some kind to Alma, but was not.) She was in a tangle with Mort, and Theo appeared to be in a similar sort of tangle with his wife, so they seemed to each other comparatively simple. That was before they had begun to accumulate history, and before Theo had moved out of his house. At that time they had been clutchers, specialists in hallways and vestibules, kissing among the hung-up coats and the rows of puddling rubbers.

Theo is a dentist, though not Alma's dentist. If he were her dentist, Alma doubts that she ever would have ended up having what she still doesn't think of as an affair with him. She feels that the inside of her mouth, and especially the insides of her teeth, are intimate in an anti-sexual way; surely a man would be put off by such evidences of bodily imperfection, of rot. (Alma doesn't have bad teeth; still, even a look inside with that little mirror, even the terminology, *orifice, cavity, mandible, molar.* . . .)

Dentistry, for Theo, is hardly a vocation. He hadn't felt called by teeth; he's told her he picked dentistry because he didn't know what else to do; he had good fine-motor coordination, and it was a living, to put it mildly.

"You could have been a gigolo," Alma said to him on that occasion. "You would have got extra in tips." Theo, who does not have a rambunctious sense of humour and is fastidious about clean underwear, was on the verge of being shocked, which Alma enjoyed. She likes making him feel more sexual than he is, which in turn makes him more sexual. She indulges him.

So, when she found herself lying on Theo's broadloom, with Theo bending over her, gratified and solicitous, saying, "Sorry, was I too rough?" she did nothing to correct his impression.

"It was like a nuclear explosion," she said, and he thought she was using a simile. Theo and Mort have one thing in common: they've both elected themselves as the cause of these little manifestations of hers. That, or female body chemistry: another good reason why women shouldn't be allowed to be airplane pilots, a sentiment Alma once caught Theo expressing.

The content of Alma's hallucinations doesn't surprise her. She suspects that other people are having similar or perhaps identical experiences, just as, during the Middle Ages, many people saw (for instance) the Virgin Mary, or witnessed miracles: flows of blood that stopped at the touch of a bone, pictures that spoke, statues that bled. As for now, you could get hundreds of people to swear they've been on spaceships and talked with extraterrestrial beings. These kinds of delusions go in waves, Alma thinks, in epidemics. Her lightshows, her blackouts, are no doubt as common as measles, only people aren't admitting to them. Most likely they're doing what she should do, trotting off to their doctors and getting themselves renewable prescriptions for Valium or some other pill that will smooth out the brain. They don't want anyone to think they're unstable, because although most would agree that what she's afraid of is something it's right to be afraid of, there's a consensus about how much. Too much fear is not normal.

Mort, for instance, thinks everyone should sign petitions and go on marches. He signs petitions himself, and brings them for Alma to sign, on occasions when he's visiting her legitimately. If she signed them during one of his sneak trips, Fran would know and put two and two

together, and by now not even Alma wants that. She
likes Mort better now that she sees less of him. Let Fran
do his laundry, for a change. The marches he goes to
with Fran, however, as they are more like social
occasions. It's for this reason that Alma herself doesn't
attend the marches: she doesn't want to make things
awkward for Fran, who is touchy enough already on the
subject of Alma. There are certain things, like parent-
teacher conferences, that Mort is allowed to attend with
Alma, and other things that he isn't. Mort is sheepish
about these restrictions, since one of his avowed reasons
for leaving Alma was that he felt too tied down.

Alma agrees with Mort about the marches and petitions, out loud that is. It's reasonable to suppose that if
only everyone in the world would sign the petitions and
go on the marches, the catastrophe itself would not
occur. Now is the time to stand up and be counted, to
throw your body in front of the juggernaut, as Mort
himself does in the form of donations to peace groups
and letters to politicians, for which he receives tax
receipts and neatly typed form letters in response. Alma
knows that Mort's way makes sense, or as much sense as
anything; but she has never been a truly sensible person.
This was one of her father's chief complaints about her.
She could never bring herself to squeeze in her two
hands the birds that flew into their plate-glass window
and injured themselves, as her father taught her to do, in
order to collapse their lungs. Instead she wanted to keep
them in boxes filled with cotton wool and feed them with
an eyedropper, thus causing them—according to her
father—to die a lingering and painful death. So he would
collapse their lungs himself, and Alma would refuse to
look, and grieve afterwards.

Marrying Mort was not sensible. Getting involved
with Theo was not sensible, Alma's clothes are not and
never have been sensible, especially the shoes. Alma
knows that if a fire ever broke out in her house, the place
would burn to the ground before she could make up her

mind about what to do, even though she's in full
possession of all the possibilities (extinguisher, fire
department's number, wet cloth to put over the nose).
So, in the face of Mort's hearty optimism, Alma shrugs
inwardly. She tries hard to believe, but she's an infidel
and not proud of it. The sad truth is that there are
probably more people in the world like her than like
Mort. Anyway, there's a lot of money tied up in those
bombs. She doesn't interfere with him or say anything
negative, however. The petitions are as constructive a
hobby as any, and the marches keep him active and
happy. He's a muscular man with a reddish face, who's
inclined to overweight and who needs to work off energy
to avoid the chance of a heart attack, or that's what the
doctor says. It's all a good enough way to pass the time.

Theo, on the other hand, deals with the question by
not dealing with it at all. He lives his life as if it isn't
there, a talent for obliviousness that Alma envies. He
just goes on filling teeth, filling teeth, as if all the tiny
adjustments he's making to people's mouths are still
going to matter in ten years, or five, or even two.
Maybe, Alma thinks in her more cynical moments, they
can use his dental records for identification when they're
sorting out the corpses, if there are any left to sort; if
sorting will be a priority, which she very much doubts.
Alma has tried to talk about it, once or twice, but Theo
has said he doesn't see any percentage in negative
thinking. It will happen or it won't, and if it doesn't the
main worry will be the economy. Theo makes investments. Theo is planning his retirement. Theo has tunnel
vision and Alma doesn't. She has no faith in people's
ability to pull themselves out of this hole, and no sand to
stick her head into. The thing is there, standing in one
corner of whatever room she happens to be in, like a
stranger whose face you know you could see clearly if
you were only to turn your head. Alma doesn't turn her
head. She doesn't want to look. She goes about her

business, most of the time; except for these minor
lapses.

Sometimes she tells herself that this isn't the first time
people have thought they were coming to the end of the
world. It's happened before, during the Black Death for
instance, which Alma remembers as having been one of
the high points of second-year university. The world
hadn't come to an end, of course, but believing it was
going to had much the same effect.

Some of them decided it was their fault and went
around flagellating themselves, or each other, or anyone
else handy. Or they prayed a lot, which was easier then
because you had some idea of who you were supposed to
be talking to. Alma doesn't think this is a dependable
habit of mind anymore, since there's an even chance
that the button will be pushed by some American
religious maniac who wants to play God and help
Revelations along, someone who really believes that he
and a few others will be raised up incorruptible afterwards, and therefore everyone else can rot. Mort says
this is a mistake unlikely to be made by the Russians,
who've done away with the afterlife and have to be
serious about this one. Mort says the Russians are better
chess players, which isn't much consolation to Alma. Her
father's attempts to teach her chess had not been too
successful, as Alma had a way of endowing the pieces
with personalities and crying when her Queen got killed.

Or you could wall yourself up, throw the corpses
outside, carry around oranges stuck with cloves. Dig
shelters. Issue instructional handbooks.

Or you could steal things from the empty houses, strip
the necklaces from the bodies.

Or you could do what Mort was doing. Or you could
do what Theo was doing. Or you could do what Alma was
doing.

Alma thinks of herself as doing nothing. She goes to
bed at night, she gets up in the morning, she takes care
of Carol, they eat, they talk, sometimes they laugh, she

sees Mort, she sees Theo, she looks for a better job, though not in a way that convinces her. She thinks about going back to school and finishing her degree: Mort says he will pay, they've both agreed he owes her that, though when it comes right down to it she isn't sure she wants to. She has emotions: she loves people, she feels anger, she is happy, she gets depressed. But somehow she can't treat these emotions with as much solemnity as she once did. Never before has her life felt so effortless, as if all responsibility has been lifted from her. She floats. There's a commercial on television, for milk she thinks, that shows a man riding at the top of a wave on a surfboard: moving, yet suspended, as if there is no time. This is how Alma feels: removed from time. Time presupposes a future. Sometimes she experiences this state as apathy, other times as exhilaration. She can do what she likes. But what does she like?

She remembers something else they did during the Black Death: they indulged themselves. They pigged out on their winter supplies, they stole food and gorged, they danced in the streets, they copulated indiscriminately with whoever was available. Is this where she's heading, on top of her wave?

Alma rests the spoon on the two edges of the glass. Now the water is cooling and the salt is coming out of solution. It forms small transparent islands on the surface that thicken as the crystals build up, then break and drift down through the water, like snow. She can see a faint white fuzz of salt gathering on the thread. She kneels so that her eyes are level with the glass, rests her chin and hands on the table, watches. It's still magic. By the time Carol comes home from school, there will be a whole winter in the glass. The thread will be like a tree after a sleet storm. She can't believe how beautiful this is.

After a while she gets up and walks through her house, through the whitish living room which Mort considers

Japanese in the less-is-more tradition but which has always reminded her of a paint-by-numbers page only a quarter filled in, past the naked-wood end wall, up the staircase from which Mort removed the banisters. He also took out too many walls, omitted too many doors; maybe that's what went wrong with the marriage. The house is in Cabbagetown, one of the larger ones. Mort, who specializes in renovations, did it over and likes to bring people there to display it to them. He views it, still, as the equivalent of an advertising brochure. Alma, who is getting tired of going to the door in her second-best dressing gown with her hair in a towel and finding four men in suits standing outside it, headed by Mort, is thinking about getting the locks changed. But that would be too definitive. Mort still thinks of the house as his, and he thinks of her as part of the house. Anyway, with the slump in house-building that's going on, and considering who pays the bills, she ought to be glad to do her bit to help out; which Mort has narrowly avoided saying.

She reaches the white-on-white bathroom, turns on the taps, fills the tub with water which she colours blue with a capful of German bath gel, climbs in, sighs. She has some friends who go to isolation tanks and float in total darkness, for hours on end, claiming that this is relaxing and also brings you in touch with your deepest self. Alma has decided to give this experience a pass. Nevertheless, the bathtub is where she feels safest (she's never passed out in the bathtub) and at the same time most vulnerable (what if she were to pass out in the bathtub? She might drown).

When Mort still lived with her and Carol was younger, she used to lock herself into the bathroom, chiefly because it had a door that closed, and do what she called "spending time with herself," which amounted to day-dreaming. She's retained the habit.

At one period, long ago it seems now, though it's really just a couple of months, Alma indulged from time to

time in a relatively pleasant fantasy. In this fantasy she
and Carol were living on a farm, on the Bruce Peninsula.
She'd gone on a vacation there once, with Mort, back
before Carol was born, when the marriage was still
behaving as though it worked. They'd driven up the
Bruce and crossed over onto Manitoulin Island in Lake
Huron. She'd noticed the farms then, how meagre they
were, how marginal, how many rocks had been pulled
out of the fields and piled into cairns and rows. It was
one of these farms she chose for her fantasy, on the
theory that nobody else would want it.

She and Carol heard about the coming strike on the
radio, as they were doing the dishes in the farm kitchen
after lunch. (Improbable in itself, she now realizes: it
would be too fast for that, too fast to reach a radio show.)
Luckily, they raised all their own vegetables, so they had
lots around. Initially Alma was vague about what these
would be. She'd included celery, erroneously, she knows
now: you could never grow celery in soil like that.

Alma's fantasies are big on details. She roughs them in
first, then goes back over them, putting in the buttons
and zippers. For this one she needed to make a purchase
of appropriate seeds, and to ask for advice from the man
in the hardware store. "Celery?" he said. (A balding,
fatherly small-town retailer, wearing braces on his pants,
a ring of sweat under each arm of his white shirt. Still,
the friendliness was tricky. Probably he had contempt for
her. Probably he told stories about her to his cronies in
the beer parlour, a single woman with a child, living by
herself out there on that farm. The cronies would cruise
by on her sideroad in their big second-hand cars, staring
at her house. She would think twice about going outside
in shorts, bending over to pull out weeds. If she got
raped, everyone would know who did it but none of
them would tell. This man would not be the one but he
would say after a few beers that she had it coming. This
is a facet of rural life Alma must consider seriously before
taking it up.)

"Celery?" he said. "Up here? Lady, you must be joking." So Alma did away with the celery, which wouldn't have kept well anyway.

But there were beets and carrots and potatoes, things that could be stored. They'd dug a large root cellar into the side of a hill; it was entered by a door that slanted and that somehow had several feet of dirt stuck onto the outside of it. But the root cellar was much more than a root cellar: it had several rooms, for instance, and electric lights (with power coming from where? It was details like this that when closely examined helped to cause the eventual collapse of the fantasy, though for the electricity Alma filled in with a small generator worked by runoff from the pond).

Anyway, when they heard the news on the radio, she and Carol did not panic. They walked, they did not run, sedately to the root cellar, where they went inside and shut the door behind them. They did not forget the radio, which was a transistor, though of course it was no use after the initial strike, in which all the stations were presumably vaporized. On the shelves built neatly into one wall were rows and rows of bottled water. There they stayed, eating carrots and playing cards and reading entertaining books, until it was safe to come out, into a world in which the worst had already happened so no longer needed to be feared.

This fantasy is no longer functional. For one thing, it could not be maintained for very long in the concrete detail Alma finds necessary before practical questions with no answers began to intrude (ventilation?). In addition, Alma had only an approximate idea of how long they would have to stay in there before the danger would be over. And then there was the problem of refugees, marauders, who would somehow find out about the potatoes and carrots and come with (guns? sticks?). Since it was only her and Carol, the weapons were hardly needed. Alma began to equip herself with a rifle, then rifles, to fend off these raiders, but she was always outnumbered and outgunned.

The major flaw, however, was that even when things worked and escape and survival were possible, Alma found that she couldn't just go off like that and leave other people behind. She wanted to include Mort, even though he'd behaved badly and they weren't exactly together, and if she let him come she could hardly neglect Theo. But Theo could not come, of course, without his wife and children, and then there was Mort's girl friend Fran, whom it would not be fair to exclude.

This arrangement worked for a while, without the quarrelling Alma would have expected. The prospect of imminent death is sobering, and Alma basked for a time in the gratitude her generosity inspired. She had intimate chats with the two other women about their respective men, and found out several things she didn't know; the three of them were on the verge of becoming really good friends. In the evenings they sat around the kitchen table which had appeared in the root cellar, peeling carrots together in a companionable way and reminiscing about what it had been like when they all lived in the city and didn't know each other, except obliquely through the men. Mort and Theo sat at the other end, drinking the Scotch they'd brought with them, mixed with bottled water. The children got on surprisingly well together.

But the root cellar was too small really, and there was no way to enlarge it without opening the door. Then there was the question of who would sleep with whom and at what times. Concealment was hardly possible in such a confined space, and there were three women but only two men. This was all too close to real life for Alma, but without the benefit of separate dwellings.

After the wife and the girl friend started to insist on having their parents and aunts and uncles included (and why had Alma left hers out?), the fantasy became over-populated and, very quickly, uninhabitable. Alma could not choose, that was her difficulty. It's been her difficulty all her life. She can't draw the line. Who is she to decide, to judge people like that, to say who must die and who is to be given a chance at life?

The hill of the root cellar, honeycombed with tunnels, too thoroughly mined, fell in upon itself, and all perished.

When Alma has dried herself off and is rubbing body lotion on herself, the telephone rings.

"Hi, what are you up to?" the voice says.

"Who is this?" Alma says, then realizes that it's Mort. She's embarrassed not to have recognized his voice. "Oh, it's you," she says. "Hi. Are you in a phone booth?"

"I thought I might drop by," says Mort, conspiratorially. "That is, if you'll be there."

"With or without a committee?" Alma says.

"Without," says Mort. What this means is clear enough. "I thought we could make some decisions." He means to be gently persuasive, but comes through as slightly badgering.

Alma doesn't say that he doesn't need her to help him make decisions, since he seems to make them swiftly enough on his own. "What kind of decisions?" she says warily. "I thought we were having a moratorium on decisions. That was your last decision."

"I miss you," Mort says, letting the words float, his voice shifting to a minor key that is supposed to indicate yearning.

"I miss you too," says Alma, hedging her bets. "But this afternoon I promised Carol I'd buy her a pink gym suit. How about tonight?"

"Tonight isn't an option," says Mort.

"You mean you aren't allowed out to play?" says Alma.

"Don't be snarky," Mort says a little stiffly.

"Sorry," says Alma, who isn't. "Carol wants you to come on Sunday to watch 'Fraggle Rock' with her."

"I want to see you alone," Mort says. But he books himself in for Sunday anyway, saying he'll double-check it and call her back. Alma says good-bye and hangs up, with a sense of relief that is very different from the feelings she's had about saying good-bye to Mort on the telephone in the past; which were, sequentially, love and desire, transaction of daily business, frustration because things weren't being said that ought to be, despair and grief, anger and a sense of being fucked over. She continues on with the body lotion, with special attention to the knees and elbows. That's where it shows up first, when you start to look like a four-legged chicken. Despite the approach of the end of the world, Alma likes to keep in shape.

She decides to take the streetcar. She has a car and knows how to drive, she can drive perfectly well, but lately she's been doing it less and less. Right now she prefers modes of transportation that do not require any conscious decisions on her part. She'd rather be pulled along, on a track if possible, and let someone else do the steering.

The streetcar stop is outside a health-food store, the window of which is filled with displays of dried apricots and carob-covered raisins, magical foods that will preserve you from death. Alma too has had her macrobiotic phase: she knows what elements of superstitious hope the consumption of such talismans involves. It would have been just as effective to have strung the raisins on a thread and worn them around her neck, to ward off vampires. On the brick wall of the store, between the window and the door, someone has written in spray paint: JESUS HATES YOU.

The streetcar comes and Alma gets on. She's going to the subway station, where she will get off and swiftly buy a pink gym suit and two pairs of summer socks for Carol and go down the stairs and get onto a subway train going

north, using the transfer she's just stuck into her purse.
You aren't supposed to use transfers for stopovers but
Alma feels reckless.

The car is a little crowded. She stands near the back
door, looking out the window, thinking about nothing in
particular. It's a sunny day, one of the first, and warm;
things are too bright.

All at once some people near the back door begin to
shout: *Stop! Stop!* Alma doesn't hear them at first, or she
hears them at the level of non-comprehension: she
knows there is noise, but she thinks it's just some
teenagers fooling around, being too loud, the way they
do. The streetcar conductor must think this too, because
he keeps on going, at a fast clip, spinning along, while
more and more people are shouting and then screaming,
Stop! Stop! Stop! Then Alma begins to shout too, for she
sees what is wrong: there's a girl's arm caught in the back
door, and the girl herself is outside, being dragged along
it must be; Alma can't see her but she knows she's there.

Alma finds herself jumping up and down, like a
frustrated child, and screaming "*Stop! Stop!*" with the
rest of them, and still the man drives on, oblivious. Alma
wants someone to throw something or hit him, why is no
one moving? They're packed in too close, and the ones at
the front don't know, can't see. This goes on for hours
which are really minutes, and finally he slows down and
stops. He gets out, walks around to the back.

Luckily there's an ambulance right beside them, so
the girl is put into it. Alma can't see her face or how
badly injured she is, though she cranes her neck, but she
can hear the noises she's making: not crying, not
whimpering, something more animal and abandoned,
more terrified. The most frightening thing must have
been not the pain but the sense that no one could see or
hear her.

Now that the streetcar has stopped and the crisis is
over, people around Alma begin muttering to one
another. The driver should be removed, they say. He

should lose his licence, or whatever it is they have. He should be arrested. But he comes back and pushes something at the front and the doors open. They will all have to get off the streetcar, he says. He sounds angry, as if the girl caught in the door and the shouting have been someone else's fault.

They aren't far from the subway stop and the store where Alma intends to do her furtive shopping: Alma can walk. At the next stoplight she looks back. The driver is standing beside the streetcar, hands in his pockets, talking with a policeman. The ambulance is gone. Alma notices that her heart is pounding. This is how it is in riots, she thinks, or fires: someone begins to shout and then you're in the middle of it, without knowing what is happening. It goes too fast, and you shut out the cries for help. If people had shouted "help" instead of "stop," would the driver have heard them sooner? But the people did shout, and he did stop, eventually.

Alma can't find a pink gym suit in Carol's size, so she buys a mauve one instead. There will be repercussions about that. She makes it onto the subway train, using her spurious transfer, and begins her short journey through the darkness she can see outside the window, watching her own face floating on the glass that seals it out. She sits with her hands clasped around the package on her lap, and begins looking at the hands of the people across from her. She's found herself doing this quite often lately: noticing what the hands are like, how they are almost luminous, even the hands of old people, knobby hands with blue veins and mottles. These symptoms of age don't frighten her as a foretaste of her own future, the way they once did; they no longer revolt her. Male or female, it doesn't matter; the hands she's looking at right now belong to a middle-aged woman of no distinction, they're lumpy and blunt, with chipped orange nail polish, they're clutching a brown leather purse.

Sometimes she has to restrain an impulse to get up,

cross the aisle, sit down, take hold of these alien hands.
It would be misunderstood. She can remember feeling
this way once, a long time ago, when she was on a plane,
going to join Mort at a conference in Montreal. They
were planning to take a mini-vacation together after it.
Alma was excited by the prospect of the hotel room, the
aroma of luxury and illicit sex that would surround them.
She looked forward to being able to use the bath towels
and drop them on the floor without having to think about
who was going to wash them. But the plane had started
to lurch around in the air, and Alma was frightened.
When it took a dip, like an elevator going down, she'd
actually grabbed the hand of the man sitting next to her;
not that it would make any difference whose hand you
were holding if there really was a crash. Still, it made her
feel safer. Then, of course, he'd tried to pick her up. He
was fairly nice in the end: he sold real estate, he said.

Sometimes she studies Theo's hands, finger by finger,
nail by nail. She rubs them over her body, puts the
fingers in her mouth, curling her tongue around them.
He thinks it's merely eroticism. He thinks he's the only
person whose hands she thinks about in this way.

Theo lives in a two-bedroom apartment in a high-rise not
far from his office. Or at least Alma thinks he lived there.
Though it makes her feel, not unpleasantly, a little like a
call girl, it's where she meets him, because he doesn't
like coming to her house. He still considers it Mort's
territory. He doesn't think of Alma as Mort's territory,
only the house, just as his own house, where his wife
lives with their three children, is still his territory. That's
how he speaks of it: "my house." He goes there on
weekends, just as Mort goes to Alma's house. Alma
suspects he and his wife sneak into bed, just as she and
Mort do, feeling like students in a fifties dorm, swearing
each other to secrecy. They tell themselves that it would
never do for Fran to find out. Alma hasn't been explicit

about Theo to Mort, though she's hinted that there's someone. That made him perk up. "I guess I have no right to complain," he said.

"I guess you don't," said Alma. It's ridiculous the way the five of them carry on, but it would seem just as ridiculous to Alma not to go to bed with Mort. After all, he is her husband. It's something she's always done. Also, the current arrangement has done wonders for their sex life. Being a forbidden fruit suits her. She's never been one before.

But if Theo is still sleeping with his wife, Alma doesn't want to know about it. He has every right, in a way, but she would be jealous. Oddly enough, she doesn't much care any more what goes on between Mort and Fran. Mort is thoroughly hers already; she knows every hair on his body, every wrinkle, every rhythm. She can relax into him with scarcely a thought, and she doesn't have to make much conscious effort to please him. It's Theo who's the unexplored territory, it's with Theo that she has to stay alert, go carefully, not allow herself to be lulled into a false sense of security: Theo, who at first glance appears so much gentler, more considerate, more tentative. For Alma, he's a swamp to Mort's forest: she steps lightly, ready to draw back. Yet it's his body—shorter, slighter, more sinewy than Mort's—she's possessive about. She doesn't want another woman touching it, especially one who's had more time to know it than she's had. The last time she saw Theo (here, in this apartment building, the impersonal white lobby of which she's now entering), he said he wanted to show her some recent snapshots of his family. Alma excused herself and went into the bathroom. She didn't want to see a picture of Theo's wife, but also she felt that even to look would be a violation of both of them; the use, by Theo, of two women to cancel each other out. It's occurred to her that she is to Theo's wife as Mort's girl friend is to her: the usurper, in a way, but also the one to be pitied because of what is not being admitted.

She knows that the present balance of power can't last. Sooner or later, pressures will be brought to bear. The men will not be allowed to drift back and forth between their women, their houses. Barriers will be erected, signs will go up: STAY PUT OR GET OUT. Rightly so; but none of these pressures will come from Alma. She likes things the way they are. She's decided that she prefers having two men rather than one: it keeps things even. She loves both of them, she wants both of them; which means, some days, that she loves neither and wants neither. It makes her less anxious and less vulnerable, and suggests multiple futures. Theo may go back to his wife, or wish to move in with Alma. (Recently he asked her an ominous question—"What do you want?"—which Alma dodged.) Mort may want to return, or he may decide to start over with Fran. Or Alma could lose both of them and be left alone with Carol. This thought, which would once have given rise to panic and depression not unconnected with questions of money, doesn't worry her much at the moment. She wants it to go on the way it is forever.

Alma steps into the elevator and is carried up. Weightlessness encloses her. It's a luxury; her whole life is a luxury. Theo, opening the door for her, is a luxury, especially his skin, which is smooth and well-fed and darker than hers, which comes of his being part Greek, a generation or two back, and which smells of brisk sweetish chemicals. Theo amazes her, she loves him so much she can barely see him. Love burns her out; it burns out Theo's features so that all she can see in the dimmed apartment is an outline, shining. She's not on the wave, she's in it, warm and fluid. This is what she wants. They don't get as far as the bedroom, but collapse onto the living-room rug, where Theo makes love to her as if he's running for a train he's never going to catch.

Time passes, and Theo's details reappear, a mole here, a freckle there. Alma strokes the back of his neck, lifting her hand to look surreptitiously at her watch: she has to be back in time for Carol. She must not forget the gym suit, cast aside in its plastic bag at the door, along with her purse and shoes.

"That was magnificent," says Alma. It's true.

Theo smiles, kisses the inside of her wrist, holds it for a few seconds as if listening for the pulse, picks up her half-slip from the floor, hands it to her with tenderness and deference, as if presenting her with a bouquet of flowers. As if she's a lady on a chocolate box. As if she's dying, and only he knows it and wants to keep it from her.

"I hope," he says pleasantly, "that when this is all over we won't be enemies."

Alma freezes, the half-slip half on. Then air goes into her, a silent gasp, a scream in reverse, because she's noticed at once: he didn't say "if," he said "when." Inside his head there's a schedule. All this time during which she's been denying time, he's been checking off the days, doing a little countdown. He believes in predestination. He believes in doom. She should have known that, being such a neat person, he would not be able to stand anarchy forever. They must leave the water, then, and emerge onto dry land. She will need more clothes, because it will be colder there.

"Don't be silly," Alma says, pulling imitation satin up to her waist like a bedsheet. "Why would we?"

"It happens," says Theo.

"Have I ever done or said anything to make you feel it would happen to us?" Alma says. Maybe he's going back to his wife. Maybe he isn't, but has decided anyway that she will not do, not on a daily basis, not for the rest of his life. He still believes there will be one. So does she, or why would she be this upset?

"No," says Theo, scratching his leg, "but it's the kind of thing that happens." He stops scratching, looks at her, that look she used to consider sincere. "I just want you to know I like you too well for that."

Like. That finishes it, or does it? As often with Theo,

she's unsure of what is being said. Is he expressing
devotion, or has it ended already, without her having
been aware of it? She's become used to thinking that in a
relationship like theirs everything is given and nothing is
demanded, but perhaps it's the other way around.
Nothing is given. Nothing is even *a given*. Alma feels
suddenly too visible, too blatant. Perhaps she should
return to Mort and become once more unseen.

"I like you too," she says. She finishes dressing, while
he continues to lie on the floor, gazing at her fondly, like
someone waving to a departing ship, who nevertheless
looks forward to the moment when he can go and have
his dinner. He doesn't care what she's going to do next.

"Day after tomorrow?" he says, and Alma, who wants
to have been wrong, smiles back.

"Beg and plead," she says.

"I'm not good at it," he says. "You know how I feel."

Once, Alma would not even have paused at this; she
would have been secure in the belief that he felt the
same way she did. Now she decides that it's a matter of
polite form with him to pretend she understands him.
Or maybe it's an excuse, come to think of it, so he will
never have to come right out on the table and affirm
anything or explain himself.

"Same time?" she says.

The last of her buttons is done up. She'll pick up her
shoes at the door. She kneels, leans over to kiss him
good-bye. Then there is an obliterating flash of light, and
Alma slides to the floor.

When she comes to, she's lying on Theo's bed. Theo is
dressed (in case he had to call an ambulance, she thinks),
and sitting beside her, holding her hand. This time he
isn't pleased. "I think you have low blood pressure," he
says, being unable to ascribe it to sexual excitement.
"You should have it checked out."

"I thought maybe it was the real thing, this time,"
Alma whispers. She's relieved; she's so relieved the bed
feels weightless beneath her, as if she's floating on water.

Theo misunderstands her. "You're telling me it's over?" he says, with resignation or eagerness, she can't tell.

"It's not over," Alma says. She closes her eyes; in a minute, she'll feel less dizzy, she'll get up, she'll talk, she'll walk. Right now the salt drifts down behind her eyes, falling like snow, down through the ocean, past the dead coral, gathering on the branches of the salt tree that rises from the white crystal dunes below it. Scattered on the underwater sand are the bones of many small fish. It is so beautiful. Nothing can kill it. After everything is over, she thinks, there will still be salt.

The Sin Eater

❦

This is Joseph, in maroon leather bedroom slippers, flattened at the heels, scuffed at the toes, wearing also a seedy cardigan of muddy off-yellow that reeks of bargain basements, sucking at his pipe, his hair greying and stringy, his articulation as beautiful and precise and English as ever:

"In Wales," he says, "mostly in the rural areas, there was a personage known as the Sin Eater. When someone was dying the Sin Eater would be sent for. The people of the house would prepare a meal and place it on the coffin. They would have the coffin all ready, of course: once they'd decided you were going off, you had scarcely any choice in the matter. According to other versions, the meal would be placed on the dead person's body, which must have made for some sloppy eating, one would have thought. In any case the Sin Eater would devour this meal and would also be given a sum of money. It was believed that all the sins the dying person had accumulated during his lifetime would be removed from him and transmitted to the Sin Eater. The Sin Eater thus became absolutely bloated with other people's sins. She'd accumulate such a heavy load of them that nobody wanted to have anything to do with her; a kind of syphilitic of the soul, you might say. They'd even avoid speaking to her, except of course when it was time to summon her to another meal."

"Hey?" I say.

Joseph smiles, that lopsided grin that shows the teeth in one side of his mouth, the side not engaged with the

206

stem of his pipe. An ironic grin, wolfish, picking up on what? What have I given away this time?

"I think of them as old women," he says, "though there's no reason why they shouldn't have been men, I suppose. They could be anything as long as they were willing to eat the sins. Destitute old creatures who had no other way of keeping body and soul together, wouldn't you think? A sort of geriatric spiritual whoring."

He gazes at me, grinning away, and I remember certain stories I've heard about him, him and women. He's had three wives, to begin with. Nothing with me though, ever, though he does try to help me on with my coat a bit too lingeringly. Why should I worry? It's not as though I'm susceptible. Besides which he's at least sixty, and the cardigan is truly gross, as my sons would say.

"It was bad luck to kill one of them, though," he says, "and there must have been other perks. In point of fact I think Sin Eating has a lot to be said for it."

Joseph's not one of the kind who'll wait in sensitive, indulgent silence when you've frozen on him or run out of things to say. If you won't talk to him, he'll bloody well talk to you, about the most boring things he can think of, usually. I've heard all about his flower beds and his three wives and how to raise calla lilies in your cellar; I've heard all about the cellar, too, I could give guided tours. He says he thinks it's healthy for his patients—he won't call them "clients," no pussyfooting around, with Joseph—to know he's a human being too, and God do we know it. He'll drone on and on until you figure out that you aren't paying him so you can listen to him talk about his house plants, you're paying him so he can listen to you talk about yours.

Sometimes, though, he's really telling you something. I pick up my coffee cup, wondering whether this is one of those occasions.

"Okay," I say, "I'll bite. Why?"

"It's obvious," he says, lighting his pipe again, spewing

out fumes. "First, the patients have to wait until they're dying. A true life crisis, no fakery and invention. They aren't permitted to bother you until then, until they can demonstrate that they're serious, you might say. Second, somebody gets a good square meal out of it." He laughs ruefully. We both know that half his patients don't bother to pay him, not even the money the government pays them. Joseph has a habit of taking on people nobody else will touch with a barge pole, not because they're too sick but because they're too poor. Mothers on welfare and so on; bad credit risks, like Joseph himself. He once got fired from a loony bin for trying to institute worker control.

"And think of the time saving," he goes on. "A couple of hours per patient, sum total, as opposed to twice a week for years and years, with the same result in the end."

"That's pretty cynical," I say disapprovingly. I'm supposed to be the cynical one, but maybe he's outflanking me, to force me to give up this corner. Cynicism is a defence, according to Joseph.

"You wouldn't even have to listen to them," he says. "Not a blessed word. The sins are transmitted in the food."

Suddenly he looks sad and tired.

"You're telling me I'm wasting your time?" I say.

"Not mine, my dear," he says. "I've got all the time in the world."

I interpret this as condescension, the one thing above all that I can't stand. I don't throw my coffee cup at him, however. I'm not as angry as I would have been once.

We've spent a lot of time on it, this anger of mine. It was only because I found reality so unsatisfactory; that was my story. So unfinished, so sloppy, so pointless, so endless. I wanted things to make sense.

I thought Joseph would try to convince me that reality was actually fine and dandy and then try to adjust me to it, but he didn't do that. Instead he agreed with me,

cheerfully and at once. Life in most ways was a big pile of
shit, he said. That was axiomatic. "Think of it as a desert
island," he said. "You're stuck on it, now you have to
decide how best to cope."

"Until rescued?" I said.

"Forget about the rescue," he said.

"I can't," I said.

This conversation is taking place in Joseph's office, which
is just as tatty as he is and smells of unemptied ash-trays,
feet, misery and twice-breathed air. But it's also taking
place in my bedroom, on the day of the funeral. Joseph's,
who didn't have all the time in the world.

"He fell out of a tree," said Karen, notifying me. She'd
come to do this in person, rather than using the phone.
Joseph didn't trust phones. Most of the message in any
act of communication, he said, was non-verbal.

Karen stood in my doorway, oozing tears. She was one
of his too, one of us; it was through her I'd got him. By
now there's a network of us, it's like recommending a
hairdresser, we've passed him from hand to hand like the
proverbial eye or tooth. Smart women with detachable
husbands or genius afflicted children with nervous tics,
smart women with deranged lives, overjoyed to find
someone who wouldn't tell us we were too smart for our
own good and should all have frontal lobotomies.
Smartness was an asset, Joseph maintained. We should
only see what happened to the dumb ones.

"Out of a *tree*?" I said, almost screaming.

"Sixty feet, onto his head," said Karen. She began
weeping again. I wanted to shake her.

"What the bloody hell was he doing up at the top of a
sixty-foot *tree*?" I said.

"Pruning it," said Karen. "It was in his garden. It was
cutting off the light to his flower beds."

"The old fart," I said. I was furious with him. It was an
act of desertion. What made him think he had the right

to go climbing up to the top of a sixty-foot tree, risking all
our lives? Did his flower beds mean more to him than we
did?

"What are we going to do?" said Karen.

What am I going to do? is one question. It can always be
replaced by *What am I going to wear?* For some people
it's the same thing. I go through the cupboard, looking
for the blackest things I can find. What I wear will be the
non-verbal part of the communication. Joseph will
notice. I have a horrible feeling I'll turn up at the funeral
home and find they've laid him out in his awful yellow
cardigan and those tacky maroon leather bedroom
slippers.

I needn't have bothered with the black. It's no longer
demanded. The three wives are in pastels, the first in
blue, the second in mauve, the third, the current one, in
beige. I know a lot about the three wives, from those off-
days of mine when I didn't feel like talking.

Karen is here too, in an Indian-print dress, snivelling
softly to herself. I envy her. I want to feel grief, but I
can't quite believe Joseph is dead. It seems like some
joke he's playing, some anecdote that's supposed to make
us learn something. Fakery and invention. *All right,
Joseph,* I want to call, *we have the answer, you can come
out now.* But nothing happens, the closed coffin remains
closed, no wisps of smoke issue from it to show there's
life.

The closed coffin is the third wife's idea. She thinks it's
more dignified, says the grapevine, and it probably is.
The coffin is of dark wood, in good taste, no showy trim.
No one has made a meal and placed it on this coffin, no
one has eaten from it. No destitute old creature,
gobbling down the turnips and mash and the heavy
secrecies of Joseph's life along with them. I have no idea

what Joseph might have had on his conscience. Nevertheless I feel this as an omission: what then have become of Joseph's sins? They hover around us, in the air, over the bowed heads, while a male relative of Joseph's, unknown to me, tells us all what a fine man he was.

After the funeral we go back to Joseph's house, to the third wife's house, for what used to be called the wake. Not anymore: now it's coffee and refreshments.

The flower beds are tidy, gladioli at this time of year, already fading and a little ragged. The tree branch, the one that broke, is still on the lawn.

"I kept having the feeling he wasn't really there," says Karen as we go up the walk.

"Really where?" I say.

"There," says Karen. "In the coffin."

"For Christ's sake," I say, "don't start that." I can tolerate that kind of sentimental fiction in myself, just barely, as long as I don't do it out loud. "Dead is dead, that's what he'd say. Deal with here and now, remember?"

Karen, who'd once tried suicide, nodded and started to cry again. Joseph is an expert on people who try suicide. He's never lost one yet.

"How does he do it?" I asked Karen once. Suicide wasn't one of my addictions, so I didn't know.

"He makes it sound so *boring*," she said.

"That can't be all," I said.

"He makes you imagine," she said, "what it's like to be dead."

There are people moving around quietly, in the living room and in the dining room, where the table stands, arranged by the third wife with a silver tea urn and a vase of chrysanthemums, pink and yellow. Nothing too funereal, you can hear her thinking. On the white tablecloth there are cups, plates, cookies, coffee, cakes. I don't know why funerals are supposed to make people hungry, but they do. If you can still chew you know you're alive.

Karen is beside me, stuffing down a piece of chocolate cake. On the other side is the first wife.

"I hope you aren't one of the loonies," she says to me abruptly. I've never really met her before, she's just been pointed out to me, by Karen, at the funeral. She's wiping her fingers on a paper napkin. On her powder-blue lapel is a gold brooch in the shape of a bird's nest, complete with the eggs. It reminds me of high school: felt skirts with appliqués of cats and telephones, a world of replicas.

I ponder my reply. Does she mean *client*, or is she asking whether I am by chance genuinely out of my mind?

"No," I say.

"Didn't think so," says the first wife. "You don't look like it. A lot of them were, the place was crawling with them. I was afraid there might be an *incident*. When I lived with Joseph there were always these *incidents*, phone calls at two in the morning, always killing themselves, throwing themselves all over him, you couldn't believe what went on. Some of them were *devoted* to him. If he'd told them to shoot the Pope or something, they'd have done it just like that."

"He was very highly thought of," I say carefully.

"You're telling *me*," says the first wife. "Had the idea he was God himself, some of them. Not that he minded all that much."

The paper napkin isn't adequate, she's licking her fingers. "Too rich," she says. "*Hers*." She jerks her head in the direction of the second wife, who is wispier than the first wife and is walking past us, somewhat aimlessly, in the direction of the living room. "You can have it, I told him finally. I just want some peace and quiet before I have to start pushing up the daisies." Despite the richness, she helps herself to another piece of chocolate cake. "*She* had this nutty idea that we should have some of them stand up and give little testimonies about him, right at the ceremony. Are you totally out of your tree? I told her. It's your funeral, but if I was you I'd try to keep it in mind that some of the people there are going to be a whole lot saner than others. Luckily she listened to me."

"Yes," I say. There's chocolate icing on her cheek: I wonder if I should tell her.

"I did what I could," she says, "which wasn't that much, but still. I was fond of him in a way. You can't just wipe out ten years of your life. I brought the cookies," she adds, rather smugly. "Least I could do."

I look down at the cookies. They're white, cut into the shapes of stars and moons and decorated with coloured sugar and little silver balls. They remind me of Christmas, of festivals and celebrations. They're the kind of cookies you make to please someone; to please a child.

I've been here long enough. I look around for the third wife, the one in charge, to say good-bye. I finally locate her, standing in an open doorway. She's crying, something she didn't do at the funeral. The first wife is beside her, holding her hand.

"I'm keeping it just like this," says the third wife, to no one in particular. Past her shoulder I can see into the room, Joseph's study evidently. It would take a lot of strength to leave that rummage sale untouched, untidied. Not to mention the begonias withering on the sill. But for her it will take no strength at all, because Joseph is in this room, unfinished, a huge boxful of loose ends. He refuses to be packed up and put away.

"Who do you hate the most?" says Joseph. This, in the middle of a lecture he's been giving me about the proper kind of birdbath for one's garden. He knows of course that I don't have a garden.

"I have absolutely no idea," I say.

"Then you should find out," says Joseph. "I myself cherish an abiding hatred for the boy who lived next door to me when I was eight."

"Why is that?" I ask, pleased to be let off the hook.

"He picked my sunflower," he says. "I grew up in a slum, you know. We had an area of sorts at the front, but it was solid cinders. However I did manage to grow this one stunted little sunflower, God knows how. I used to get up early every morning just to look at it. And the little bugger picked it. Pure bloody malice. I've forgiven a lot of later transgressions but if I ran into the little sod tomorrow I'd stick a knife into him."

I'm shocked, as Joseph intends me to be. "He was only a child," I say.

"So was I," he says. "The early ones are the hardest to forgive. Children have no charity; it has to be learned."

Is this Joseph proving yet once more that he's a human being, or am I intended to understand something about myself? Maybe, maybe not. Sometimes Joseph's stories are parables, but sometimes they're just running off at the mouth.

In the front hall the second wife, she of the mauve wisps, ambushes me. "He didn't fall," she whispers.

"Pardon?" I say.

The three wives have a family resemblance—they're all blondish and vague around the edges—but there's something else about this one, a glittering of the eyes. Maybe it's grief; or maybe Joseph didn't always draw a totally firm line between his personal and his professional lives. The second wife has a faint aroma of client.

"He wasn't happy," she says. "I could tell. We were still very close, you know."

What she wants me to infer is that he jumped. "He seemed all right to me," I say.

"He was good at keeping up a front," she says. She takes a breath, she's about to confide in me, but whatever these revelations are I don't want to hear them. I want Joseph to remain as he appeared: solid, capable, wise, and sane. I do not need his darkness.

I go back to the apartment. My sons are away for the weekend. I wonder whether I should bother making dinner just for myself. It's hardly worth it. I wander around the too-small living room, picking things up. No longer my husband's: as befits the half-divorced, he lives elsewhere.

One of my sons has just reached the shower-and-shave phase, the other hasn't, but both of them leave a deposit every time they pass through a room. A sort of bathtub ring of objects—socks, paperback books left facedown and open in the middle, sandwiches with bites taken out of them, and, lately, cigarette butts.

Under a dirty T-shirt I discover the Hare Krishna magazine my younger son brought home a week ago. I was worried that it was a spate of adolescent religious mania, but no, he'd given them a quarter because he felt sorry for them. He was a dead-robin-burier as a child. I take the magazine into the kitchen to put it in the trash. On the front there's a picture of Krishna playing the flute, surrounded by adoring maidens. His face is bright blue, which makes me think of corpses: some things are not cross-cultural. If I read on I could find out why meat and sex are bad for you. Not such a poor idea when you think about it: no more terrified cows, no more divorces. A life of abstinence and prayer. I think of myself, standing on a street corner, ringing a bell, swathed in flowing garments. Selfless and removed, free from sin. Sin is this world, says Krishna. This world is all we have, says Joseph. It's all you have to work with. It is not too much for you. You will not be rescued.

I could walk to the corner for a hamburger or I could phone out for pizza. I decide on the pizza.

"Do you like me?" Joseph says from his armchair.

"What do you mean, do I *like* you?" I say. It's early on; I haven't given any thought to whether or not I like Joseph.

"Well, do you?" he says.

"Look," I say. I'm speaking calmly but in fact I'm outraged. This is a demand, and Joseph is not supposed to make demands of me. There are too many demands being made of me already. That's why I'm here, isn't it? Because the demands exceed the supply. "You're like my dentist," I say. "I don't think about whether or not I like my dentist. I don't *have* to like him. I'm paying him to fix my teeth. You and my dentist are the only people in the whole world that I don't *have* to *like*."

"But if you met me under other circumstances," Joseph persists, "would you like me?"

"I have no idea," I say. "I can't imagine any other circumstances."

This is a room at night, a night empty except for me. I'm looking at the ceiling, across which the light from a car passing outside is slowly moving. My apartment is on the first floor: I don't like heights. Before this I always lived in a house.

I've been having a dream about Joseph. Joseph was never much interested in dreams. At the beginning I used to save them up for him and tell them to him, the ones I thought were of interest, but he would always refuse to say what they meant. He'd make me tell him, instead. Being awake, according to Joseph, was more important than being asleep. He wanted me to prefer it.

Nevertheless, there was Joseph in my dream. It's the first time he's made an appearance. I think that it will please him to have made it, finally, after all those other dreams about preparations for dinner parties, always one plate short. But then I remember that he's no longer around to be told. Here it is, finally, the shape of my bereavement: Joseph is no longer around to be told. There is no one left in my life who is there only to be told.

I'm in an airport terminal. The plane's been delayed, all the planes have been delayed, perhaps there's a strike, and people are crammed in and milling around. Some of them are upset, there are children crying, some of the women are crying too, they've lost people, they push through the crowd calling out names, but elsewhere there are clumps of men and women laughing and singing, they've had the foresight to bring cases of beer with them to the airport and they're passing the bottles around. I try to get some information but there's no one at any of the ticket counters. Then I realize I've forgotten my passport. I decide to take a taxi home to get it, and by the time I make it back maybe they'll have everything straightened out.

I push towards the exit doors, but someone is waving to me across the heads of the crowd. It's Joseph. I'm not at all surprised to see him, though I do wonder about the winter overcoat he's wearing, since it's still summer. He also has a yellow muffler wound around his neck, and a hat. I've never seen him in any of these clothes before. Of course, I think, he's cold, but now he's pushed through the people, he's beside me. He's wearing a pair of heavy leather gloves and he takes the right one off to shake my hand. His own hand is bright blue, a flat tempera-paint blue, a picture-book blue. I hesitate, then I shake the hand, but he doesn't let go, he holds my hand, confidingly, like a child, smiling at me as if we haven't met for a long time.

"I'm glad you got the invitation," he says.

Now he's leading me towards a doorway. There are fewer people now. To one side there's a stand selling orange juice. Joseph's three wives are behind the counter, all in identical costumes, white hats and frilly aprons, like waitresses of the forties. We go through the doorway; inside, people are sitting at small round tables, though there's nothing on the tables in front of them, they appear to be waiting.

I sit down at one of the tables and Joseph sits opposite me. He doesn't take off his hat or his coat, but his hands are on the table, no gloves, they're the normal colour again. There's a man standing beside us, trying to attract our attention. He's holding out a small white card covered with symbols, hands and fingers. A deaf-mute, I decide, and sure enough when I look his mouth is sewn shut. Now he's tugging at Joseph's arm, he's holding out something else, it's a large yellow flower. Joseph doesn't see him.

"Look," I say to Joseph, but the man is already gone and one of the waitresses has come instead. I resent the interruption, I have so much to tell Joseph and there's so little time, the plane will go in a minute, in the other room I can already hear the crackle of announcements, but the woman pushes in between us, smiling officiously. It's the first wife; behind her, the other two wives stand in attendance. She sets a large plate in front of us on the table.

"Will that be all?" she says, before she retreats.

The plate is filled with cookies, children's-party cookies, white ones, cut into the shapes of moons and stars, decorated with silver balls and coloured sugar. They look too rich.

"My sins," Joseph says. His voice sounds wistful but when I glance up he's smiling at me. Is he making a joke?

I look down at the plate again. I have a moment of

panic: this is not what I ordered, it's too much for me, I might get sick. Maybe I could send it back; but I know this isn't possible.

I remember now that Joseph is dead. The plate floats up towards me, there is no table, around us is dark space. There are thousands of stars, thousands of moons, and as I reach out for one they begin to shine.

The Sunrise

❦

Yvonne follows men. She does this discreetly and at a
distance, at first; usually she spots them on the subway,
where she has the leisure to sit down and look about her,
but sometimes she will pass one on the street and turn
and walk along behind him, hurrying a little to keep up.
Occasionally she rides the subway or goes walking just
for this purpose, but more often the sighting is acciden-
tal. Once she's made it, though, she postpones whatever
she's doing and makes a detour. This has caused her to
miss appointments, which bothers her because she's
punctual as a rule.

On the subway, Yvonne takes care not to stare too
hard: she doesn't want to frighten anyone. When the
man gets off the train, Yvonne gets off too and walks to
the exit with him, several yards behind. At this point she
will either follow him home to see where he lives and lie
in wait for him some other day, when she's made up her
mind about him, or she'll speak to him once they're out
on the street. Two or three times a man has realized he's
being shadowed. One actually began to run. Another
turned to confront her, back against a nearby drugstore
window, as if cornered. One headed for a crowd and lost
her in it. These, she thinks, are the ones with guilty
consciences.

When the time is right, Yvonne quickens her pace,
comes up beside the man, and touches him on the arm.
She always says the same thing:

"Excuse me. You're going to find this strange, but I'd
like to draw you. Please don't mistake this for a sexual
advance."

Then there's an interval, during which they say *What*? and Yvonne explains. There's no charge, she says, and no strings. She just wants to draw them. They don't have to take their clothes off if they don't want to; the head and shoulders will do nicely. She really is a professional artist. She is not mad.

If they've listened to her initial appeal at all, and most do, it's very hard for them to say no. What does she want from them, after all? Only a small amount of their time, so that they can let her had access to something only they can give. They've been singled out as unique, told they are not interchangeable. No one knows better than Yvonne how seductive this is. Most of them say yes.

Yvonne isn't interested in men who are handsome in the ordinary way: she's not drawing toothpaste ads. Besides, men with capped-looking teeth and regular features, men even remotely like Greek gods, are conscious of the surface they present and of its effect. They display themselves as if their faces are pictures already, finished, varnished, impermeable. Yvonne wants instead whatever it is that's behind the face and sees out through it. She chooses men who look as if things have happened to them, things they didn't like very much, men who show signs of the forces acting upon them, who have been chipped a little, rained on, frayed, like shells on the beach. A jaw slightly undershot, a nose too large or long, eyes of different sizes, asymmetry and counterpoise, these are the qualities that attract her. Men of this kind are not likely to be vain in any standard way. Instead they know that they must depend on something other than appearance to make an impact; but the mere act of being drawn throws them back upon their own unreliable bodies, their imperfect flesh. They watch her as she draws, puzzled, distrustful, yet at the same time vulnerable and oddly confiding. Something of theirs is in her hands.

Once Yvonne gets the men into her studio she is very delicate with them, very tactful. With them in mind she has purchased a second-hand armchair with a footstool to match: solid, comforting, wine velvet, not her usual taste. She sits them in it beside the large window, and turns them so that the light catches on their bones. She brings them a cup of tea or coffee, to put them at ease, and tells them how much she appreciates what they are doing for her. Her gratitude is real: she's about to eat their souls, not the whole soul of course, but even a small amount is not to be taken lightly. Sometimes she puts on a tape, something classical and not too noisy.

If she thinks they're relaxed enough she asks them to take off their shirts. She finds collar-bones very expressive, or rather the slight hollow at the V, the base of the throat; the wish-bone, which gives luck only when broken. The pulse there says something different from the pulse at wrist or temple. This is the place where, in historical movies set in mediaeval times, the arrow goes in.

When Yvonne has arranged her materials and started to draw, she goes quickly: for the sake of the men, she doesn't like to stretch things out. Having been subjected to it herself in her student days, when people posed for each other, she knows how excruciating it is to sit still and let yourself be looked at. The sound of the pencil travelling over the paper raises the small hairs on the skin, as if the pencil is not a pencil at all but a hand being passed over the body, half an inch from the surface. Not surprisingly, some of the men connect this sensation— which can be erotic—with Yvonne, and ask to take her out or see her again or even sleep with her.

Here Yvonne becomes fastidious. She asks if the man is married, and if he is, she asks if he's happy. She has no wish to get involved with an unhappily married man; she doesn't want to breathe anyone else's black smoke. But if he's happy, why would he want to sleep with her? If he isn't married, she thinks there must be some good reason why not. Mostly, when these invitations are issued, Yvonne refuses, gently and continuing to smile. She discounts protestations of love, passion, and undying friendship, praise of her beauty and talent, claims on her charity, whining, and bluster; she's heard these before. For Yvonne, only the simplest-minded rationale will do. "Because I want to" is about all she'll accept.

Yvonne's studio is right downtown, near the water-front, in an area of nineteenth-century factories and warehouses, some of which are still used in the original way, some of which have been taken over by people like her. In these streets there are drunks, derelicts, people who live in cardboard boxes; which doesn't bother Yvonne, since she hardly ever goes there at night. On the way to her studio in the mornings she has often passed a man who looks like Beethoven. He has the same domed forehead, overgrown brow bones, gloomy meditative scowl. His hair is grey and long and matted, and he wears a crumbling jeans suit and sneakers tied on with pieces of parcel string, even in winter, and carries a plastic-wrapped bundle that Yvonne thinks must contain everything he owns. He talks to himself and never looks at her. Yvonne would very much like to draw him, but he's far too crazy. She has a well-developed sense of self-protection, which must be why she hasn't landed in serious trouble with any of the men she picks up. This man alarms her, not because she thinks he's dangerous, but because he's a little too much like what she could become.

Nobody knows how old Yvonne is. She looks thirty and dresses as if she were twenty, though sometimes she looks forty and dresses as if she were fifty. Her age depends on the light, and what she wears depends on how she feels, which depends on how old she looks that day, which depends on the light. It's a delicate interaction. She wears her bronze-coloured hair cut short at the back and falling slantwise across her forehead, like Peter Pan's. Sometimes she rigs herself out in black leather pants and rides a very small motorcycle; on the other hand, sometimes she pins on a hat with a little veil, sticks a beauty mark on her cheek with an eyebrow pencil, and slings a second-hand silver fox with three tails around her neck.

She sometimes explains her age by saying she's old enough to remember garter belts when they were just ordinary articles of women's clothing. You wore them when you were young, before you were forced to put on girdles and become rubberized, like mothers. Yvonne remembers the advent of panty-hose, the death of the seamed stocking, whereas for younger women these events are only mythology.

She has another way of dating herself, which she uses less often. Once, when she was young but adult, she had a show of her paintings closed down by the police. It was charged with being obscene. She was one of the first artists in Toronto that this happened to. Just before that, no gallery would even have dared to mount the show, and shortly afterwards, when chains and blood and body parts in supermarket trays had become chic, it would have been considered tame. All Yvonne did at the time was to stick the penises onto men's bodies more or less the way they really were, and erect into the bargain. "I don't see what the big deal was," she can say, still ingenuously. "I was only painting hard-ons. Isn't that what every man wants? The police were just jealous." She goes on to add that she can't make out why, if a penis is a good thing, calling someone a penis-brain is an insult. She has this conversation only with people she knows very well or else has just met. The shocking thing about Yvonne, when she intends to be shocking, is the contrast between certain elements of her vocabulary and the rest of it, which, like her manner, is reserved and even secretive.

For a while she became a sort of celebrity, but that was because she was too inexperienced to know better. People made her into a cause, and even collected money for her, which was nice of them but got in the way, she now feels, of her reputation as a serious artist. It became boring to be referred to as "the penis lady." There was one advantage though: people bought her paintings, though not for ultra-top prices, especially after magic realism came back in. By this time she has money put away: she knows too much about the lives of artists to spend it all and have nothing to fall back on when the wind shifts and the crunch comes, though she sometimes worries that she'll be one of those old women found dead in a pile of empty cat-food cans with a million dollars stashed in her sock. She hasn't had a show now for several years; she calls it "lying low." The truth is she hasn't been producing much except her drawings of men. She has quite a few of them by now, but she isn't sure what she's going to do with them. Whatever she's looking for she hasn't yet found.

At the time of her revolutionary penises, she was more interested in bodies than she is now. Renoir was her hero, and she still admires him as a colourist, but she now finds his great lolloping nudes vapid and meaningless. Recently she's become obsessed with Holbein. A print of his portrait of Georg Gisze hangs in her bathroom, where she can see it while lying in the tub. Georg looks out at her, wearing a black fur coat and a wonderful pink silk shirt, each vein in his hands, each fingernail perfectly rendered, with a suggestion of darkness in his eyes, a wet shine on his lip, the symbols of his spiritual life around him. On his desk stands a vase, signifying the emptiness and vanity of mortal existence, with one carnation in it, signifying the Holy Ghost, or possibly betrothal. Earlier in her life Yvonne used to dismiss this kind of thing as the Rosemary for Remembrance school of flower arranging: everything had to mean something else. The thing about painting penises was that no one ever mistook them for phallic symbols, or indeed for symbols at all. But now she thinks it would be so handy if there were still some language of images like this, commonly known and understood. She would like to be able to put carnations between the fingers of the men she draws, but it's far too late for that. Surely Impressionism was a mistake, with its flesh that was merely flesh, however beautiful, its flowers that were merely flowers. (But what does she mean by "merely"? Isn't that enough, for a flower to be itself? If Yvonne knew the answer. . . .)

Yvonne likes to work in the late mornings, when the light is at its best in her studio. After that she sometimes has lunch, with various people she knows. She arranges these lunches from pay phones. She doesn't have a phone herself; when she did have one, she felt she was always at its mercy, whether it was ringing or not; mostly when it was not.

She doles out these lunches to herself like pills, at intervals, when she thinks she needs them. People living alone, she believes, get squirrelly if they go too long without human contact. Yvonne has had to learn how to take care of herself; she didn't always know. She's like a plant—not a sickly one, everybody comments on how healthy she always is—but a rare one, which can flourish and even live only under certain conditions. A transplant. She would like to write down instructions for herself and hand them over to someone else to be carried out, but despite several attempts on her part this hasn't proved to be possible.

She prefers small restaurants with tablecloths; the tablecloth gives her something to hold on to. She sits opposite whoever it is that day, her large green eyes looking out from behind the hair that keeps falling down over her forehead, her chin tilted so that the left side of her head is forward. She's convinced that she can hear better with her left ear than with her right, a belief that has nothing to do with deafness.

Her friends enjoy having lunch with Yvonne, though

probably they wouldn't enjoy it as much if they did it more often. They would find themselves running out of things to say. As it is, Yvonne is a good listener: she's always so interested in everything. (There's no deception here: she *is* interested in everything, in a way.) She likes to catch up on what people are doing. Nobody gets around to catching up on what she is doing, because she gives the impression of being so serene, so perfectly balanced, that their minds are at rest about her. Whatever she's doing is so obviously the right thing. When they do ask, she has a repertoire of anecdotes about herself which are amusing but not very informative. When she runs out of these, she tells jokes. She writes down the punch lines and keeps them on filing cards in her purse so she won't forget them.

She eats out alone, but not often. When she does, it's usually at sushi bars, where she can sit with her back to the rest of the room and watch the hands of the chefs as they deftly caress and stroke her food. As she eats, she can almost feel their fingers in her mouth.

Yvonne lives on the top floor of a large house in an older but newly stylish part of the city. She has two big rooms, a bathroom, a kitchenette concealed by louvred folding doors which she keeps closed most of the time, and a walk-out deck on which there are several planters made from barrels sawed in two. These once contained rosebushes, not Yvonne's. This floor used to be the attic, and although Yvonne has to go through the rest of the house to get to it, there's a door at the bottom of her stairs that she can lock if she wants to.

The house is owned by a youngish couple named Al and Judy, who both work for the town planning department of City Hall and are full of talk and projects. They intend to expand their own living area into Yvonne's floor when their mortgage is paid off; it will be a study for Al. Meanwhile, they are delighted to have a tenant like

Yvonne. These arrangements are so fragile, so open to incompatibility and other forms of disaster, so easily destroyed by stereo sets and mud on the rugs. But Yvonne is a gem, says Judy: they never hear a peep out of her. She's almost too quiet for Al, who would rather hear the footsteps when someone comes up behind him. He refers to Yvonne as "The Shadow," but only when he's had a hard day at work and a couple of drinks.

Anyway, the advantages far outweigh the disadvantages. Al and Judy have a year-old baby named Kimberly, who is at day-care in the mornings and Judy's office in the afternoons, but if they want to go out in the evenings and Yvonne is in, they have no hesitation about leaving Kimberly in her charge. They don't ask her to put Kimberly to bed herself, however. They have never said she's just like one of the family; they don't make that mistake. Sometimes Yvonne comes down and sits in the kitchen while Kimberly is being fed, and Judy thinks she can spot a wistful expression in Yvonne's eyes.

At night when they're lying in bed or in the morning when they're getting dressed, Al and Judy sometimes talk about Yvonne. Each has a different version of her, based on the fact that she never has men over, or even women. Judy thinks she has no sex life at all; she's given it up, for a reason which is probably tragic. Al thinks she does have a sex life, but carries on elsewhere. A woman who looks like Yvonne—he's not specific—has to be getting it somehow. Judy says he's a dirty old man, and pokes him in the midriff.

"Who knows what evil lurks in the hearts of men?" Al says. "Yvonne knows."

As for Yvonne, the situation suits her, for now. She finds it comforting to hear the sounds of family life going on beneath her, especially in the evenings, and when she goes away Judy waters her plants. She doesn't have many of these. In fact, she doesn't have much of anything, in Judy's opinion: an architectural drawing board, a rug and some cushions and a low table, a couple of framed prints, and, in the bedroom, two futons, one on top of the other. Judy speculated at first that the second was for when some man slept over, but none ever does. Yvonne's place is always very tidy, but to Judy it looks precarious. It's too portable, she feels, as if the whole establishment could be folded up in a minute and transported and unfolded almost anywhere else. Judy tells Al that she wouldn't be surprised one morning to find that Yvonne has simply vanished. Al tells her not to be silly: Yvonne is responsible, she'd never go without giving notice. Judy says she's talking about a feeling, not about what she thinks objectively is really going to happen. Al is always so literal.

Al and Judy have two cats, which are very curious about Yvonne. They climb up to her deck and meow at the french doors to be let in. If she leaves her door ajar, they are up her stairs like a shot. Yvonne has no objection to them, except when they jump on her head while she's resting. Sometimes she will pick up one of them and hold it so that its paws are on either side of her neck and she can feel its heart beating against her. The cats find this position uncomfortable.

Once in a while Yvonne disappears for days, maybe even a week at a time. Al and Judy don't worry about her, since she says when she'll be back and she's always there at the time stated. She never tells them where she's going, but leaves a sealed envelope with them which she claims contains instructions for how she could be reached in case of an emergency. She doesn't say what would constitute an emergency. Judy sticks the envelope carefully behind the wall telephone in the kitchen; she doesn't know it's empty.

Al and Judy have incorporated these absences of Yvonne's into the romances they have built up about her.

In Al's, she's off to meet a lover, whose identity must remain secret, either because he's married or for reasons of state, or both. He imagines this lover as much richer and more important than he is. For Judy, Yvonne is visiting the child or children Judy is convinced she has. The father is a brute, and more strong-willed than Yvonne, who anyone can see is the kind of woman who couldn't stand up to either physical violence or a long court battle. This is the only thing that can excuse, for Judy, Yvonne's abandonment of her children. Yvonne is allowed to see them only at infrequent intervals. Judy pictures her meeting them in restaurants, in parks, the constraint, the anguish of separation. She spoons applesauce into the wet pink oyster-like mouth of Kimberly and bursts into tears.

"Don't be silly," says Al. "She's just off having a roll in the hay. It'll do her a world of good." Al thinks Yvonne has been looking too pale.

"You think sex with a man is the big solution to everything, don't you?" says Judy, wiping her eyes with the sleeve of her sweater.

Al pats her. "Not the only one," he says, "but it's better than a slap with a wet noodle, eh?"

Sometimes it *is* a slap with a wet noodle, thinks Judy, who has been over-tired recently and feels too many demands are being made upon her. But she smiles up at Al with fondness and appreciation. She knows she's lucky. The standard against which she measures her luck is Yvonne.

Thus the existence of Yvonne and her slightly weird behaviour lead to marital communication and eventual concord. If she knew this, Yvonne would be both pleased and a little scornful; but deep down underneath she would not give a piss.

When everything has been smooth and without painful incident for some time, when the tide has gone out too far, when Yvonne has been wandering along the street, looking with curiosity but no great interest at the lighting fixtures, the coral-encrusted bottles and the bridesmaids' dresses, the waterlogged shoes and the antique candle-holders held up by winged nymphs and the gasping fish that the receding waters have left glistening and exposed in all their detail, when she's gone into the Donut Centre and sat down at the counter and seen the doughnuts under glass beneath her elbows, their tentacles drawn in, breathing lightly, every grain of sugar distinct, she knows that up on the hills, in the large suburban yards, the snakes and moles are coming out of their burrows and the earth is trembling imperceptibly beneath the feet of the old men in cardigans and tweed caps raking their lawns. She gets up and goes out, no faster than usual and not forgetting to leave a tip. She's considerate of waitresses because she never wants to be one again.

She heads for home, trying not to hurry. Behind her, visible over her shoulder if she would only turn her head, and approaching with horrifying but silent speed, is a towering wall of black water. It catches the light of the sun, there are glints of movement, of life caught up in it and doomed, near its translucent crest.

Yvonne climbs the stairs to her apartment, almost running, the two cats bounding up behind her, and hits the bed just as the blackness breaks over her head with a force that tears the pillow out of her hands and blinds and deafens her. Confusion sweeps over and around her, but underneath the surface terror she is not too frightened. She's done this before, she has some trust in the water, she knows that all she has to do is draw her knees up and close everything, ears, eyes, mouth, hands. All she has to do is hold on. Some would advocate that she let go instead, ride with the current, but she's tried it. Collision with other floating objects does her no good. The cats jump on her head, walk on her, purr in her ear; she can hear them in the distance, like flute music on a hillside, up on the shore.

Yvonne can think of no reason for these episodes. There's no trigger for them, no early warning. They're just something that happens to her, like a sneeze. She thinks of them as chemical.

Today Yvonne is having lunch with a man whose collarbone she admires, or did admire when it was available to her. Right now it isn't, because Yvonne is no longer sleeping with this man. She stopped because of the impossibility of the situation. For Yvonne, situations become impossible quickly. She doesn't like situations.

This is a man with whom Yvonne was once in love. There are several such men in Yvonne's life; she makes a distinction between them and the men she draws. She never draws men she's in love with; she thinks it's because she lacks the necessary distance from them. She sees them, not as form or line or colour or even expression, but as concentrations of the light. (That's her version of it when she's in love; when she isn't, she remembers them as rarified blurs, like something you've spilled on a tablecloth and are trying to wash out. She has occasionally made the mistake of trying to explain all this to the men concerned.) She's no stranger to addiction, having once passed far too many chemical travelogues through her body, and she knows its dangers. As far as she's concerned love is just another form of it.

She can't stand too much of this sort of thing, so her affairs with such men don't last long. She doesn't begin them with any illusions about permanence, or even about temporary domestic arrangements; the days are gone when she could believe that if only she could climb into bed with a man and pull the covers over both their heads, they would be safe.

However, she often likes these men and thinks that something is due them, and so she continues to see them afterwards, which is easy because her separations from them are never unpleasant, not anymore. Life is too short.

Yvonne sits across from the man, at a table in a small restaurant, holding on to the tablecloth with one hand, below the table where he can't see it. She's listening to him with her customary interest, head tilted. She misses him intensely; or rather, she misses, not him, but the sensations he used to be able to arouse in her. The light has gone out of him and now she can see him clearly. She finds this objectivity of hers, this clarity, almost more depressing than she can bear, not because there is anything hideous or repellant about this man but because he has now returned to the ordinary level, the level of things she can see, in all their amazing and complex particularity, but cannot touch.

He's come to the end of what he's been saying, which had to do with politics. Now it's time for Yvonne to tell him a joke.

"Why is pubic hair curly?" she says.

"Why?" he says; as usual, he attempts to conceal the shock he feels at hearing her say words like *pubic*. Nice men are more difficult for Yvonne than pigs. If a man is piggish enough, she's glad to see him go.

"So you won't poke your eyes out," says Yvonne, clutching the tablecloth.

Instead of laughing he smiles at her, a little sadly. "I don't know how you do it," he says. "Nothing ever bothers you."

Yvonne pauses. Maybe he's referring to the fact that, in their withdrawal from each other, there were no frantic phone calls from her, no broken dishes, no accusations, no tears. She's tried all these in the past and found them lacking. But maybe he wanted those things, as proof of something, of love perhaps; maybe he's disappointed by her failure to provide them.

"Things bother me," says Yvonne.

"You have so much energy," he goes on, as if he hasn't heard her. "Where do you get it from? What's your secret?"

Yvonne looks down at her plate, on which there is half

an apple and walnut and watercress salad and a crust of
bread. To touch his hand, which is there in plain view, on
the tablecloth a mere six inches away from her wine
glass, would be to put herself at risk again, and she is
already at risk. Once she delighted in being at risk; but
once she did everything too much.

She looks up at him and smiles. "My secret is that I
get up every morning to watch the sunrise," she says.
This *is* her secret, though it's not the only one; it's only
the one that's on offer today. She watches him to see if
he's bought it, and he has. This is enough in character for
him, it's what he thinks she's really like. He's satisfied
that she's all right, that there will be no trouble, which is
what he wanted to know. He orders another cup of coffee
and asks for the bill. When it comes, Yvonne pays half.

They walk out into the March air, warmer than usual
this year, a fact on which they both comment. Yvonne
avoids shaking hands with him. It occurs to her that he is
the last man she will ever have the energy to love. It's so
much work. He waves good-bye to her and gets onto a
streetcar and is borne away, towards a set of distant
stoplights, along tracks that converge as they recede.

Near the streetcar stop there's a small flower shop where
you can buy one flower at a time, if one flower is all you
want. It's all Yvonne ever wants. Today they have tulips,
for the first time this year, and Yvonne chooses a red one,
the inside of the cup an acrylic orange. She will take this
tulip back to her room and set it in a white bud vase in
the sunlight and drink its blood until it dies.

Yvonne carries the tulip in one hand, wrapped in its
cone of paper, held stiffly out in front of her as if it's
dripping. Walking along past the store windows, into
which she peers with her usual eagerness, her usual
sense that maybe, today, she will discover behind them
something that will truly be worth seeing, she feels as if
her feet are not on cement at all but on ice. The blade of

the skate floats, she knows, on a thin film of water, which it melts by pressure and which freezes behind it. This is the freedom of the present tense, this sliding edge.

Yvonne is drawing another man. As a rule, she draws only men who fall well within the norm: they dress more or less conventionally, they turn out, when asked, to have jobs recognized and respected by society, they're within ten years of her own age, shooting either way. This one is different.

She began to follow him about three blocks past the flower shop, trotting along behind him—he has long legs—with her tulip held up in front of her like a child's flag. He's young, maybe twenty-three, and on the street he was carrying a black leather portfolio, which is now leaning against the wall by her door. His pants were black leather too, and his jacket, under which he was wearing a hot-pink shirt. His head is shaved up the back and sides, leaving a plume on top, dyed fake-fur orang-outang orange, and he has two gold earrings in his left ear. The leather portfolio means that he's an artist or a designer of some sort; she suspects he's a spray-painter, the kind that goes around at night and writes things on brick walls, things like *crunchy granola sucks* and *Save Soviet Jews! Win Big Prizes!* If he ever draws at all, it's with pink and green fluorescent felt pens. She'd bet ten dollars he can't draw fingers. Yvonne's own renderings of fingers are very good.

In the past she's avoided anything that looked like another artist, but there's something about him, the sullenness, the stylistic belligerence, the aggressive pastiness and deliberate potato-sprouting-in-the-cellar lack of health. When she caught sight of him, Yvonne felt a shock of recognition, as if this was what she'd been looking for, though she doesn't yet know why. She ran him to earth outside a submarine shop and said her piece. She expected a rejection, rude at that, but here he is, in her studio, wearing nothing at the moment but his pink shirt, one bloodless leg thrown over the arm of the wine velvet chair. In his hand is the tulip, which clashes violently with the shirt and the chair and his hair, which all clash with each other. He's like a welding-shop accident, a motorcycle driven full tilt into a cement wall. The look he's focussing on her is pure defiance, but defiance of what? She doesn't know why he agreed to come with her. All he said was, "Sure, why not?" with a look she read as meaning that she totally failed to impress him.

Yvonne draws, her pencil moving lightly over his body. She knows she has to go quickly or he will get restless, he will escape her. She can put the tulip in later, when she paints him. Already she's decided to paint him; he will be her first real painting for years. The tulip will become a poppy; it's almost the right colour anyway.

She's only down to the collar-bone, half visible under the open shirt, when he says, "That's enough," and pulls himself out of the chair and comes over and stands behind her. He puts his hands on her waist and presses himself against her: no preliminaries here, which would suit Yvonne fine—she likes these things to be fast— except that she's uneasy about him. None of her usual mollifications, coffee, music, gratefulness, have worked on him: he's maintained a consistent level of surliness. He's beyond her. She thinks of Al and Judy's cat, the black one, and the time it got its foot caught in the cord of her Venetian blind. It was so enraged she had to throw a towel over it to get it untangled.

"That's *art*," he says, looking over her shoulder.

Yvonne mistakes this for a compliment, until he says, "Art sucks." There's a hiss in the last word.

Yvonne gasps: there is such hatred in his voice. Maybe if she just stands there nothing will happen. He turns away from her and goes to the corner near the door: he wants to show her what he's got in his portfolio. What he does are collages. The settings are all outdoors: woods, meadows, rocks, seashores. Onto them he has pasted women, meticulously cut from magazines, splayed open-legged torsoes with the hands and feet removed, sometimes the heads, over-painted with nail polish in various shades of purple and red, shiny and wet-looking against the paper.

Yet as a lover he is slow and meditative, abstracted, somnambulent almost, as if the motions he's going through are only a kind of afterthought, like a dog groaning in a dream. The violence is all on the cardboard; it's only art, after all. Maybe everything is only art, Yvonne thinks, picking her sky-blue shirt up off the floor, buttoning it. She wonders how many times in the future she will find herself doing up these particular buttons.

When he's gone out, she locks the door behind him and sits in the wine velvet chair. It's herself she's in danger from. She decides to go away for a week. When she comes back she will buy a canvas the size of a doorway and begin again. Though if art sucks and everything is only art, what has she done with her life?

In her medicine cabinet Yvonne keeps several bottles of pills, which she has collected from doctors on one pretext or another over the years. There was no need to do this, to go through the rigmarole of prescriptions, since anything you want is available on the street and Yvonne knows who from; yet the prescriptions gave her a kind of sanction. Even the actual pieces of paper, with their illegible Arabic-textured scrawls, reassured her, much as a charm would if she believed in them.

At one time she knew exactly how many pills to take, of which kinds, at which precisely timed intervals, to keep from either throwing up or passing out before the right dose had been reached. She knew what she would say ahead of time to fend off those who might otherwise come looking for her, where she would go, which doors she would lock, where and in what position she would lie down; even, and not least importantly, what she would wear. She wanted her body to look well and not be too troublesome to those who would eventually have to deal with it. Clothed corpses are so much less disturbing than naked ones.

But lately she's been forgetting much of this arcane knowledge. She should throw the pills out: they've become obsolete. She's replaced them with something much simpler, more direct, faster, more failure-proof, and, she's been told, less painful. A bathtub full of warm water, her own bathtub in the bathroom she uses every day, and an ordinary razor blade, for which no prescriptions are necessary. The recommendation is that the lights be turned out, to avoid panic: if you can't see the spreading red, you hardly know it's there. A stinging at the wrists, like a minor insect. She pictures herself wearing a flannel nightgown, printed with small pink flowers, that buttons up to the neck. She has not yet bought this.

She keeps a razor blade in her paintbox; it could be for slicing paper. In fact she does slice paper with it, and when it gets dull she replaces it. One side of the blade is taped, since she has no desire to cut her fingers by accident.

Yvonne hardly ever thinks about this razor blade and what it's really doing in her paintbox. She is not obsessed with death, her own or anybody else's. She doesn't approve of suicide; she finds it morally distasteful. She takes care crossing the street, watches what she puts into her mouth, saves her money.

But the razor blade is there all the time, underneath everything. Yvonne needs it there. What it means is that she can control her death; and if she can't do that, what control can she ever possibly achieve over her life?

Perhaps the razor blade is only a kind of *memento mori*, after all. Perhaps it's only a pictorial flirtation. Perhaps it's only a dutiful symbol, like the carnation on the desk of Holbein's young man. He isn't looking at the carnation anyway, he's looking out of the picture, so earnestly, so intently, so sweetly. He's looking at Yvonne, and he can see in the dark.

The days are getting longer, and Yvonne's alarm clock goes off earlier and earlier. In the summers she takes to having afternoon naps, to make up for the sleep she loses to these dawn rituals. She hasn't missed the sunrise for years; she depends on it. It's almost as if she believes that if she isn't there to see it there will be no sunrise at all.

And yet she knows that her dependence is not on something that can be grasped, held in the hand, kept, but only on an accident of the language, because *sunrise* should not be a noun. The sunrise is not a thing, but only an effect of the light caused by the positions of two astronomical bodies in relation to each other. The sun does not really rise at all, it's the earth that turns. The sunrise is a fraud.

Today there's no overcast. Yvonne, standing out on her deck in her too-thin Japanese robe, holds on to the wooden railing to keep from lifting her arms as the sun floats up above the horizon, like a shimmering white blimp, an enormous kite whose string she almost holds in her hand. Light, chilly and thin but light, reaches her from it. She breathes it in.

Unearthing Suite

❧

My parents have something to tell me: something apart from the ordinary course of conversation. I can guess this from the way they sit down first, both on the same chair, my mother on the arm, and turn their heads a little to one side, regarding me with their ultra-blue eyes.

As they have grown older their eyes have become lighter and lighter and more and more bright, as if time is leeching them of darkness, experience clarifying them until they have reached the transparency of stream water. Possibly this is an illusion caused by the whitening of their hair. In any case their eyes are now round and shiny, like the glass-bead eyes of stuffed animals. Not for the first time it occurs to me that I could not have been born, like other people, but must have been hatched out of an egg. My parents' occasional dismay over me was not like the dismay of other parents. It was less dismay than perplexity, the bewilderment of two birds who had found a human child in their nest and have no idea what to do with it.

My father takes a black leather folder from the desk. They both have an air of suppressed excitement, like children waiting for a grown-up friend to open a present they have wrapped; which will contain a joke.

"We went down and bought our urns today," my father says.

"You what?" I say, shocked. There is nothing wrong with my parents. They are in perfect health. I on the other hand have a cold.

"It's best to be prepared," my mother says. "We looked at plots but they're so expensive."

"They take up too much space," says my father, who has always been conscious of the uses to which the earth is wrongly in his opinion put. Conversation around the dinner table when I was growing up concerned itself more than once with how many weeks it would take a pair of fruit flies breeding unchecked to cover the earth to a depth of thirty-two feet. Not many, as I recall. He feels much the same about corpses.

"They give you a little niche too," says my mother.

"It's in here," says my father, indicating the folder as if I am supposed to remember about all this and deal with it at the right time. I am appalled: surely they aren't leaving something, finally, up to me?

"We wanted to be sprinkled," says my mother. "But they told us it's now illegal."

"That's ridiculous," I say. "Why can't you be sprinkled if you want to?"

"The funeral-parlour lobby," says my father, who has been known to be cynical about government decisions. My mother concedes that things might get a bit dusty if everyone were to be sprinkled.

"I'll sprinkle you," I say bravely. "Don't worry about a thing."

This is a rash decision and I've made it on the spur of the moment, as I make all my rash decisions. But I fully intend to carry it out; even though it will mean action, a thing I avoid when possible. Under pretense of a pious visit I will steal my parents from their niche, substituting sand if necessary, and smuggle them away. The ashes part doesn't bother me; in fact I approve of it. Much better than waiting, like the Christians, for God to grow them once more instantaneously from the bone outward, sealed meanwhile rouged and waxed and wired, veins filled with formaldehyde, in cement and bronze vaults, a prey to mould and anaerobic bacteria. If God wants to make my parents again the molecules will do just as well to start with, same as before. It is not a question of matter, which turns over completely every seven years anyway, but of form.

We sit for a minute, considering implications. We are way beyond funerals and mourning, or possibly we have by-passed them. I am thinking about the chase, and being arrested, and how I will foil the authorities: already I am concocting fictions. My father is thinking about fertilizer, in the same tone in which other people think about union with the Infinite. My mother is thinking about the wind.

Photographs have never done justice to my mother. This is because they stop time; to really reflect her they would have to show her as a blur. When I think of her she is often on skis. Her only discoverable ambition as a child was to be able to fly, and much of her subsequent life has been spent in various attempts to take off. Stories of her youth involve scenes in trees and on barn roofs, break-neck dashes on frothy-mouthed runaway horses, speed-skating races, and, when she was older, climbs out of windows onto forbidden fire escapes, done more for the height and adventure than for the end result, an after-hours college date with some young man or other who had been knocked over by her, perhaps literally. For my mother, despite her daunting athleticism and lack of interest in frilly skirts, was much sought after. Possibly men saw her as a challenge: it would be an accomplishment to get her to pause long enough to pay even a fleeting amount of attention to them.

My father first saw her sliding down a banister—I imagine, in the 1920s, that she would have done this sidesaddle—and resolved then and there to marry her; though it took him a while to track her down, stalking her from tree to tree, crouching behind bushes, butterfly net at the ready. This is a metaphor but not unjustified.

One of their neighbours recently took me to task about her.

"Your poor mother," she said. "Married to your father."

"What?" I said.

"I see her dragging her groceries back from the supermarket," she said. (True enough, my mother does this. She has a little cart with which she whizzes along the sidewalk, hair wisping out from her head, scarf streaming, exhausting anyone foolhardy enough to make the trip with her; by that I mean myself.) "Your father won't even drive her."

When I told her this story, my mother laughed.

My father said the unfortunate woman obviously didn't know that there was more to him than met the eye.

In recent years my mother has taken up a new winter exercise. Twice a week she goes dancing on figure skates: waltzes, tangos, foxtrots. On Tuesday and Thursday mornings she can be observed whirring around the local arena to the tune of "A Bicycle Built For Two" played over the scratchy sound system, speed undiminished, in mittens which do not match her skirt, keeping perfect time.

My father did what he did because it allows him to do what he does. There he goes now, in among the trees, battered grey felt hat—with or without a couple of trout flies stuck in the band, depending on what year we're talking about—on his head to keep things from falling into his hair, things that are invisible to others but which he knows all too well are lurking up there among the innocent-looking leaves, one or two or a clutch of children of any age tagging along after him, his own or his grandchildren or children attracted at random, as a parade attracts followers, as the sun attracts meteors, their eyes getting larger and larger as wonder after wonder is revealed to them: a sacred white larva that will pupate and fly only after seven years, a miraculous beetle that eats wood, a two-sexed worm, a fungus that crawls. No freak show can hold a candle to my father expounding Nature.

He leaves no stone unturned; but having turned it, to see what may be underneath—and at this point no squeals or expressions of disgust are permitted, on pain of his disfavour—he puts everything carefully back: the grub into its hollow, the woodborer beneath its rotting bark, the worm into its burrow, unless needed of course for fishing. He is not a sentimentalist.

Now he spreads a tarpaulin beneath a likely-looking tree, striped maple let us say, and taps the tree trunk with the pole of his axe. Heaven rewards him with a shower of green caterpillars, which he gathers tenderly in, to carry home with him and feed on leafy branches of the appropriate kind stuck into quart jars of water. These he will forget to replace, and soon the caterpillars will go crawling over our walls and ceiling in search of fodder, to drop as if on cue into the soup. My mother is used to this by now and thinks nothing of it.

Meanwhile the children follow him to the next tree: he is better than magicians, since he explains everything. This is indeed one of his purposes: to explain everything, when possible. He wants to see, he wants to know, only to see and know. I'm aware that it is this mentality, this curiosity, which is responsible for the hydrogen bomb and the imminent demise of civilization and that we would all be better off if we were still at the stone-worshipping stage. Though surely it is not this affable inquisitiveness that should be blamed.

Look, my father has unearthed a marvel: a slug perhaps, a snake, a spider complete with her sack of eggs? Something educational at any rate. You can't see it from here: only the backs of the children's heads as they peer down into his cupped hands.

My parents do not have houses, like other people. Instead they have earths. These look like houses but are not thought of as houses, exactly. Instead they are more like stopping places, seasonal dens, watering holes on some caravan route which my nomadic parents are always following, or about to follow, or have just come back from following. Much of my mother's time is spent packing and unpacking.

Unlocking the door of one of their earths—and unlike foxes they get rid of the bones, not by burial but by burning, the right thing to do unless you want skunks—I am greeted first by darkness, then by a profusion of objects heaped apparently at random but actually following some arcane scheme of order: stacks of lumber, cans of paintbrush cleaner with paintbrushes soaking in them, some of these dry and stiff or glued to the insides of the cans by the sticky residue left by evaporation, boxes of four-inch spikes, six-quart baskets filled with an assortment of screws, hinges, staples, and roofing-nails, rolls of roofing, axes, saws, brace-and-bits, levels, peevees, spokeshaves, rasps, drills, post-hole diggers, shovels, mattocks, and crowbars. (Not all of these things are in the same place at the same time: this is a collective memory.) I know what each of these tools is for and may even at some time have used it, which may go part way towards explaining my adult slothfulness. The smell is the smell of my childhood: wood, canvas, tar, kerosene, soil.

This is my father's section of the house. In my mother's, things are arranged, on hooks and shelves, in inviolable order: cups, pots, plates, pans. This is not because my mother makes a fetish of housekeeping but because she doesn't want to waste time on it. All her favourite recipes begin with the word *quick*. Less is more, as far as she is concerned, and this means everything in its place. She has never been interested, luckily, in the house beautiful, but she does insist on the house convenient.

Her space is filled. She does not wish it altered. We used to give her cooking pots for Christmas until we realized that she would much rather have something else.

My father likes projects. My mother likes projects to be finished. Thus you see her, in heavy work gloves, carting cement blocks, one by one, or stacks of wood, from one location to another, dragging underbrush which my father has slashed, hauling buckets of gravel and dumping them out, all in aid of my father's constructionism.

Right now they are digging a large hole in the ground. This will eventually be another earth. My mother has already moved a load of cement blocks to the site, for lining it with; in the mornings she goes to see what animal tracks she can find on the fresh sand, and perhaps to rescue any toads and mice that may have tumbled in.

Although he is never finished, my father does finish things. Last summer a back step suddenly appeared on our log house up north. For twenty years my mother and I had been leaping into space whenever we wanted to reach the clothesline, using biceps and good luck to get ourselves back up and in. Now we descend normally. And there is a sink in the kitchen, so that dirty dishwater no longer has to be carried down the hill in an enamel pail, slopping over onto one's legs, and buried in the garden. It now goes down a drainhole in the approved manner. My mother has added her completing touch: a small printed sign Scotch-taped to the counter, which reads:

PUT NO FAT DOWN SINK.

A jar of dried bacteria stands nearby: one teaspoonful is poured down at intervals, so the stray tea leaves will be devoured. This prevents clogging.

Meanwhile my father is hard at work, erecting cedar logs into vertical walls for the new outhouse, which will contain a chemical toilet, unlike the old one. He is also building a fireplace out of selected pink granite boulders which my mother steps over and around as she sweeps the leaves off the floor.

Where will it all end? I cannot say. As a child I wrote small books which I began with the words *The End*. I needed to know the end was guaranteed.

My own house is divided in two: a room full of paper, constantly in flux, where process, organicism, and fermentation rule and dustballs breed; and another room, formal in design, rigid in content, which is spotlessly clean and to which nothing is ever added.

As for me, I will die no doubt of inertia. Though witness to my parents' exhausting vitality, I spent my childhood learning to equate goodness with immobility. Sitting in the bottoms of canoes that would tip if you lurched, crouching in tents that would leak if you touched them in rainstorms, used for ballast in motorboats stacked precariously high with lumber, I was told not to move, and I did not. I was thought of as being well-behaved.

At intervals my father would bundle the family and the necessary provisions into the current car—*Studebaker* is a name I remember—and make a pilgrimage of one kind or another, a thousand miles here, a thousand miles there. Sometimes we were in search of saw-flies; at other times, of grandparents. We would drive as long as possible along the almost empty post-war highways, through the melancholy small towns of Quebec or northern Ontario, sometimes down into the States, where there were more roadside billboards. Long after the minor-key sunsets late at night, when even the White Rose gasoline stations were closed, we would look for a motel; in those days, a string of homemade cottages beside a sign that read FOLDED WINGS, or, more somberly, VALHALLA, the tiny clapboard office festooned with Christmas-tree lights. Ever since then, *vacancy* has been a magic word for me: it means there is room. If we did not find a vacancy my father would simply pull over to the side of the road in some likely-looking spot and put up a tent. There were few campgrounds, no motorcycle gangs; there was more emptiness than there is now. Tents were not so portable then; they were heavy and canvas, and sleeping bags were dank and filled with kapok. Everything was grey or khaki.

During these trips my father would drive as fast as he could, hurling the car forward it seemed by strength of will, pursued by all the unpulled weeds in his gardens, all the caterpillars uncollected in his forests, all the nails that needed to be hammered in, all the loads of dirt that had to be shifted from one place to another. I, meanwhile, would lie on a carefully stowed pile of baggage in the back seat, wedged into a small place beneath the roof. I could see out of the window, and I would watch the landscape, which consisted of many dark trees and of the telephone poles and their curves of wire, which looked as if they were moving up and down. Perhaps it was then that I began the translation of the world into words. It was something you could do without moving.

Sometimes, when we were stationary, I held the ends of logs while my father sawed them, or pulled out designated weeds, but most of the time I lived a life of contemplation. In so far as was possible I sneaked off into the woods to read books and evade tasks, taking with me supplies filched from my mother's tin of cooking raisins and stash of crackers. In theory I can do almost anything; certainly I have been told how. In practice I do as little as possible. I pretend to myself that I would be quite happy in a hermit's cave, living on gruel, if someone else would make the gruel. Gruel, like so many other things, is beyond me.

What is my mother's secret? For of course she must have one. No one can have a life so apparently cheerful, so seemingly lacking in avalanches and swamps, without having also a secret. By *secret* I mean the price she had to pay. What was the trade-off, what did she sign over to the Devil, for this limpid tranquillity?

She maintains that she once had a quick temper, but no one knows where it has gone. When she was forced to take piano lessons as part of a young lady's battery of accomplishments, she memorized the pieces and played them by rote while reading novels concealed on her lap. "More *feeling*," her teacher would say to her. Pictures of her at four show a shy-looking ringleted child bedecked in the lacey lampshade dresses inflicted on girls before the First World War, but in fact she was inquisitive, inventive, always getting into trouble. One of her first memories is of sliding down a red clay bank in her delicate white post-Victorian pantaloons. She remembers the punishment, true, but she remembers better the lovely feeling of the mud.

Her marriage was an escape from its alternatives. Instead of becoming the wife of some local small-town professional and settling down, in skirts and proper surroundings, to do charity work for the church as would have befitted her status, she married my father and took off down the St. John's river in a canoe, never having slept in a tent before; except once, just before the wedding, when she and her sisters spent a weekend practising. My father knew how to light fires in the rain and what to do about rapids, which alarmed my mother's friends. Some of them thought of her as having been kidnapped and dragged off to the wilderness, where she was imprisoned and forced to contend with no electricity, no indoor plumbing, and hordes of ravening bears. She on the other hand must have felt that she had been rescued from a fate worse than death: antimacassars on the chairs.

Even when we lived in real houses it was something like camping out. There was an improvisational quality to my mother's cooking, as if the ingredients were not bought but scavenged: what we ate depended on what was at hand. She made things out of other things and never threw anything out. Although she did not like dirt, she could never take housecleaning seriously as an end in itself. She polished the hardwood floors by dragging her children over them on an old flannelette blanket. This sounds like fun until I reflect: they were too poor for floor polishers, maids, or babysitters.

After my birth she developed warts, all over both her hands. Her explanation was the ammonia: there were no disposable diapers then. In those days babies wore knitted woollen sweaters, woollen booties, woollen bonnets, and woollen soakers, in which they must have steamed like puddings. My parents did not own a wringer washer; my mother washed everything by hand. During this period she did not get out much to play. In the photographs, she is always posed with a sled or a carriage and one or two suspicious-looking infants. She is never alone.

Possibly she got the warts from being grounded; or, more particularly, from me. It's a burden, this responsibility for the warts of one's mother, but since I missed out on the usual guilts this one will have to do. The warts point towards my mother's secret but do not reveal it. In any case they went away.

My mother lived for two years in the red-light district of Montreal without knowing what it was. She was informed only afterwards, by an older woman who told her she ought not to have done it. "I don't know why not," said my mother. That is her secret.

My father studies history. He has been told by Poles that he knows more Polish history than most Poles, by Greeks that he knows more Greek history than most Greeks, by Spaniards that he knows more Spanish history than most Spaniards. Taking the sum total of worldwide *per capita* knowledge into consideration this is probably so. He alone, among my acquaintances, successfully predicted the war in Afghanistan, on the basis of past examples. Who else indeed was paying any attention?

It is his theory that both Hiroshima and the discovery of America were entomological events (the clue is the silkworm) and that fleas have been responsible for more massacres and population depletions than have religions (the clue is the bubonic plague). His overview is dire, though supported, he would hasten to point out, by the facts. Wastefulness, stupidity, arrogance, greed, and brutishness unroll themselves in technicolour panorama across our dinner table as my father genially carves the roast.

Should civilization as we know it destroy itself, he informs us, ladling the gravy—as is likely, he adds—it will never be able to rebuild itself in its present form, since all available surface metals have long since been exhausted and the extraction of deeper ones is dependent upon metal technologies, which, as you will remember, will have been demolished. There can never be another iron age, another bronze age; we will be stuck—if there is any *we*, which he doubts—with stone and bone, no good for aeroplanes and computers.

He has scant interest in surviving into the twenty-first century. He knows it will be awful. Any person of sense will agree with him (and lest you make the mistake of thinking him merely quaint, let me remind you that many do).

My mother, however, pouring out the tea and forgetting as usual who takes milk, says she wants to live as long as possible. She wants to see what happens.

My father finds this naïve of her, but lets it pass and goes on to discuss the situation in Poland. He recalls to our memories (paying his listeners the compliment, always, of pretending he is merely reminding them of something they have of course already known, long and well) the Second World War Polish cavalry charge against the German tanks: foolishness and bravery. But foolish. But brave. He helps himself to more mashed potato, shaking his head in wonder. Then, changing the subject, he delivers himself of one of those intricate and reprehensible puns he's so fond of.

How to reconcile his grim vision of life on earth with his undoubted enjoyment of it? Neither is a pose. Both are real. I can't remember—though my father could, without question, ferreting among his books to locate the exact reference—which saint it was who, when asked what he would do if the end of the world were due tomorrow, said he would continue to cultivate his garden. The proper study of mankind may be man, but the proper activity is digging.

My parents have three gardens: one in the city, which produces raspberries, eggplants, irises, and beans; another halfway up, which specializes in peas, potatoes, squash, onions, beets, carrots, broccoli, and cauliflower; and the one up north, small but lovingly cherished, developed from sand, compost, and rations of sheep and horse manure carefully doled out, which yields cabbages, spinach, lettuce, long-lasting rhubarb, and Swiss chard, cool-weather crops.

All spring and summer my parents ricochet from garden to garden, mulching, watering, pulling up the polyphiloprogenitive weeds, "until," my mother says, "I'm bent over like a coat hanger." In the fall they harvest, usually much more than they can possibly eat. They preserve, store, chill, and freeze. They give away the surplus, to friends and family, and to the occasional stranger whom my father has selected as worthy. These are sometimes women who work in bookstores and have demonstrated their discernment and intelligence by recognizing the titles of books my father asks for. On these he will occasionally bestow a cabbage of superior size and delightfulness, a choice clutch of tomatoes, or, if it is fall and he has been chopping and sawing, an elegant piece of wood.

In the winter my parents dutifully chew their way through the end products of their summer's labour, since it would be a shame to waste anything. In the spring, fortified with ever newer and more fertile and rust-resistant varieties from the Stokes Seed Catalogue, they begin again.

My back aches merely thinking about them as I creep out to some sinful junk-food outlet or phone up Pizza Pizza. But in truth the point of all this gardening is not vitaminization or self-sufficiency or the production of food, though these count for something. Gardening is not a rational act. What matters is the immersion of the hands in the earth, that ancient ceremony of which the Pope kissing the tarmac is merely a pallid vestigial remnant.

In the spring, at the end of the day, you should smell like dirt.

Here is a fit subject for meditation: the dock. I myself use it, naturally, to lie down on. From it I can see the outlines of the shore, which function for me like a memory. At night I sit on it, in a darkness which is like no other, watching stars if there are any. At dusk there are bats; in the mornings, ducks. Underneath it there are leeches, minnows, and the occasional crayfish. This dock, like Nature, is permanently crumbling away and is always the same.

It is built on cribs of logs weighted down by granite boulders, which are much easier to move around underwater than they are on land. For this venture my father immersed himself in the lake, which he otherwise prefers to stay out of. No wonder; even on good days, at the height of summer, it is not what you would call warm. Scars go purple in it, toes go white, lips go blue. The lake is one of those countless pot-holes left by the retreating glaciers, which had previously scraped off all the topsoil and pushed it south. What remained is bedrock, and when you dip yourself into this lake you know that if you stay in it long enough or even very long at all you will soon get down to the essentials.

My father looks at this dock (his eyes narrowing in calculation, his fingers itching) and sees mainly that it needs to be repaired. The winter ice has been at it, the sun, the rain; it is patched and treacherous, threads of rot are spreading through it. Sometime soon he will take his crowbar to it, rip apart its punky and dangerous boards and the logs excavated by nesting yellow-jackets, and rebuild the whole thing new.

My mother sees it as a place from which to launch canoes, and as a handy repository for soap and towel when, about three in the afternoon, in the lull between the lunch dishes and reactivating the fire for supper, she goes swimming. Into the gelid, heart-stoppingly cold water she wades, over the blackened pine needles lying on the sand and the waterlogged branches, over the shells of clams and the carapaces of crayfish, splashing the tops of her arms, until she finally plunges in and speeds outward, on her back, her neck coming straight up out of the water like an otter's, her head in its white bathing cap encircled by an aureole of blackflies, kicking up a small wake behind her and uttering cries of:

Refreshing! Refreshing!

Today I pry myself loose from my own entropy and lead two children single-file through the woods. We are looking for anything. On the way we gather pieces of fallen birchbark, placing them in paper bags after first shaking them to get out the spiders. They will be useful for lighting the fire. We talk about fires and where they should not be lit. There are charcoal-sided trunks crumbling here and there in the forest, *mementi mori* of an ancient burnout.

The trail we follow is an old one, blazed by my brother during his trail-making phase thirty years ago and brushed out by him routinely since. The blazes are now weathered and grey; hardened tree blood stands out in welts around them. I teach the children to look on both sides of the trees, to turn once in a while and see where they have come from, so that they will learn how to find their way back, always. They stand under the huge trees in their raincoats, space echoing silently around them; a folklore motif, these children in the woods, potentially lost. They sense it and are hushed.

The Indians did that, I tell them, pointing to an old tree bent when young into knees and elbows. Which, like most history, may or may not be true.

Real ones? they want to know.

Real, I say.

Were they alive? they ask.

We go forward, clambering up a hill, over boulders, past a fallen log ripped open by a bear in search of grubs. They have more orders: they are to keep their eyes open for mushrooms, and especially for puffballs, which even they like to eat. Around here there is no such thing as just a walk. I feel genetics stealing over me: in a minute I will be turning over stones for them, and in fact I am soon on my hands and knees, grubbing a gigantic toad out from under a fallen cedar so old it is almost earth, burnt orange. We discuss the fact that toads will not give you warts but will pee on you when frightened. The toad does this, proving my reliability. For its own good I put it into my pocket and the expedition moves forward.

At right angles there's a smaller trail, a recent one, marked not by blazes but by snapped branches and pieces of fluorescent pink tape tied to bushes. It leads to a yellow birch blown down by the wind—you can tell by the roots, topsoil and leaf-mould still matted on them—now neatly sawn and stacked, ready for splitting. Another earthwork.

On the way back we circle the burn-heap, the garden, going as quietly as we can. The trick, I whisper, is to see things before they see you. Not for the first time I feel that this place is haunted, by the ghosts of those not yet dead, my own included.

Nothing goes on forever. Sooner or later I will have to renounce my motionlessness, give up those habits of reverie, speculation, and lethargy by which I currently subsist. I will have to come to grips with the real world, which is composed, I know, not of words but of drainpipes, holes in the ground, furiously multiplying weeds, hunks of granite, stacks of more or less heavy matter which must be moved from one point to the other, usually uphill.

How will I handle it? Only time, which does not by any means tell everything, will tell.

This is another evening, later in the year. My parents have returned yet once again from the north. It is fall, the closing-down season. Like the sun my parents have their annual rhythms, which, come to think of it, are not unrelated to that simile. This is the time of the withering of the last bean plants, the faltering of the cabbages, when the final carrot must be prized from the earth, tough and whiskered and forked like a mandrake; when my parents make great altars of rubbish, old cardboard boxes, excess branches lopped from trees, egg cartons, who knows?—and ignite them to salute the fading sun.

But they have done all that and have made a safe journey. Now they have another revelation to make: something portentous, something momentous. Something has happened that does not happen every day.

"I was up on the roof, sweeping off the leaves—" says my mother.

"As she does every fall—" says my father.

It does not alarm me to picture my seventy-three-year-old mother clambering nimbly about on a roof, a roof with a pitch so steep that I myself would go gingerly, toes and fingers suctioned to the asphalt roofing like a tree-frog's, adrenaline hazing the sky, through which I can see myself hurtling earthward after a moment of forgetfulness, a mis-step, one of those countless slips of the mind and therefore of the body about which I ought to have known better. My mother does these things all the time. She has never fallen off. She will never fall.

"Otherwise trees would grow on it," says my mother.

"And guess what she found?" says my father.

I try to guess, but I cannot. What would my mother have found on the roof? Not a pine cone, not a fungus, not a dead bird. It would not be what anyone else would find there.

In fact it turns out to be a dropping. Now I have to guess what kind of dropping.

"Flying squirrel," I hazard lamely.

No, no. Nothing so ordinary.

"It was about this big," says my father, indicating the length and the circumference. It is not an owl then.

"Brown?" I say, stalling for time.

"Black," says my father. They both regard me, heads a little on one side, eyes shining with the glee of playing this ancient game, the game of riddles, scarcely able to contain the right answer.

"And it had hair in it," says my father, as if now light will break upon me, I must surely guess.

But I am at a loss.

"Too big for a marten," says my father, hinting, waiting. Then he lowers his voice a little. "Fisher," he says.

"Really?" I say.

"Must be," says my father, and we all pause to savour the rarity of this event. There are not many fishers left, not many of those beautiful arboreal voracious predators, and we have never before found the signs of one in our area. For my father, this dropping is an interesting biological phenomenon. He has noted it and filed it, along with all the other scraps of fascinating data he notes and files.

For my mother however, this is something else. For her this dropping—this hand-long, two-fingers-thick, black, hairy dropping—not to put too fine a point on it, this deposit of animal shit—is a miraculous token, a sign of divine grace; as if their mundane, familiar, much-patched but at times still-leaking roof has been visited and made momentarily radiant by an unknown but by no means minor god.

ABOUT THE AUTHOR

Born in Ottawa, MARGARET ATWOOD spent much of her early life in the northern bushlands of Ontario and Quebec, where her father worked as a forest entomologist. She has also lived in Sault Ste. Marie, Boston, Vancouver, Edmonton, Montreal, France, Italy, and London, England. Author of more than twenty volumes of poetry, fiction, and non-fiction, Atwood is perhaps best known for her five novels, *The Edible Woman*, *Surfacing*, *Lady Oracle*, *Life Before Man*, and *Bodily Harm*.

Her work has been published in more than fifteen countries.

Margaret Atwood lives in Toronto with writer Graeme Gibson and their daughter.

SEAL BOOKS

Offers you a list of outstanding fiction, non-fiction and classics of Canadian literature in paperback by Canadian authors, available at all good bookstores throughout Canada.

THE CANADIAN ESTABLISHMENT	Peter C. Newman
THE IVORY SWING	Janette Turner Hospital
A JEST OF GOD	Margaret Laurence
LADY ORACLE	Margaret Atwood
THE SNOW WALKER	Farley Mowat
ST. URBAIN'S HORSEMAN	Mordecai Richler
MALICE IN BLUNDERLAND	Allan Fotheringham
THE STONE ANGEL	Margaret Laurence
THE BACK DOCTOR	Hamilton Hall
JAKE AND THE KID	W. O. Mitchell
ZEMINDAR	Valerie Fitzgerald
DADDY'S GIRL	Charlotte Vale Allen
BODILY HARM	Margaret Atwood
PREPARING FOR SABBATH	Nessa Rapoport
SUNDAY'S CHILD	Edward Phillips
THE DIVINERS	Margaret Laurence
HIGH CRIMES	William Deverell
THE ESTABLISHMENT MAN	Peter C. Newman
THE HAUNTED LAND	Val Cleary
ROSEGARDEN	Kurt Palka
THE CANADIANS (six volumes)	Robert E. Wall
COMEBACK	Dan Hill
MURDER ON LOCATION	Howard Engel
NEVER CRY WOLF	Farley Mowat
LIFE BEFORE MAN	Margaret Atwood
WHO HAS SEEN THE WIND	W. O. Mitchell
GOING THROUGH THE MOTIONS	Katherine Govier
THE ACQUISITORS	Peter C. Newman
MEET ME IN TIME	Charlotte Vale Allen
THE SERPENT'S COIL	Farley Mowat
BODILY HARM	Margaret Atwood
PERPETUAL MOTION	Graeme Gibson
JOSHUA THEN AND NOW	Mordecai Richler

The Mark of Canadian Bestsellers

F I V E   B Y

MITCHELL

A sophisticated thinker, playwright, raconteur and creative teacher, W. O. Mitchell writes novels of innocence overwhelmed by experience in his fictional documentaries of Canadian small-town life.

His first book, WHO HAS SEEN THE WIND is a permanent Canadian classic. A work of brilliance, sheer beauty and rare perception, this tells of a child's search for "the ultimate meaning of the cycle of life."

In JAKE AND THE KID Mitchell shows his special skill in capturing the peculiar individuality of his characters. This is the story of a hired man, a ten-year old boy and their homely, whimsical adventures.

THE VANISHING POINT presents the complex dilemma of native peoples and the well-meaning whites who try to help them. Much of the power of this novel lies in the rendering of the Indian characters, authentic and strong.

Remarkable for its descriptive beauty, humour and original characterization, THE KITE is written with vitality and affection, and will warm the reader's heart in its presentation of time and old age.

What begins as a dream of boyhood in HOW I SPENT MY SUMMER HOLIDAYS ends in a nightmare of corruption and insanity. Most somber of Mitchell's novels, this is a haunting, powerful tale of lost innocence.

 Available in Seal paperbacks at all good bookstores throughout Canada.